THE RO MURL ER

Tom Walsingham Mysteries
Book One

C. P. Giuliani

SAPERE
BOOKS

THE ROAD TO MURDER

Published by Sapere Books.

20 Windermere Drive, Leeds, England, LS17 7UZ,
United Kingdom

saperebooks.com

ISBN: 978-1-80055-627-0

To the memory of my beloved grandmother, Bruna Giuliani, who first made me a teller of stories.

ACKNOWLEDGEMENTS

I was once told (a little testily) that the internet has made things easy for writers of my generation — and indeed, it has made accessible an abundance of invaluable resources. Without it, I would never be able to research and write my historical fiction from a little village in the plains of Northern Italy, with or without the pandemics.

That said, it still has taken the help, support, and generosity of many flesh-and-blood individuals to bring this novel where it is now — in a reader's hands.

Many thanks go to those who assisted with my research. Craig Lambert, of **medievalandtudorships.org**, provided the information that went into the creation of Guion Benabic's *Meance*. Jean-François Graillot, from the Musée de France Roger Rodière in Montreuil-sur-mer, greatly helped me when it came to moving Tom and Skeres around the Montreuil of 1581 — and thanks also go to the Mayor of Montreuil, and the whole Municipalité de la ville, for allowing me to view the old cadastral maps. And then the libraries! What would we do without libraries and librarians? Thank you to Special Collection Assistant Sarah Moxey, at the National Library of Scotland in Edinburgh, and the very efficient and helpful staff there, and also to the staff at the Biblioteca Baratta here in Mantova, who never bat an eyelash at my requests for outlandish international interlibrary loans.

Once a novel is researched and written, there is still the little matter of publishing it... For this I'm very, very thankful to the lovely people at Sapere Books — especially to Amy Durant who actually suggested that I should write mysteries in the first place, and has made the whole journey a very pleasant one.

And, last but not least, writing historical fiction is not quite the solitary endeavour it may seem. Many friends have offered enthusiasm, cheering, support, and patience during the whole process — but I have two people to thank in particular. Thank you, Milla, for much idea-bouncing, the early reading, the countless phone-calls — and for yelling me out of procrastination bouts and assorted quagmires. And thank you, Mother, for all the listening, the patience, the tea and cake on bad days, the good humour, the sound-boarding, the 16th century French judicial system at meal-times, and most of all for the unwavering faith. Cliché though it is, I wouldn't have made it without you.

PROLOGUE

4th of November 1581, London — just before dawn

Hissing, whispering, bringing out stenches, making clothes cling cold to body and limbs… Nance hated rain. She drew the wet shawl tighter around her head and tried to squint at the man in the dark. One of these days she was going to have herself a cloak, a fine one, of thick wool, with a proper hood. Very soon, if this one little bargain went the way she meant.

Of which she was no longer all that sure…

Straightening up against a shiver, she took a gulp of cold air — thick with piss and wet, rotting things. Hugh wasn't going to like this…

"He was too drunk to make up things," she insisted. "All swaying-like, and cross-eyed, and tapping his nose —"

"Men can pretend," said the man.

Nance snorted. He didn't believe that any more than she did, but still…

"And why would he name names to the likes of you?" he asked.

She stamped a pattened foot in the mud. "He never! The other one did, the servant-lad as came to fetch him. And my gentleman wasn't none too pleased."

The man shifted at that. Just a very little, almost invisible in the black alley — but it was enough that Nance took a small step away, back against the nearest wall, cold and damp through her clothes. A graveyard wall — but no, she must not think of that.

"And then off they went, muttering to each other." She shrugged in a show of unconcern. "But one thing more I heard: they were to leave this morning." When nothing came, she shrugged again and held out her hand, palm up for the money, as steady as she knew. Not a beggar's gesture, but one awaiting payment. "Only, mind — Hugh mustn't know."

"No, that would never do."

A rustle of thick wool, the muffled jingling of a fat purse.

Nance's guts danced in her belly. She held up her chin, for all that he couldn't see it, or the way she tucked a lock of red hair under the shawl. *Red like the Queen's*, they said.

"And so." The faceless voice had a cat-like, lazy alertness. There was more jingling in the darkness. "You thought that I would pay for this?"

Victory washed all through Nance. He wasn't fooling her — at all. "You think, because I'm a whore, I've no wits? Oh ay, you'll pay for this — and well." *Or others will*, she was going to say — but didn't.

The man hummed, very mildly, like one who understood and was a little sorry. He took a step forward, and something hissed harsher than the whispering rain.

Nance tried to jolt away and stumbled in her pattens — then an arm slammed into her throat, pinning her to the mouldy wall, squeezing, crushing. Bright lights flickered at the corners of her eyes. At first she didn't even know the pain, then it came, red and blinding, and she crumpled in the cold, as wet steps faded away in the rain.

And there were thoughts of Hugh — what would he do, poor Hugh? — but the last thought was, she'd never have her cloak now…

CHAPTER 1

10th of November, 1581

"Poor, poor Tom!" Ursula, Lady Walsingham, fastened the knot, and snipped the blue thread with her tiny scissors, chuckling to herself as she eyed critically the back of her new tapestry. "All the way to Paris with that annoying little man... Let us hope he has better weather than we have, at least."

Past the diamond-patterned windows she could hear the cold November rain, straight and unrelenting, batter the poor little walled garden, and the whole, sprawling pile of Barn Elms.

"I doubt it, my dear," her husband, Sir Francis Walsingham, said from where he sat across the cavern of a fireplace, hardly glancing up from his book. "I rather doubt it."

In truth, so did Ursula — but she couldn't help the motherly wish, for the sake of her husband's young cousin. She remembered only too well being swept across the Channel in a bad gale, back in her husband's ambassadorly days, with nothing but a creaky ship and the Lord's mercy between herself and the sea. "At least he has the sort of stomach that doesn't upset easily."

"Well, he is nineteen," her husband murmured. "And they will have crossed days ago, now. If anything plagues Thomas, it will be that man Litcott, rather than the weather."

When Ursula looked up from the tapestry, it was to find an amused gleam in the dear man's dark grey eyes.

"Well, shepherding tailors is hardly what one imagines to do as a courier..." Ursula turned the tapestry to frown at the figure of a blue-caparisoned steed.

"Litcott is a glover, my dear — in fact, a glove-maker," Sir Francis gently corrected. "And what one should imagine to do as a courier, is the Queen's bidding."

"The Queen's — or Monsieur's?" Ursula always found herself growing a little tart when it came to the Queen's French suitor, the Duke of Anjou. "Don't they have glove-makers in Navarre?"

Sir Francis closed his book and raised an eyebrow. "It is not every day that the French will acknowledge English superiority — if only in the making of riding gloves. Besides, if Queen Marguerite can make them a fashion, think how good it will be for trade!"

Ursula huffed in laughter at the notion of foolish, fussy Simon Litcott promoting the welfare of England in foreign courts. "And to demand a change of courier, too — poor Citolini!"

"Well, we can only hope that was more on account of the letters Tom is carrying than the glover," Sir Francis said. "The Duke of Anjou, it appears, has no trust in Italians."

"With one for a mother!"

"Because of that, quite possibly." Sir Francis leant forward, studying the crackling flames in the hearth. "At all events, Her Grace allowed it. She's letting the Duke sound just how far he can push. So far, she denies him nothing."

"Nothing except her hand in marriage?" There went the tartness again.

Her husband tutted — not that he liked the French Match any better than she did. "So far, yes, thank the Lord," he murmured, nodding to himself. "A most extraordinary courtship, truly."

More like the training of a hound pup, was Ursula's irreverent thought — one she kept to herself. Ah well, as long

as the pup was shipped back to his kingly brother in the end…
"I hope you told poor Tom," she said, after a little silence.

"That he's dealing with the destinies of kingdoms, more than
the whims of princelings?" The smile was clear in Sir Francis's
voice. "After two years of training, he should need no telling."

Without looking up, Ursula hummed. "Oh, not that he does
— but he would appreciate the words from you." A pup
himself, dear Tom, so bright, so worshipping of his great
cousin, so boyishly pleasant — and shaping up to be well-
looking, too, now that he was no longer all knees and ears and
elbows… Of the Walsingham young cousins, he was her
favourite by far.

"He's not training badly," Sir Francis said, thumbing through
his book. "It won't be long before he can make himself useful
here in London."

Ursula kept her eyes firmly on her unstitching. "Perhaps…"
she murmured, slowly, and with some regret. "Perhaps he
could stay in Paris a while longer?"

The dear man only hummed a little, already engrossed in his
reading again. *He must be tired*, Ursula decided. Surely it was
restful, after spending his days in Richmond as Mr. Secretary,
thinking for everyone and most of all for the Queen, to be able
to devote his mind to one thing at a time… Only, now she
wanted that one thing to be their only daughter.

"Frances…" she ventured, looking at her husband sideways.
"She's grown quite fond of him."

"They're children both…"

Oh, Lord bless all men — most urgently all fathers of girls of
fourteen!

"Not children at all, my dear," Ursula explained. "In a year or
two, Frances will be of an age to marry. And Tom is out there,

in charge of himself and others, dealing with the destiny of kingdoms — and, I'm sure — charged with your trust…"

This time Sir Francis sat up, closing the book and frowning. Ursula watched him, wondering whether, when you were Mr. Secretary, you had enough of your mind left to notice certain small things.

Things like their quiet, serious child lighting up at the very mention of her cousin, saying as of a great authority that Tom says this, Tom thinks that. And Tom bowing to the girl, laughing blue eyes belying the show of ceremony…

Sir Francis, a loving father but bearing the weight of a great realm on his shoulders, frowned vaguely. "He quizzes her Latin grammar," he murmured — as though there should be any sort of safety in that!

"No, my dear," said Ursula. "Or he used to — but lately Frances and Tom have been discussing the poetry of Virgil."

It was with some relief that she saw her husband's face grow thoughtful. Thoughtful of Tom, no doubt — only a third son, and penniless, with no prospects beyond what Sir Francis himself might offer, and, to be quite frank, a boy of no consequence at all…

Ursula sighed to herself as her husband thought, and shook her head a little, and went back to her tapestry — and to wishing, very hard, that poor dear Tom might have a smooth journey.

In the early-morning gloom of the Post stables in Amiens, Thomas Walsingham swatted his damp hat against the nearest stall's door, making the post-horse inside nicker in protest, and wondered what he had done, dear Lord, to deserve it all. "How the devil do you mean, gone?" he asked through gritted teeth, and glared at his ad interim servant.

Sturdy, squat Nick Skeres, eighteen and built like a scantling minotaur, scratched at the reddish wisps he liked to call a beard, and didn't look much perturbed. "That I can't find 'im, I mean," he said with a shrug.

Tom pinched the bridge of his nose, and counted to ten in Latin. *Unus. Duo. Tres.* "He can't have lost his way between the inn and here, can he?"

Skeres only pursed his lips, and wasn't wrong, either — for all that the inn was just across the street from the post-stables. After travelling for four days with Simon Litcott, maker of gloves to lords and foreign princes, there was little that Tom put beyond the man's lack of wit.

"'E did scuddle, the last night in London," Skeres said — and then he stopped, throwing a scowl past Tom's shoulder.

At a reappearing Litcott, for a miracle? Tom spun around, ready to give the dunce a piece of his mind, and found himself facing Jouvet instead, the Postmaster's man, wet as a dog from the rain outside.

"So, do you think to leave before night?" was the man's greeting. "I have so many horses out, what with the Fair coming, and all the couriers in Christendom scurrying around like mice, and you won't leave, and will leave, and then won't... Mind, Monsieur Walsn'am — let anyone come asking for horses, and he'll have them!"

Tom's stomach clenched. Now that was all he lacked — losing the horses, delaying even more. What would Sir Francis say — and, worse, think?

Jouvet looked wary — clearly expecting to be tongue-lashed for hindering the Queen's service. Not that, in truth, he was to blame: he'd had the mounts and packhorse saddled for nearly an hour now — all the luggage hauled down to the stables by Skeres, for the good Lord forfend that Litcott should raise anything heavier than a needle, or lead his own packhorse. It was hardly the Post-man's fault that they could not leave.

Tom swallowed his angry words. "You haven't seen my other fellow, have you?" he asked in French.

"Ah, you mean the one with the yellow hat?" Jouvet asked, all mock innocence, waving both hands around his head. "I've not seen him since yesterday."

Nick Skeres, who had been quiet until then, pushed at Tom's side. "Scurvy frog-eater!" he growled, ears scarlet and fists clenched. "What's 'e say?"

"Nothing you can't guess," Tom snapped, reverting to English, and stepping in Skeres's way. "Go find Litcott, instead of picking quarrels with the Post-folk."

Skeres grumbled a little under his breath, but off he stalked, crushing his shapeless hat on his head, and rushing out in the pelting rain.

Tom watched him go and threw a look at the saddled horses waiting under the awning in the courtyard. Three mounts and a packhorse... Three. Ah, so he *could* yell at Jouvet, after all! "What the devil, Jouvet! What if I wanted to leave now? Where's my guide?"

Not that he needed a guide to tell him the way to Paris — he'd ridden often enough these past two years, London to Paris and back again. No Queen's courier needed a guide on this route, except to bring back the post horses. He found some satisfaction when Jouvet startled, looked this way and that, and went scarlet from neck to pockmarked jowls.

"Crétins!" the man bellowed, and stalked away — as likely as not to bite off the head of some errant stable-hand, not to mention the missing guide.

Good. Let someone else look like a fool, for a change — for all that it meant more delay, even supposing Skeres ran to earth

16

the cursed glove-maker. More delay to add to the worst journey in Tom's two years of couriering, and more still if Jouvet made good on his threat. Oh, there were plenty of horses to hire in Amiens, as a rule — although costlier than post-horses — but with the Fair of Saint Remi starting on the morrow, there was no saying…

Tom ambled along the row of mostly empty stalls, watching the ostlers scurry about under Jouvet's fulminations, and sighed to himself. In all conscience, no matter what his mother might say, he didn't think he'd earned half of it. The wretched crossing, and being swept to Boulogne instead of Calais, he could have blamed on his own swearing — or perhaps the ceaseless rain since leaving London — or else Simon Litcott … but not all of it, surely? A man must do something worse than the occasional oath to deserve such a miserable journey? Then again, he should have known from the moment Sir Francis summoned him in haste.

"Oy, Master!"

Oh yes — and then there was Nick Skeres. Skeres, shouting Stentor-like from the awning, dripping wet, shaking water from his cloak, and not minding where it went, spattering stableboy and saddled horses.

To look at him, there wasn't much cheer to expect.

"Not even the smell of 'im!" the lad bellowed, for the whole of Amiens to hear.

Tom hastened to the door, and beckoned him closer. "Have you asked the host? The tapsters?" he inquired.

Skeres shrugged. "There ain't much asking, with these 'eathens as don't speak a word of God's own English."

Right. Foolish of him to ask. Tom kicked a mounting block, scuffing further an already scuffed boot. To think it shouldn't even have been him making this ride… "And now they'll say I've lost Monsieur's glove-maker!"

"Who will? Your uncle?"

"Cousin," Tom bit back irritably. "Sir Francis is my father's cousin." As though it made any difference what sort of relation he was to Mr. Secretary.

Skeres shrugged — again. He did that a lot.

"And ay, Sir Francis will, for one — and wonder what I've done with the Duke's packet, and with the glover, and with myself, and…" Tom stopped, spun away, and bit down the rest.

It had seemed such an honour to be chosen when the Royal guest — a French Duke, and the Queen's own suitor — had wanted an especially trusted courier, and he barely nineteen. A little less so to be entrusted with the glove-maker — Monsieur's present for his sister the Queen of Navarre — but still. And then… Tom fingered the hem of his doublet, a little on the right, where Sir Francis's own letter lay, carefully sewn under the lining, meant for the Ambassador in Paris.

Skeres hummed like one who had no cares in this world. "Ay, well, blame it on the rain."

"And say what? That Litcott was made of sugar, and melted away?"

"Made of sugar — and don't 'e look it!" The lad boomed with laughter, loud enough to make horses shy. Easily amused fellow. He was still cackling when the guide appeared from the stables' depths, leading another ready horse, of a straw colour so bright, it gleamed.

"So now we go, Master?" Jeannot Jouvet, nephew of the elder Jouvet, through no fault of his — in his thirties, gangly, missing a few teeth — and one of the few Frenchmen Tom knew who'd bothered to learn some words of English.

Tom wanted to laugh bitterly — only restrained by the thought of Sir Francis's dislike of such displays. "No, we do not, Jeannot," he said. "We do not leave, because I'm missing one of my men."

Jeannot stared, and looked about — as if the glover might have been dropped in the straw. "Missing, Monsieur? But … how have you lost him?"

A question many people were going to ask, no doubt — Dukes, and Queens, and Secretaries of State among them.

Tom ignored Skeres's snort. "You haven't seen him, have you? A short, thin fellow in a yellow hat…"

"Oh, that one." Jeannot's opinion of Litcott must not have been very high, judging by the twist of his mouth. "But yes, when he came in with you last night."

Tom twitched in hopeful impatience. "And what of today?"

Jeannot sucked his teeth, thinking hard. "No, I can't say that I've seen him," was the reply at long last. "But me, I'd leave him behind, Monsieur."

Skeres grunted in approval. Indeed, waiting on the fancies of the likes of Litcott seemed a waste of time — if only Litcott weren't a fancy of the Duke of Anjou, who was himself the fancy of the Queen — or perhaps he wasn't, who could tell…?

"Tempted as I am, Jeannot…" Tom began, only for the guide to tug at his sleeve and point.

"But yes, we must go: before *mon oncle* gives the horses to that one, you see?"

And sure enough, by the post-house's back door across the stable-yard, Jouvet was in earnest conversation with a tall man muffled in a cloak, and wearing a black hat. The Post-man kept pointing at the saddled beasts under the awning, and nodding at what the other said.

"He is a courier, too," Jeannot said. "Italian, or the like. And if we don't leave now —"

"Oy, you!" bellowed Skeres, and would have charged off like the Cretan Bull, hadn't Tom grabbed him by the sleeve.

"What are you going to do, you lack-wit? Break his arms, so he can't ride?"

"Why not?" Skeres shrugged free, lowering and so obviously spoiling for a fight that Tom wished he hadn't mentioned breaking arms. "D'you want to lose the 'orses to some mangy Papist?"

Tom hissed the lad quiet. The violence between Catholics and Huguenots might have dwindled down in the last year or so, but that didn't mean one went and hollered his dislike of the other side in the middle of the post-station. Who on earth had thought that loud, pugnacious, thoughtless Skeres would ever make a good Service man — or a good servant, at that?

Tom glanced around: the stableboy had no English, and Jeannot, who did, seemed little concerned — but still…

Right then Jouvet and the other courier, having rushed across the yard with their heads lowered against the rain, bustled through the stable door.

The supposed Italian smacked into Tom, reaching out to steady him as he shook his dripping cloak. "Crave your pardon," he began in French — and stopped short. Italian, indeed — and not.

"Oh, look, it's Monsieur Paul," greeted Jeannot. "I hadn't known you."

The man never bothered with the guide, too busy raising eyebrows at Tom. "So it *is* you!" he said, switching to English. "I would not believe it when Jouvet told me…"

Tom stiffened. Of all the men to have in one's hair! "What are you doing here, Citolini?" he asked — rather more sharply than was civil, perhaps.

The Italian didn't look any more pleased. "Going back — with letters," he announced, cocking his head to look down on Tom. Not that he truly needed to, being half a head taller — but it could be safely said that Paolo Citolini, long-limbed, hawk-faced, eternally black-clad, lived in a pose. "But you — you should be in Paris by now, surely?"

He even had a good, dark voice, with a touch of Italian to his speech, and a knack for rubbing a fellow the wrong way.

Tom bit his tongue for a heartbeat before it all came spilling out — the ugly crossing, Litcott, and nothing but rain these three past days. But he was not going to explain or whine. Not to Paolo Citolini, who was to have done this journey — until Monsieur had wanted a different courier, one who enjoyed Mr. Secretary's full trust. One, in truth, who wasn't Italian. Which meant that Citolini had been in London a week past. "When did *you* leave?"

"The day after you did," was the answer. "And I never thought that I would catch up."

"And just how the devil did you?" Tom snapped, before remembering they had an audience.

Jeannot gaped, Nick Skeres lowered, while Jouvet and the stableboy stared in gleeful — if uncomprehending — fascination, as the two couriers barked at each other. Or at least Tom barked. Citolini just leant back against the doorpost, crossing his arms and raising an eyebrow.

"I crossed to Boulogne," Citolini said — as though he'd meant to go to Boulogne in the first place. "Then I followed — and when it stopped raining, late this night, I took my chances and just arrived."

Of course. *Of course.* Leave it to Citolini to ride at night, and travel a day faster even in the miserable weather — and not quite boast about it. The Italian never boasted — just made you look lacking by comparison. Tom swallowed bitter words.

"So, if it is not asking too much," Citolini said, "I would have some bread and wine, and then leave with you. So we can share a guide."

And leave it to Citolini, also, to be right, and reasonable, and thrifty — and to be so with that manner of thankless patience that made a man's blood boil.

At Tom's shoulder, Skeres made a noise — but what way was there to refuse without appearing petty and churlish?

"Good," Tom ground out, with as much good grace as he could muster. "Go and have your breakfast at the Coq — and don't be long about it."

And that earned another raised eyebrow from Citolini — who, of course, had never been known to tarry over breakfast — and more noise from Skeres, and a shuffling of feet from Jeannot. And right they were, because when Citolini came back from the Coq, ready to leave, and there was no Litcott, what was Tom going to tell him?

For a few heartbeats the Italian gazed at Tom, and fiddled with the reddish hilt of the long Venetian stiletto he always wore. Then he twisted his mouth in a small, bitter smile, and stood up straight. "As you say," he murmured, and bowed his head just a little, in a way that said *Look what I have to bear.* Still, he gathered his cloak around him, and off he strode.

Tom sighed. "Off with you — and this time, find him," he quietly ordered Skeres, and then, ignoring the lad's mutterings, he turned to the Post-man. "A horse for Monsieur Paul, Jouvet," he ordered, with the sort of cool jollity he sometimes practised by himself. "*Another* one."

And then he wished he had waited for Citolini to be out of earshot, because Jouvet, quite unlike the people in Tom's imaginings, instead of scurrying to obey, threw up his hands.

"Another horse, says he! Another horse — where am I to find another horse, just like that?"

Tom crossed his arms and looked pointedly at the two beasts a few stalls away — a grey gelding and an ugly, big-headed roan.

"But no!" Jouvet protested, jowls a-quiver. "I can't remain with only one horse! If an *Inspecteur des Postes* from Paris should come by…"

Careful not to glance towards the door, where Citolini lingered to observe the exchange, Tom laughed. "Oh, I'm sure he'd wonder how you come to be this short of horses just on Fair days," he said. "Have the roan saddled, Jouvet. This minute."

"But bless you!" cried the man. "You can't even leave — not without that fellow of yours!"

If curses could kill, Jouvet would have been on his way to Tartarus.

"What fellow?" called Citolini, striding back.

Tom took a deep breath. "He's not —"

Citolini wasn't to be deterred. "Never the glover, is it?"

And, there being nothing for it, Tom told him.

The Italian spread his hands in a great show of disbelief. "You have lost the Duke's glover?"

"I've done nothing of the sort!" protested Tom, a little too loud.

Citolini grabbed him by the arm, and drew him away from the Frenchmen. "So the Duke of Anjou sends a glover to the Queen of Navarre — and picks you to escort him, and you lose him in Amiens!" he hissed. "What do you think Mr. Secretary will say? Or Her Majesty, when this reaches her ear?"

Tom shook free of Citolini's grasp. "I haven't lost him! My man is finding him right now, and…" He stopped when a sideways glance revealed Skeres not finding anyone at all, but standing a few yards away, chewing a blade of straw and uselessly looking daggers at the Italian.

Citolini glanced in turn. "Finding him, where — under the straw?" He turned back to Tom, and shook his head in disgusted disbelief. "See what comes of entrusting you with the Duke's man because of the name you bear, because you were born English — while…!" *While I'm thrust aside to carry ordinary letters*, he didn't say — but there was no need, that being his eternal grievance, and now more than ever.

"Monsieur…" came shyly.

It amused Tom when both he and Citolini waved the interruption aside with identical gestures. Then the Italian shook his head — as one not crediting Tom's stupidity. "Two years under Mr. Secretary's tutelage — and…" he murmured — and if he was trying to suppress his glee at Tom's blunder, he quite failed.

And — indeed. Tom's heart sank.

"Monsieur Walsn'am!" came again, together with a tug at his sleeve.

"What is it?" Tom turned to find the stable boy shying at his elbow. Tom repeated the question in French, and softer.

"Is it the one with the yellow hat that you're looking for, Monsieur?" asked the lad.

"What!" Tom jumped, grabbing him by the arm. "You saw him? Where?"

The lad gaped in round-eyed perplexity. "But in the alley, Monsieur. Behind the stables," he said, jerking a thumb over his shoulder, as though only the dim-witted didn't know that the alley behind the stables was where one found waylaid Englishmen.

With an exclamation, and with Skeres following, Tom sprinted out of the door, across the courtyard, and around the post-station, into the narrow, ill-smelling alley — and sure enough, there he was: the glove-maker, flapping his cloak as he picked his fussy way through mud and churned straw on thin booted legs, looking for all the world like a flustered crane. He looked wet through and through.

"Litcott!" Tom roared with all the fury of relief. "Simon Litcott, where the devil have you been?"

The man startled satisfyingly, and squinted in the rain beneath the brim of his yellow hat. He opened his mouth to speak, closed it again, then drew a chest-puffing breath and called: "'Tis *Master* Litcott, if you please." And the rest he let go, with another blink.

Tom took a deep, deep breath. *Unus. Duo. Tres. Quattuor...*

"Do I trounce 'im for you, Master?" Skeres asked, around the bit of straw he was chewing.

"No, you don't," Tom said bitterly — lest Skeres take silence for assent — and then beckoned to the glove-maker. "Come on, Master Litcott."

The man hopped along the alley, stumbled, and bumped into Tom, who grabbed two handfuls of soggy cloak to steady him. Skeres, leave it to him, stepped out of the way before he was drenched in turn.

"Do you know how late it is? What were you doing out there?" Tom asked, shaking cold rain from his sleeves as they trotted back the way they'd come.

Litcott shrugged and blinked — he was always blinking, which was annoying, until one remembered all the stitches that went in a pair of gloves — and pointed a vague hand backwards. "Waiting," he said.

"Ay, waiting!" Skeres gave the man a rough poke in the ribs. "Waiting like 'e waited the other night in London, eh? So a fellow can't sit by the fire in peace, no — 'e 'as to trudge in the rain, and 'im *waiting* with a whore at the King's 'Ead…"

Another poke — and Litcott yelped and shoved back. Skeres didn't budge, and took a mulish air.

"Enough!" Tom stepped between the two. "What Master Litcott does at night is his own business — but —" he turned to regale the glove-maker with the kind of dispassionate glare Sir Francis might have used — "*but* by day he does as he is told — for his own safety, and for the Queen's Service." Both men, he was pleased to notice, muttered assent and looked away — though Skeres, perhaps, a little smugly.

"And now we leave." Tom pressed his hat on his head and strode for the stableyard, with Skeres at his elbow and Litcott, hopefully, behind. He resisted the temptation to check.

"Waiting my foot!" Skeres grumbled as they went. "Another whore, 'e 'ad, I tell you."

Which Tom rather doubted. The alley was narrow enough that the buildings on either side sheltered it from the worst of the rain — and yet the man was soaking wet. He must have been out in the heavy rain — and surely one didn't fornicate in broad daylight in the public street under the rain — not even in France? But never mind Litcott's pastimes — they were leaving, at last! With any luck tomorrow they'd be in Paris, and he could deliver the man into Ambassador Cobham's care. And be upbraided for being late, rather than for losing Monsieur's man — which was some manner of consolation.

Once back in the stables, Tom found that Jouvet was having a horse saddled under Citolini's directions. And not the ugly roan, either, but the grey.

"You have found the glover," said the Italian, as he handed his one bag to the stableboy — and was Tom imagining that he looked disappointed?

"Glove-maker," piped up Litcott from behind, and then he stopped short like one elbowed in the ribs — no matter how innocent Skeres looked.

Tom didn't bother to answer. Wasn't the cursed glover — glove-maker — there in the flesh to see?

Citolini didn't wait for an answer. "*Bene*," he said. "Now we can leave."

Taking command — which wasn't unreasonable, seeing just how well Tom had acquitted himself.

Still Tom made an attempt. "Go and have that wine and bread, while —"

The Italian met this with a disbelieving stare. "Have you not lost time enough?" he asked, and, again waiting for no answer, he took the reins and led his grey out in the rain.

Time enough, indeed. Tom crammed his hat as low on his forehead as it would go, and slipped on his gloves.

"Why can't we wait?" whined Litcott, sullenly worrying at the silver ring on his forefinger, one of those in the shape of two clasped hands. "See how hard it rains…"

Oh, very hard. Hard enough to drench a man to the bone, and to turn the road into a quagmire, and to make travelling a torment. "So it did yesterday, Master Litcott," Tom said. "And the day before."

He led his own mount out of the awning, a black mare that had looked lively inside, but flattened her ears in sullen displeasure the moment the first drops hit her — and small blame to her.

The stable boy was busy shoving the glover in the saddle, and Citolini was already mounted, looking down on the rest of the group like a dissatisfied Caesar.

Skeres, leading horse and packhorse, threw a black glare at the Italian. "'Oity-toity bugger!" he grumbled. "Why do you travel with an Italian courier?"

Why, indeed? "He is not…" Tom began, in what he hoped was a meaningfully low voice — and stopped, and shook his head. "He *is* Italian, but he rides for us. Ambassador Cobham's man." And he set foot to stirrup and mounted — in a show of finality meant to quell Skeres.

"Still a filthy Papist," grunted the lad, not quelled in the least, and loud enough to be heard over the pelting rain. Loud enough to earn a black look even from the peaceable Jeannot.

Oh Lord — were they all in league to make Tom's life a misery?

"Once and for all, Skeres," Tom growled, loose-mouthed servants being as good a target as any, "when you ride for the Service, you do and you say nothing that makes the locals want to put a blade in you!" After which he set spurs to the mare's flanks, and followed Citolini through the gate and out into the grey, muddy street.

Behind him Litcott gave a jangling, high-pitched laugh — and what he found so amusing, Heaven knew.

CHAPTER 2

Litcott and the black mare had not been wrong, in their own
way — for Jove Pluvius had no mercy to spare for those
trudging on the roads of Picardy, that day. The highway itself
would have been punishment enough for a whole life misspent
as, ill-kept and rutted, lined with nothing but the stumps of the
elms that should have sheltered it, it wound its miserable way
around the humps of hillock after muddy hillock.

It was no help that a stiff wind blew the pelting rain askew,
cold and insistent, and by the time they'd cleared the last of
Amiens, Tom felt as though he'd taken a plunge in the Thames
in his clothes. Hat and cloak, jerkin and doublet, hose and
gamashes — all clung to him, sodden and chill, in that way that
made a fellow despair of ever being dry and warm again.

He was used enough to it, having ridden this particular route
for two years in all manners of haste and weather. His charges
were not.

Aldgate-born and raised, Skeres must have travelled very
little in his life, and kept grumbling like a summer storm, partly
at himself for seeking adventure and gain abroad, partly at the
hard-necked packhorse he dragged — which, with that white
hind leg, anyone with an ounce of wit should have known for
an evil-minded beast — and partly at fine gentlemen who cared
naught for their underlings' comfort.

Litcott, perched unhappily atop his sturdy mount, his silly
hat soaked shapeless, kept regaling all and no one in particular
with the delights of travelling with some previous master.

"Never went about in foul weather, his Lordship did," the
fellow whined again and again, making Tom wonder why on

earth would anyone take a glove-maker on his travels — most of all this one. "And he would always say to me, his Lordship: good roads, good company, and good weather, Litcott — that's the way."

Now and then Litcott's litany would break in a choked yelp, when his horse stumbled yet again, and "All is well, Monsieur, all is well," would soothe Jeannot in his sing-song English — using a tone that, Tom suspected, would be equally used on skittish horses and dim-witted children.

Once Skeres drew up at Tom's side, packhorse in tow.

"Should have stayed at 'ome, that one!" the servant groused. "What was your uncle thinking, sending 'im about like this?"

"Cousin," Tom corrected. "My cousin — and it happens that he much agreed with you." Sir Francis's look of weary amusement as he told of the Duke's whim flashed through Tom's mind. "Had it been for Mr. Secretary, Master Litcott would be sitting safe and dry at home." He shut up when he caught a disapproving gaze from Citolini — who, of course, would never discuss his orders with a loose-mouthed servant.

Tom swallowed a sigh. They would never be friends, he and the Italian — but did they need the ill will? Why couldn't they discuss Ovid (for this son of a Venetian scholar was quite erudite) instead of each waiting for the other to blunder?

It was a most fleeting thought, dispelled into vexation when the Italian trotted by, aloof and resentful — as though Tom were to blame for all the ills in life.

In truth, though, no amount of Ovid could have made the travelling less tiresome, as the horses kept either stumbling in the muddy ruts, or slipping on some loose stone of the worn pavement — the supposedly evil-minded packhorse most of all. Again and again Skeres had to drag the brute ahead, as it stood quivering, crook sliding askew and eyes rolling, up to the fetlocks in the mire — to the music of Jeannot's advice, as voluble as it was pointless, and Litcott's shrilling over his truss, his truss, his truss...

And then came the cart — a largish, ox-drawn, covered waggon, Amiens-bound, loaded full, and black with water, whose churl of a driver had to dispute the use of the road's centre.

In all fairness, in the carter's place Tom would have wanted the paved centre too, bad as it was, rather than the strip of rutted and churned mud on either side, with its crumbling banks — a trap for heavy wheels if ever there was one.

But when Jeannot, being after all his uncle's nephew, managed to get the carter in a tiff, shouting with a Titan's vigour, red-faced and puffing, and as insolent as can be, Tom didn't like to back down — not with Citolini's disdainful eye on him.

"Tell the fellow to draw aside, Jeannot," he ordered in English — carefully not glancing at the Italian. "Enough that we can file by."

A greatly sensible notion, he thought, and one Sir Francis himself would have approved — no matter that the carter, lacking both philosophy and diplomacy, only yielded to it out of arithmetic, there being five of them to one of him. And all the same, French highways and human temper being what they were, it all ended with the cart down to the axle in a rut, and the packhorse's crook wrecked, and Litcott's truss strewn about half of Picardy — to much wailing, and fulminations in two languages.

Tom quashed the commotion as best he could, with no help whatsoever from Citolini, tipped the carter (and how was he going to put down that particular expense for the Ambassador?), and resigned himself to yet more delay.

It took some doing before they were able to trudge on, sodden and muddied and disgruntled, and carrying Litcott's bundles like a band of nomads.

By the time they reached the village of Dury, Tom was fit for the Bedlam. There was no changing horses there — still the accursed Fair — and Jeannot and the mounts were paid for to the next station anyway. In fact, Tom had not planned to stop in Dury at all — but now there was no helping it.

They had to wait while a cobbler looked at the crook's broken harness, and hummed and hawed a good deal before he pronounced it past mending, much to Jeannot's dismay. Thus another harness had to be procured, and the Postmaster of Dury, being no friend of Jouvet, set out to make matters difficult. He would not loan, nor hire, nor sell — and so it was that, well past noon, Tom waited alone in the musty parlour of the village's one inn, while Jeannot haggled for the hire of an old harness with the ostler.

He sat in a worn high-backed chair by the narrow fireplace, shivering hard — now let him not be coming down with an ague! — and grimly considered Jeannot's adamant protestations that the broken harness should be repaid to his uncle. Which wasn't unfair, Tom reckoned, bending down to warm his hands at the sputtering flames — but would Ambassador Cobham see that, or would the money have to come from Tom's own rather lean purse? He had been counting on this journey's fee to settle some little debts he had in Paris — if not the larger ones in London — but, at this rate, there would be precious little left. Would Father be generous, should worse come to worst? Would his brothers? On Guildford there was no counting, and Edmund, even with his fatter purse, and his inheritance forthcoming... Somehow, Tom rather doubted he'd help.

He was busy adding sums with half his mind — the other half contemplating the melancholy plight of younger sons — when the parlour's door opened, and Nick Skeres barged in.

"There's bread and meat," the lad announced, as he picked at his teeth with a fingernail. "Wine's as bad as they come. The picket one."

Tom swallowed the urge to say he wasn't hungry — and the wine was *piquette*. It wouldn't do to seem as though he were sulking. He nodded and rose — but not before Skeres saw his hesitation, and mistook it for something else.

"Ay, 'e's there too," he said, with a twist of his lips. "'Ow come the Ambassador keeps 'im? 'As 'e no Englishmen to do 'is running?"

Tom struggled a little, and fairness won. "He's very good at it," he said. "Trustworthy. Besides, I think he must be an English citizen, by now. He's been over many years."

Skeres clicked his tongue. "Foreign-born, foreign stays, I say. And Papist foreign's twice foreign."

"I doubt he's much of a Papist, seeing that he fled to England from the Inquisition…"

"Ay? Fled from where?" Skeres asked.

"Venice, I think."

"And Venice's Popish places!" was the lad's triumphant conclusion. "So, you want to eat or not?"

Ah, well. Tom gathered his wet cloak, hoping that it might dry faster by the bigger taproom fire, and preceded Skeres into the passage.

The servantman, though, wasn't done yet on the subject of the Italian. "Knows it 'imself," he explained. "Near forty and long in the Service, still 'as to bow down to pups 'alf 'is age, 'e says — all on account of 'im not being English-born."

Tom snorted. "Ay — he bows down about as well as the Tower, that one!" Not that he should, if one was to be fair — not to Tom, all of nineteen, and still green at the game — and not that either the Ambassador or Sir Francis ever showed that they expected him to. But Paolo Citolini liked to think he was ill used. Still, to complain to a servant...! "Has he been telling you?"

"No, that other fellow. Says 'e's travelled with — Oy!"

Tom stopped on the taproom's threshold, so abruptly that Skeres bumped into him. "What other fellow?"

The lad pointed with his chin. At a table by the fireplace, the Italian sat before the remains of his dinner, deep in conversation with another man. This one was busy demolishing a wedge of cheese, while Litcott sat a little apart, sulking to himself, turning and turning his ugly ring.

They all looked up when Tom approached.

"Are we ready?" Citolini asked, in that manner he had, at times even with Cobham, that made it hard to say whether he was taking orders or issuing them. It never failed to nettle Tom.

"No, we are not," he answered curtly.

Citolini raised an eyebrow, and sat back. That he looked a good deal warmer and dryer than Tom felt, might have been a further cause for irritation — but Tom was distracted by the Italian's new companion. Where had he met him? Because surely he had met him, this narrow ferret of a man, with the keen eyes set deep into bruised sockets, and the tense shoulders...

"You know Jack Dennis, Walsingham?" asked Citolini — and Tom remembered, if vaguely.

"Crossing to Rouen, was it?" Tom nodded, the minutest bow, as tendrils of memory snatched together. "The Merchant Strangers' post?"

The man nodded back with a thin, squinting smile. "About Michaelmas, last year," he said. "Good of you to remember — for all that I've no famous name, I."

Tom never knew too well what to answer to this sort of talk, for all that he'd heard enough of it through his two years in the Service. A good thing that Dennis pushed upright well before the hesitation became awkward.

"I was asking Mastro Paolo, here," he said, still chewing cheese. "May I travel on with you? You're bound for Paris, so am I — and I mistrust riding alone, these days."

Tom wondered a little at that, for in truth Picardy had never quite settled down after the war, but Dennis did not strike him as timid … unless perhaps he was carrying valuables?

Citolini leant forward, elbows on the table. "*I* have nothing against it, but it is for Walsingham to say."

Skeres snorted, and even Litcott looked up from his empty tankard.

Why, oh why couldn't the Italian have been half a day late, with all his playing at ill-deserved patience? And sharp Jack Dennis, too, who looked as though he hadn't missed the game, and was being greatly amused. It was a very good thing that Tom hadn't much against it, either — because refusing now, even to a man of the Merchant Strangers, would have seemed — no, would have *been* downright petty.

"Then join us," Tom said, striving for the little sideways nod Sir Francis had for matters of no great importance.

Dennis nodded back — and if he was minded to offer thanks, he never got to do it, because right at that moment the two guides bustled through the door — Jeannot and another of Jouvet's fellows — shaking rain from their cloaks, and stamping muddy boots in the straw.

"The harnais is old as Herod, Monsieur Walsn'am," Jeannot announced, "but ready we are."

Oh, thanks be! Tom slapped the man's shoulder with a laugh of relief. "It may be as old as all the world, if it serves," he said. "Let us go."

Litcott blinked and moaned, but rose with the others in a great flurry of cloaks and hats.

Tom threw his still wet cloak around his shoulders — and, once he'd settled the score with the innkeeper, followed the others out and across the inn's muddy courtyard, hunched like a hammer-less Vulcan against the rain.

Onwards, at last — and glory be!

Right after Dury, the hillocks grew a denser fleece of trees and shrubs — woods of sort, through which the highway thrust. It had been a pleasant, shady place in the summer, when Tom had travelled to Paris with Sir Francis on his diplomatic mission; November turned it in one more manner of misery. Bare trees, black with rain, loomed over the road. Growing roots and long neglect had undone edges and pavement, crumbling the stones in the mud. The horses misliked having to pick their way on and off the paved strip, shying and snorting at every splash, every creak, every gust of wind among the trees. It was unchancy going, and wearisome, and slow as Lent, and Skeres kept grumbling that they should have stayed at the inn. Once or twice Tom silenced him half-heartedly — not that the lad was wrong. Paris seemed a thousand miles away, and hardly an inch nearer than it had been from Dury. And by the way the sky darkened beyond the tangle of black branches, before long they'd be forced to put up for the night.

Tom was reckoning miles, and leagues and hours, and wondering what consolation was to be found in that Citolini was just as hampered as himself, when it happened.

They appeared out of the rain and the trees, as though from behind a curtain. Came in twos and threes, a few of them mounted, all grim and clamouring.

"*Arrêtez!*" they shouted. "*Arrêtez!*"

They wore big cloaks and big-brimmed, ragged hats. Brigands, one would think, until the dull gleam of morions hanging from the saddles gave the lie to that.

"*Soldats!*" cried Jeannot, reverting to French, and jerking his yellow horse to a halt. "Stop, stop, for God's sake!"

And if not all understood the words, there was no mistaking the quiver of unease, the stiffening of shoulders.

Tom drew up, letting the mare dance so he could look around as he reached for the rapier under his cloak. More of the rogue-like soldiers were spilling out of the trees from behind and from the left. Perhaps a score of them, a good half carrying pikes, and among them a blunderbuss or two. Perhaps on lawful business — more likely not.

Either way, Tom had known since his very first French trip that there was little point in resisting them. No point on earth, in fact — and possibly much danger. With a fleeting thought that Dennis had been both right and wrong, he left his rapier alone, and checked his party.

They'd all stopped, for a blessing, and drawn closer in a loose knot.

"King's soldiers," Tom said, in hushed urgency. "Do nothing foolish. Say nothing foolish." His eye fell on chin-jutting Skeres, and he amended: "Do nothing at all."

Citolini, Dennis and the guides needed no telling; Litcott inched closer to Tom, a nervous eye on the ring of hostile, rapacious-looking men. "Oh, thank the Lord!" he exclaimed, loud with relief.

Tom hissed him quiet — or tried.

"But I'd taken them for brigands," the glover insisted, louder still.

On the man's other side, Jack Dennis snorted quietly. "Ay, well, you weren't wrong."

Tom shushed them both, just as one of the soldiers on horseback detached himself from his pack. Indeed, there was no other word for them: wolf-like, they had closed around the English party, lean, and sharp, and grey with water. And their leader, as he rode a step in front, bared white teeth in a hungry grin. An officer of some sort, judging by his big-boned horse, and the bedraggled plumes on his hat.

"What business have you on the King's road?" he called, rough and hoarse.

"We are —" Tom began, and could have kicked himself for the way his voice cracked. It was no more than a heartbeat — but...

"We are couriers of Her Majesty, the Queen of England." Trust Citolini to step in, even-voiced and assured, kneeing his horse just one perfect step forward, so that he stood before the soldiers.

Not that they were impressed. The clang of eased swords chimed clear even in the pelting rain, and the officer cocked an eyebrow at the Italian, then at the rest.

"What, all of you?" he asked.

"Not I," Jack Dennis hastened to say. "I ride for the Merchant Strangers, not the English Queen."

The weasel — and he asking for the company of the Queen's men not an hour since.

"The two of us, though." Tom urged the black mare forward. "Bound for Paris, with servants and a guide."

The officer scowled, rain streaming down his beard. "Travel in force, do you?" he sneered, and held out a hand. "Passports."

Of course. Tom swallowed a groan — though the request was small surprise. Postmasters, provosts, soldiers, town officials — half of France had a right to inspect a traveller's passport, and pick fault if they pleased — and Tom had yet to meet a Frenchman who enjoyed a scrap of power and didn't use it. Yet, refusing was to borrow trouble. He reached under his cloak for the papers — not the English licence to travel, but the French courier's passport — just as Citolini and Dennis did the same, and again a few of the soldiers put hand to hilt, and pointed their pikes, and a blunderbuss was trained on Tom — though what they thought he'd do, he didn't know. He hesitated as he took out the passport, grimacing at the bare, dripping trees. No shelter to be had, and the papers would get soaked.

"Come, come!" With a curse, the Frenchman pushed his horse against Tom's mare, snatching the passport from his hand.

And that was when Nick Skeres decided it stood upon him to defend the honour of England. "Oy, you Papist lout!" the lad shouted, barging forward — and never mind Tom's hand raised in warning.

At a bark from their officer, three of the soldiers came forward, to seize Skeres roughly and drag him from the saddle, kicking and cursing.

"Stop! *Assez!*" Tom shouted. "Plague take you, Skeres — be quiet! And you, call off your men, Monsieur."

And he could have spoken Greek, for all Skeres or the Frenchman heeded him — but at least the soldiers stopped, though holding their prisoner down on his knees in the mud.

The officer turned an unpleasant look on Tom. "Your man, here, he assaulted the King's soldiers," he said.

Tom held the Frenchman's glare with one of his own. "Ay — after you assaulted a Queen's courier."

They glowered at each other until the officer nodded for his men to release Skeres — but he shoved Tom's passport in his sleeve.

Oh Lord! So now the next soul who took it into his head to ask for Tom's papers between here and Paris, could have him imprisoned for travelling without leave…

"The Queen's ambassador will have something to say to that," Tom retorted, kneeing the mare a step forward.

If you must make empty threats, make them as though they weren't, was one of Sir Francis's tenets. But no amount of cold glaring was going to serve with these brigands.

The Frenchman snorted — and small blame to him, for who was going to see justice exacted from these men, if they only refrained from killing?

A jerk of their officer's head was all it took: the soldiers closed in, hemming in the English party, shoving away the two guides at sword's point. Rough hands grabbed at Tom's reins — and not his alone. Citolini called in French, and there went Litcott, yowling that they leave alone his truss, slapping gamely — and stupidly — at the soldier who yanked on his stirrup.

Oh, devil take it! "Litcott, don't!" Tom called. "He'll only thrash you…"

And, taking his own good counsel, he dismounted before the Frenchmen dragged him down. He splashed ankle-deep in mud, right into the grabbing hands of a large, gap-toothed soldier. The fellow stank wet and unwashed as he shoved Tom against the black mare's flank, tearing at cloak and jerkin. A few steps away, Dennis swore in French with a fishwife's fluency, while a bemired and puffing Skeres tried to shake off three Frenchmen at once, most mastiff-like. Litcott alone was still in the saddle, hanging on to mane and pommel for dear life — while Citolini was on foot too, held by both arms before the officer, and...

Tom froze.

The officer had dismounted and, teeth bared and eyes cold, pointed the Italian's own thin, wicked stiletto at the man's throat.

"*Assez!*" Tom tore free of his captor long enough to reach inside his doublet. "We ride for your Duke of Anjou —!" That was as far as he went before the big soldier caught him, and slammed him to the ground.

He landed on his back on the muddy grass, winded more by the surprise than the fall, and tried to roll away from the startled mare's hooves. Alarm flashed on Citolini's face — another surprise — and there was a bellow of "Master!" from Skeres, cut short, as though by a blow.

If nothing else, the officer no longer had a blade at the Italian's throat. He loomed over Tom, instead, and jerked his chin at the gap-toothed soldier.

Not wolves — well trained wolf-hounds, these were... At the merest sign, the huge man bent to roughly tear open Tom's doublet, and ripped out the packets — one English, one French — together with Tom's purse.

The officer took them, and glowered at the Royal lilies on the French packet's seal. "What's this?" he barked.

Tom sat up, and would have stood, but rough hands held him back. "If you don't give a straw for my Ambassador, perhaps you will for your Duke — and for your King, who awaits those letters."

The man paused, face bunching in anger and doubt. One of his men leant close to whisper, too low for Tom to hear — but it was nothing the officer liked.

He scowled blacker. "Leave 'em be!" he ordered. He thrust Citolini's stiletto in his own belt, threw packets and purse at Tom, and stalked away to his horse.

The ring of glowering faces dissolved. A whorl of grey cloaks and calls, a splashing of cantering hooves, and the French hounds were gone — vanished in the woods.

The guides came back, calling on all the Saints, and reviling the soldiers for rogues and thieves... *Now* they found their courage!

"Lord a-mercy!" whined Litcott. "If these are soldiers, I don't want to know what thieves are like!" Alone of them all, he still perched on horseback.

Tom began in a huff of laughter, and ended shivering. He caught Jack Dennis's proffered hand, and let the man drag him to his feet, for all that... "Know the Queen's men again now, do you?" he sniped.

Dennis's thin, squinting smile was strained. "Much good it did me..." he said. "Still, I reckon you saved us all a beating — for all it could have come to you a tad sooner..."

"It should not have come to him at all! Bandying about his Royal packet..." groused Citolini, striding near to grip Tom's shoulder. "Are you well?"

There — that was Paolo Citolini for you: instead of thanks, a scolding! Teach him to save the fellow's hide. "Are you afraid Sir Francis will blame you if I'm not?" Tom shrugged off the Italian's hand, and stomped away in search of his mare. "Let us —"

He stopped short. The mare was well enough, shuddering and tossing her mane a few yards off the road, in the company of the shaken packhorse. Skeres, on the other hand, sat in the mud with his arms around his ribs, one eye swollen shut, blood on his face. All of it earned for trying to go to Tom's aid.

Tom bent to pat a bunched, sodden shoulder. "Did they knap your nose for you, Nick Skeres?"

The servantman waved him away. "Gave as good as I got," he slurred, before turning away to spit blood.

"I'm sure," Tom frowned. "Are you much hurt?"

Skeres squinted at him a moment, then snorted in disgust. "Bit me cursed tongue," he announced, and made a grab for Tom's wrist — missing it by inches. A second attempt he managed better, and tried to haul himself up. With a hiss of pain he fell back on his rear-side, nearly dragging Tom with him.

Jeannot came to help, and somehow managed to hoist Skeres to his feet, and then on the piebald horse, with much name-calling in two tongues.

Tom shook his head. They weren't going much farther that day.

It was Dennis's guide who picked the passports from the mud, all crumpled and soaked, but still folded. The officer hadn't had a glance to spare for the papers. At least he hadn't kept them, though much good they'd do now, with the writing all but washed out. Tom wished he could have mopped the mud from the paper — if only he had a dry stitch on him…

"Common thieves, that's what they are!" Litcott hunched in the saddle like a wet hen, mournfully blinking at his yellow hat, trampled to a rag in a puddle. "They tried to take my purse…"

"Mine, they took," Skeres announced glumly, echoed by Dennis.

"And my stiletto," said Citolini.

Apparently, only so much protection extended beyond the bearer of the Royal seal. "Let's count our blessings," Tom said, as he hauled his mire-covered self in the saddle. "It could have been much worse. Jeannot, what's the next place, Halcourt?"

"What if it is?" Citolini came to stand at Tom's stirrup, and made a great show of not quite lowering his voice. "You never want to stop, do you? We have gone ... what? Two leagues all day? Three?"

"Devil seize you — can't you see?" Tom snapped, bending to whisper angrily in the Italian's face. "It's growing dark, we're all soaked to the marrow, and my man's fit to fall off the saddle! You go ahead if you like. The first inn I find, I'm stopping." And with a savage tug at the reins, he wheeled the none-too-pleased mare back on the road and trotted away, without checking who followed.

Surely, *surely* it couldn't get any worse.

CHAPTER 3

Could it not get worse — indeed? One should never tempt the fates — not even in thought.

Once in Halcourt, the inn of the Trois Poissons was packed to the eaves — Lord smite all fairs and fair-goers! And Tom had long outgrown all those glib travellers' accounts of snug, clean French inns where the landlord's pretty daughter met the guests with a kiss, but he still could have done without the bony inn-keeper with her voice high in her nose, who kept throwing up her hands and wondering loudly how on earth and heaven was she going to accommodate seven men... For Citolini, much against Tom's hopes, had not ridden ahead after all, and nor had Jack Dennis, while the two guides, who would have ridden back to Amiens, had to be coaxed, bullied, and bribed into staying.

And still, "*Mais voyons,*" the hostess shrilled, twisting her apron in her hands, "where should I put you all?"

Tom would have thought the woman's cries a ploy to squeeze the last sol out of them — but perhaps she'd truly had her fill of travellers for the day, or else she misliked their battered looks. Whatever the reason, nothing they said seemed to move her.

In fairness, a number of men crowded the tables in the sooty, ill-lit common room, some locals and some not, by the look of them, nursing pots of wine, and watching the landlady shake her head at the bedraggled Englishmen.

And so, Halcourt being so puny a place that the Trois Poissons was its one inn, and even the piddling post-station, where the horses had been grudgingly stabled, had no beds...

"Ah, curse it." Tom pinched the bridge of his nose. "So you'll have it your way, Citolini. We ride ahead."

From the fireplace where he'd retreated to hunch and sulk, Litcott exclaimed in dismay, and poor Skeres squinted through his one good eye. Even the Italian grimaced, less than happy to have his way after all.

Tom was asking Jeannot how far to the next village, when an English voice spoke up.

"Come, come, Madame Mirault! My room will take a few more."

They all looked to see a Hercules of a man rise from a nearby table and saunter close.

The hostess gestured at the group. "But all of them, Monsieur?"

The man shrugged broad shoulders. "Those who won't fit can share the hayloft with my man," he said.

The landlady threw her hands to the heavens once more, griping that all Englishmen were in league to take advantage of a poor widow, and stalked off, beckoning that they follow. Tom could have embraced her in his relief. He stopped to thank their benefactor, and the man, a huge, red-faced fellow, twice as big as Tom in his padded jerkin, said it would be a sad day when an Englishman failed to assist another in such a heathen place.

"Ralph Garrard," he offered, holding out a hand like a spade.

"Thomas Walsingham," Tom said, and waited for the raised eyebrow, the jest, the question… But the man's gaze remained steady, brown eyes round and earnest in a bloated face.

They shook hands, and then, "*Allez, Monsieur, Allez!*" called Madame Mirault from the staircase, clucking like a poultry-wife shepherding chickens — and Tom hastened to follow.

Garrard's room, it turned out, was not Garrard's alone. It was large enough, damp as the Sirens' lair, and men occupied it two or three to a bed. Tom counted at least three yellow-haired foreigners — Flemings by the sound of them — and one chubby, timid fellow.

From under one of the beds, a maid was dragging out a pallet when they entered — a plump, black-haired young woman, who threw a saucy smile at the newcomers when the widow shooed her from the room.

Tom ended up sharing a mouldy straw mattress on the pallet with Citolini. There was some scuffle over who would be their third companion. Tom would have greatly preferred to keep Litcott where he could see him — but the glover had a good deal to say of the stinking room, the lice, the Fleming roommates... Until Dennis sat on the corner of the pallet.

"I don't travel with lords — I'm not particular," he said, with cheerful malice. "Those used to high company can have the hay."

When Litcott gasped in outrage, Tom counted in Latin, and mustered patience. "It's either this or the hayloft, Master Litcott," he explained. "Your choice."

The glover looked none too pleased. "On my Lord's travels," he sniffed, turning and turning his ring, "we never slept but in the best inns, and we were made welcome in the great houses."

Which might well be true, but it didn't mean that my Lord's glove-maker hadn't slept in a hayloft before — so Tom paid no mind when Litcott, grumbling that the hay would be warmer and cleaner, stomped off to share the loft with Skeres, the guides, and whoever else would be there — nor when Dennis laughed in triumph and stretched on his portion of the pallet.

Instead, Tom paid the widow to provide some salve for Skeres's bruises and black eye. More money that he wouldn't see again — but then, the lad was short a purse for coming to Tom's aid — or trying…

On hearing this, Skeres sucked his teeth and nodded slowly as he considered Tom. "I'd manage some more miles, if *you* want to ride on," he said gruffly.

Ay — now that they had a roof over their heads… Still, as likely as not, it was the most Tom would get in the way of thanks. So he nodded, dismissed the fellow, and went to claim his third of the pallet. It was where servants would sleep as a rule — musty, creaky, and exposed to all sort of draughts — but, once he'd sunk to sit on it with his back against the wall, idly undoing the buckles of his tall gamashes, Tom thought he'd never rise again. Even the prospect of supper in the common room seemed hardly lure enough. Now, if only someone would help him out of his sodden buskins… Skeres — but Skeres was off somewhere. Could it be hoped he would at least come back to sponge the mud from Tom's cloak…?

He wanted to laugh at himself — so spent for trotting half-a-dozen miles in a whole day! What would Sir Francis think? Then again, Sir Francis hadn't had to ferret out Simon Litcott first thing in the morning, and argue with Jouvet of the Amiens Post — and that even before Citolini turned up… Nor had Sir Francis crept along the most wretched highway in Christendom under the rain, with a glover's lamentations in his ear, until the guide had fought with a cart-man … oh, and the cursed harness, and the hours squandered in Dury, and Citolini's smugness, and then the soldiers holding them up — there being no other word for it — and spoiling them, and beating Skeres, and tearing Tom's second best travelling doublet —

Tom jolted upright.

Tearing his doublet — and he'd never once thought of checking... He clawed frantic fingers at the lining of his doublet, near the hem, a little on the right.

Across the pallet, Citolini looked up sharply from the jerkin he was brushing. "What is it?"

Tom didn't answer. The lining was torn — and empty.

Citolini narrowed his eyes. "You never... What were you carrying?"

"Sir Francis —" Tom clamped his mouth shut. It was no business of the Italian — nor was it a great secret that Mr. Secretary liked to entrust his young kinsman with any private correspondence between himself and Ambassador Cobham.

"*Diavolo!*" cursed Citolini, a flash of rancorous satisfaction clear as day in the black eyes. "See? See what comes of wagging your tongue — and that packet of yours!"

Anger boiled inside Tom. "Don't be a fool!" he snapped, too angry for caution. "That was *after* that lout manhandled me." *Or was it?*

"But are you certain?" The Italian frowned in doubt, as though he had any right to question.

"And whenever it was, it saved your —!" Tom stopped short when Citolini's eyes darted in warning at something across the room.

Tom looked over his shoulder. Jack Dennis stood leaning against the doorjamb, squint-eyed and amused.

"Don't mind me, go ahead." He waved a hand. "I never tire of watching how you Queen's fellows work."

Small wonder no one liked the Merchant Strangers' Post! Tom glared at the man, and was sure Citolini was doing the same. Dennis stretched his lips and sniffed, before he pushed himself off the door and sauntered away.

"*Diavolo!*" muttered Citolini again, just as the three straw-haired Flemish merchants stumbled through the door, laughing and jostling each other, ruddy-cheeked with Madame Mirault's claret.

Outside, Jove Pluvius still poured his hissing displeasure on Picardy — and small blame to him.

The widow's claret proved indifferent, but the rabbit stew was, if nothing else, hot and plentiful. Like everything else in the Trois Poissons' common room, it smelt and tasted like soot and woodsmoke. Litcott was nowhere to be seen, and Skeres, when questioned, gave a sullen shrug. Had the glover taken in snuff yet again, or had he found himself a woman? Too tired, and too miserable, to care much, Tom ate distractedly, and felt he had to invite Ralph Garrard to share a flagon of wine for his assistance.

He was soon glad that he had. The man — well clad in fine broadcloth — had a ready, barking laugh and a cheerful manner, and it was a welcome change from Citolini's purse-lipped grimness, and Tom's own grimmer thoughts, to be discussing the many miseries of travel. Being on his way from Paris — bound for Amiens first, he said, and then back home to Dover — Garrard was more than ready to commiserate on the state of the roads. He listened with his fixed, intent stare, chewing his upper lip as Tom told the tale of their brush with the soldiers.

"Packs of bandits, that's what they are," was the merchant's comment. "It happens all the time, and not a soul will lift a finger about it. First time it happened to me, I went to the Prévôts in Paris. They laughed in my face."

Tom shook his head in sympathy, but was not overly surprised. "Oh, I'm sure they let them loose on foreign travellers, these days," he said — trying to copy Sir Francis's wry tone. "With the war over, soldiers must live somehow."

Garrard's laugh rang fiercely loud in the sooty room. "Still," he said, reaching to pour himself more piquette, "count yourselves lucky. I had a guide, once, who took objection. There was a pond nearby, and would you believe it? They up and threw him in. Poor fellow nearly drowned."

Tom had loosened enough, by then, to remember an oft-heard story, and he turned to Citolini, who sat across the table, cross-armed and frowning. "Didn't they dunk you too, once?" he asked, and then he turned to Garrard. "Master Citolini swims like a fish, though, and..." And why the Italian must take it in bad part, Tom didn't know — but he rose stiffly, and bid a stiffer goodnight, and stalked away like one grievously offended.

Only by a whisker Tom caught himself short of shrugging in answer to Garrard's raised eyebrow — because truly, squabbling before a stranger! He schooled his expression to blandness instead, and drained the last of his wine. It tasted sour and watery, and his briefly lifted spirit fell again, under the weight of all the day's mischances.

Afterwards, with no better consolation than the assurance that Litcott, at least, was accounted for, and sulking in the hayloft above the stables, Tom trudged wearily up the stairs.

He stopped when he reached the gallery, propping his elbows on the banister to watch the common room downstairs. The Flemings had gone back there, drinking and laughing in a pool of candlelight, like three straw-haired satyrs painted in gold. Good company to each other, by the look of them, and with no cares in this world. Then again, they were unlikely to have lost their powerful cousin's letter — one that

51

could make or unmake the ties of kingdoms — all through their own careless stupidity…

"My, my — but you look full of megrims, Monsieur!"

Tom startled, and turned to find someone at his elbow. A young woman — the black-haired maid he'd seen earlier, stood there, watching him in frowning sympathy. She carried a sputtering rushlight. "Thinking of your sweetheart back at home, are you?" she asked in a soft, purring voice.

Tom couldn't help a small huff. "Oh, I wish it were that simple — or that pretty!"

The woman clicked her tongue. "*Pauvre garçon!*" she murmured, and drew closer to touch his arm. In the rushlight's dim glow, her round-cheeked face was the colour of cream. "Do tell all to Luchette!"

And for a heartbeat, Tom wanted nothing better. He wanted to pour his woes into the ears of this kindly creature with the smiling eyes… Until the thought of Sir Francis occurred — one eyebrow raised at the notion of his kinsman, his courier, the Queen's courier, unburdening his heart to a French tavern nymph.

Tom failed to swallow a huff of laughter, and ran a hand down his face. Oh Lord — Citolini was right about him. A simpleton — that's what he was!

The woman — Luchette — clicked her tongue again. "Or else tell nothing — not a word," she said, taking his hand and tugging.

Tom held fast. "No, I…"

Luchette smiled, and tugged again. Cooing under her breath, she led him along the gallery.

"Truly, I should…" Tom tried, casting a look towards the door to his shared room as they went past — his heart not quite in it.

Luchette smiled again, and continued along the gallery, where it looked on the narrow inner yard. The flame of her rushlight flickered in a gust of rain-laden air, spitting greasy smoke. They went past the blackness of another stairwell, and then Luchette let them into a small, airless room. Shelves and cupboards lined the walls, crammed with white bundles. There was a small table with an array of wax-encrusted candlesticks, and on the floor lay a pile of what looked like sacking — and there the woman made them both sit. She undid the linen cloth that bound her head, shaking her hair loose in a gleaming black fall — and she smiled, and reached out to touch Tom's cheek.

"*Mais vous êtes fort joli,*" she whispered in a singsong voice, barely louder than the hiss of the rain on the roof.

Tom slid an arm around her waist and drew her close. She smelt of lye, and milk — and a little of soot, and her smile was saucy again. He smiled back. Oh, plague take it, there were ways of lightening one's heart — without telling a word…

In this world, Tom's mother always said, contentment was a short-lived thing.

Tom rather agreed with her, when he slipped back into the shared room in utter dark. He groped his way to his side of the pallet, and lowered himself on the corner the others had left for him. He was stiff and tired, all the warmth of his little interlude gone — and, had he been asked later, he would have said he hadn't slept a wink all night.

He lay in the dark, bone-tired and cold against the damp wall, shivering in the draught, listening to the rain outside, and to the Flemings snoring in concert — or were that Garrard and his fidgety bedfellow? Bone-tired — and yet, whenever he began to drift, questions started to dance a pavane in his mind, asking themselves in Sir Francis's even, cut-glass voice.

Item: Was the letter lying trampled in the mire in the forest of Dury, or in the hand of those wolfish soldiers?

Item: If the latter, would they have English enough to read it? Possibly not — but then...

Item: Even if they hadn't, would they scent a chance for money in selling it?

Item: If so, to whom?

Item: What were the chances of the letter reaching the hands of someone who'd know what to do with it?

Item: Should worse come to worst, how much damage could they inflict...?

Tom half-awoke at a creak of wood. Was it steps on the floor — someone coming in or going out? He couldn't tell in the dark, and the haze of fatigue.

And then another voice joined Sir Francis's ghostly questioning — voluble, impatient, soft with an accent.

Item: Had Tom truly waved about Monsieur's packet only after that French boor began to search him?

Item: Had Tom, by his outburst, piqued the interest of the soldiers?

Item: Should Tom, the next time a rogue threatened to slit Citolini's throat, step back and allow it?

Item: How could Tom have failed to check for the letter right away? Because he was a fool — but then...

Item: Even if he had, and found it missing, what could he have done?

Item: Was any consolation to be found in the officer's utter disregard for their passports? Surely, if he hadn't spared a glance for those, he'd have little time for letters in foreign tongues?

Item: Could it be hoped that the soldiers had been only intent on spoil and plunder — and the taking of the letter was a stroke of chance?

Item: Had Tom's stupidity exposed and wrecked Sir Francis's work of years?

CHAPTER 4

"Master! Oy, Master!"

Tom awoke to leaden morning light, an aching neck, and Nick Skeres's bruised and swollen face, hovering over him. So he must have slept, after all...

Turning to lie on his back, he groaned, and ground both fists in his eyes. "What do you want, Skeres?" he asked around a yawn.

The lad sat back on his heels. "It's Litcott, Master."

Lord give him patience! Tom propped himself on an elbow to glare at the servantman. "If you've lost him again, I swear..."

Skeres's thick features twisted to glum solemnity. "Lost 'im? No," he said. "I've found 'im. Found 'im dead."

At least it wasn't raining anymore... And that was all that Tom could bring himself to think for quite a long time, as he watched poor Simon Litcott, huddled face down in the mud against the low wall, across from the kitchen door — one hand outstretched, mouth open, the one visible eye vacant and bulging.

He seemed to gape like a dying carp in the yellow flicker of the stableboy's tallow candle. Tom shivered and looked away.

It did not help that, at his elbow, the Veuve Mirault kept whingeing that she was ruined, Monsieur, ruined — and would she'd never taken them in at all, and she'd known it too, felt it in her bones, and look what came of giving charity to foreigners...

Tom didn't bother to answer.

"We should…" he murmured instead, and stopped, not quite knowing what they should do. Perhaps send for … for whom, in fact? Who would deal with murder out here? In Paris one would send to the Châtelet — but in Picardy…? Picardy was, for the most part, a place you passed through as quickly as you could. "We should see what killed him…"

At his side, Citolini nodded, looking as grim as Tom felt — and, for a wonder, not a whit more certain.

Ah, well. Tom beckoned to Skeres, who stood back a few steps, scowling as though the glover had died just to bother him. "Let's turn him, poor fellow."

When Skeres ambled close in no great haste, Tom joined him. Not that it took two men to shift a body — much less that of crane-like Litcott — but it was one of Sir Francis's maxims that men were best led by example. So Tom crouched down with only the smallest shiver — one he could perfectly well blame on the grey, chilly dawn — grasped a handful of drenched sleeve, and hauled.

The body flopped on its back like a sack of flour, limbs sprawling, head lolling aside to show a cheek and brow caked with reddish mud.

Tom blinked at the stench of stale urine, and blood, and wet wool. Somehow, like a fool, he'd half hoped that Litcott could not be dead after all. But there was no doubting, nor wondering how he'd died — not with the man's unlaced doublet showing a shirt drenched with blood, and more of it in the puddle around the body.

A sharp intake of breath, and a mutter of "*Dannazione!*" came from behind, and Tom looked up in irritation at the Italian's white face. What did the man have to whine about? Surely he was not breathless with grief over the glover? "Don't fret," Tom snapped, uncharitable as it sounded to his own ears. "It's me they'll blame for this — and with good reason. I should never have let him out of my —" and there he stopped short. Citolini wasn't listening to him, not even staring at the corpse. He followed the man's gaze, and… "Light, Skeres!" he ordered.

The lad bent down, holding a rushlight — surely snatched from the stableboy. He swung it about like Hermes's torch.

"Keep it steady!" Bracing himself on Skeres's knee, Tom reached across the body — so intent on not touching it again, he almost went sprawling. But there was something against the wall, where the man had been lying. Something reddish, a glint of steel…

Hissing in disgust, he picked the thing from the cold, stinking mud, and pushed himself back to crouch on his heels.

Citolini made to take the object, but Tom moved it out of reach. Well worn, reddish wood, carved in elegant curves, like three knots atop each other. A narrow crossguard. Two inches of broken blade…

"Cuds-me!" Nick Skeres exclaimed, far too loud in the close courtyard. "That's —" He yelped when Tom elbowed him quiet, and lost his balance, and went down on his backside, dropping the rushlight in the mud. "Oy, what was that for?" he grumbled, as he picked himself up, slapping the rear of his breeches.

Tom didn't answer. He looked from the broken hilt to Litcott's blood-stained chest, and from there to Citolini, grey-faced in the growing light, as he gaped at the broken hilt of his own Venetian dagger.

"Those rogues had this…" the Italian whispered.

Tom shook his head. "Ay — but why would they…?"

Citolini held out his hand again to take the hilt.

Restraining from wiping his fingers on his breeches, Tom made himself look at Litcott again. It was nearly full daylight by then, as much of it as they were going to have under the clouds — and by it the body's throat showed bruises. Would one stab a man *and* strangle him?

Tom reached to tug aside Litcott's open collar — and right then a voice called out in French: "You, there! What the devil are you doing?"

Across the yard, a man stood by the kitchen door — fierce-eyed above a ruddy, bearded face, with big shoulders and an enormous pair of boots. Luchette, a kerchief tied over her loose hair, was half squeezing between the man and the doorjamb to point to them.

And of course, as these things will go in Picardy as in England, they'd gathered a crowd by then. The stableboy, the young woman, one of the Flemings, Jeannot and the other guide, Dennis, and Garrard's chubby bed-fellow, and a few more Tom didn't know … all a-quiver with the novelty of a killed man lying in the mud.

Tom rose as the newcomer strode across the yard, raising fans of muddy water with each step. He was grizzled, seen closer, and big-boned, wearing a faded leathern jack, a plain two-handed tuck banging against his thigh, and an old soldier's casual belligerence. And while rather better groomed than their friends from the forest…

"Oh, not another one!" Tom muttered between his teeth — and he heard Citolini swear under his breath.

"What's this, Madame Mirault?" the man asked of the innkeeper for all greeting, and the widow launched herself into a nose-voiced recital of the many ills the Englishmen had brought down on her head and house…

And on the Englishmen the soldier turned a baleful glare. "*Anglais?*" he barked.

Only it seemed to Tom that, before being barked at, he'd ask at least one question of his own. So he took a step forward and, before Citolini did, he demanded, "Who asks?" — and was passably pleased with the way it turned out.

The man grunted in some acknowledgement, straightening his jack to show two liveries. One was the King's crowned H. The other Tom didn't know. "Regnauld Burry," he said. "Maître d'Archers — on behalf of the Prévôt des Maréchaux de Picardie."

So the Maréchaussée was here, after all — sent for, one could only imagine, by Madame Mirault.

Ah, well. Tom introduced himself and his companions. "Couriers of Her Majesty, the Queen of England. Travelling to join the English Ambassador in Paris," he concluded, trying to look and sound as though that settled most things.

To see Burry twist his mouth, one wouldn't think he much liked foreign couriers — or was it just the English? "What, all of you?" he asked, so much like that ragged officer in the forest that Tom had to clamp down hard on a burst of laughter. Mad, that's what he'd end up...

Before he (or Citolini, for that matter) could think of anything sane to say, Madame Mirault gave vent again, pointing at Jack Dennis and then in turn at the guides, who were not, mind you, English, but with the English had come — clearly no great merit.

Tipping back his big-brimmed felt hat, Maître Burry threw a glance at Jack Dennis who, perhaps not liking to be discussed in absentia, was ambling closer. The archer looked very much like a housewife who'd found a nest of mice in her clothespress.

"*Anglais?*" he asked again, with the same brisk disgust he'd had for them.

"Not a Queen's courier, though. The Merchant Strangers' Post," Tom supplied, wondering if the Prévôt's man would know what that was.

That he asked for no explanation, did not mean he did, not of a necessity. "I want a look at your papers," he said, of course, and then crossing his arms, he turned to give poor Litcott a good look. "Now, what about this one?"

Tom took a deep breath — mostly to see whether Citolini would step in, but of course, he didn't. Why should he? Tom had said so himself: the glover's death was his own trouble. His to explain, if he could. His to sink under if he could not. He might as well try with Maître Burry, man of the Prévôt des Maréchaux, to begin with.

"Simon Litcott, of London. A glove-maker," he said.

One of Burry's grizzled eyebrows went up in question.

"Travelling to Paris under my care, and then to Navarre — and yes, I've papers to prove it."

The other eyebrow reached its fellow — and, with a sceptical grunt, Burry bent double, hands on knees, tuck thrust aside, to observe the corpse closely. He reached out to touch the shirt, where the stain had turned the colour of rust at the edges. There was a tear in the centre.

The hushed chatter had all but stopped — though one Flemish voice could be heard grousing across the yard. Tom, Citolini, Skeres, the widow and now Jack Dennis all crowded around as Burry took his time humming and inspecting and tugging at his beard.

When at last he braced himself upright, he looked pleased. "Well, Monsieur … Wals'nam, is it? There is a blade inside your man."

Tom didn't bother to correct him — he'd yet to meet the Frenchman who could wrap his tongue around his name — but he had to wonder what there was to make the man happy.

"Murder, that's what I call it. Murder in a private dwelling — no matter for the Prévôt des Maréchaux."

They all began at once — the widow calling to all the saints, Tom wanting to know whose matter was it then, Skeres asking what had the cocklorel said, and the stableboy running up to tug at his mistress's sleeve...

Because someone else was entering the yard of the Trois Poissons by the carriage gate — and quite an entrance it was. The little crowd parted for the smallish, flabby, curly-headed, curly-bearded man on horseback, clearly some deity in the local Pantheon, in spite of the mud-spatters on a dark cloak and a velvet beret worn slightly askew. It helped, of course, that he had at each elbow a City sergent in corselet and plumed hat.

Maître Burry nodded his chin at this small Jupiter. "That's the one you want," he said. And then, raising his voice in salutation: "Monsieur l'Échevin."

There now! Tom threw an unfriendly glare at the innkeeper. Madame Mirault, it seemed, had gone all the way when it came to summoning the authorities.

"Maître Burry." Monsieur l'Échevin traded stiff nods with the archer, dismounted, and only advanced as far as the middle of the courtyard with his escort in tow. Burry made no move to meet him halfway — oh no: he just pushed back his hat a little, rocked back on his heels, and waited.

Oh, curse it! Two mastiffs with a bone... Now they'd never see the last of Halcourt!

"Who's that?" asked Nick Skeres at Tom's elbow, in what perhaps the lad fondly thought was a whisper.

"A magistrate of sorts," Tom murmured. "Mayor's Man."

Skeres looked from one Frenchman to the other the way he would size the beasts at the bear-baiting. "And who's the bigger dog?"

Tom and Citolini huffed in unison. If only if were that simple!

But lest the two Frenchmen thought he'd wait while they out-officed each other, Tom took a step away from Burry — who had yet to budge — and called out to the échevin across the yard.

Jupiter the Small fumed through a sketchy introduction, and named himself, as Guillaume de Briet, Échevin of the City of Amiens, in a whitish, droning voice that would, no doubt, make him a nightmare at council meetings…

"One of my party was slain, Monsieur," Tom called, just a little louder for the benefit of what, by then, looked like half the village gathered. "An Englishman. I — and with me Ambassador Cobham on behalf of Her Majesty the Queen, expect the City's justice to —"

That's how far he went before, blushing the colour of summer plums, de Briet waved him quiet and stomped across, his sergents clanging on his heels.

Behind Tom, Maître Burry grunted — small and amused it sounded, though Tom resisted the urge to make sure. Perhaps Sir Francis would have been amused too — and approving of the small manoeuvre?

"Monsieur —"

"Tut, man!" De Briet silenced him again. "Slain, you say? Here in the inn?"

Tom pointed at Litcott, lying in the mud.

"And he was lodging here? At the Trois Poissons?"

"We all were, this night past," Tom said — and, of course, that set Madame Mirault off with the litany of her woes again.

De Briet ignored her altogether, and instead beamed at Tom. "Ah well, then," he said, spreading his plump hands in all benevolence. "I am much afraid there's nothing that the City can do."

"Why, Monsieur l'Échevin!" Burry took a step towards De Briet, pushing his hilt forward like a Capitano in an Italian play. "Wilful murder in a private dwelling, this is right up your alley."

De Briet, a full head smaller, took a step back — and it was a wonder that he didn't crash into the sergents. "But no, Maître Burry!" He clicked his tongue, shaking a pudgy forefinger. "A roadside inn is most certainly no private dwelling. Certainly it makes this a grave crime committed on the road — and therefore…" He forged on over Burry's snort. "And therefore under the jurisdiction of the Maréchaussée."

Burry shook his head. "Road's the road. Village's the village — and one under Amiens —"

"But out of City bounds… Most definitely not ours."

"If it's not yours, perhaps it's the Bailli's. These ones…" Burry jerked his head towards the English party. "They carry Royal letters." He turned abruptly to Tom. "Don't you?"

Tom swallowed his first answer. He felt Citolini's burning glare — but the Italian might have spared himself the trouble. After the disaster in the forest and the loss of his letter, Tom had no great desire to discuss what he carried. "What we carry is no concern of —" he began, and might have been speaking to the cobbles underfoot, for all the good it did.

Burry gave a told-you-so sort of grunt. "A Royal case, for sure."

"Well…" De Briet hummed, with all the looks of liking the notion. "There's some merit to that — although foreigners' misdeeds are still a matter for the Maréchaux…"

Tom had a sense, most unpleasant, that the matter was slipping through his fingers. "We did no misdeed!" he exclaimed. "Why, it was done to us!"

They both turned to consider him, Burry sucking his teeth, de Briet tugging at his curly beard. No, not Jupiter — a faun, a satyr...

"Ah, but — for all we know," de Briet murmured, running small, porcine eyes from Englishman to Englishman, "it could well have been any of you."

Tom gaped. "What? No! Of course not! How would we —?" And the rest he bit off — because what would it look like to these ones, Citolini's dagger inside the dead man, even though...? At Tom's elbow, the Italian shifted. It was easy to imagine white knuckles gripping a worn, red hilt. "Why would we kill him?" Tom concluded, and it sounded quite, quite lame to his own ears.

"Ah..." Burry shrugged as one wondering, why did one kill his fellow man? "But then, come to that, why would anyone in Halcourt?"

"Well, there's always the soldiers!"

Of course. Tom had as good as forgotten Jack Dennis, but the man had been there all the time, without a word to say until now — and, of course, it had to be *this*.

"What soldiers?" asked de Briet, who already seemed to like this better than Burry did.

Jack Dennis gave that twitchy, cock-headed shrug of his. "A score of them or so. Held us up yesterday, not far out of Dury. And, seeing as you are here, I'm telling you: they filched my purse, the lousy priggers..."

Burry turned to Tom, for all the world like a master displeased with a lacking pupil. "Held you up?" he asked.

Tom sighed and explained the soldiers' ambush in the woods.

"Adventurers, more like," said Burry. "Disbanded soldiers — but they keep together, rob travellers... *Et bien*, you've seen it."

"And these ones have brought them to my door!" wailed the innkeeper, twisting her hands.

"We don't know that, Madame Mirault," Burry snapped. "For all we know..."

"And yet it's quite likely, I think?" de Briet was bouncing on his toes. "And whether it was soldiers or adventurers, Maître Burry..."

"Yes — yes, it is a headache for the Prévôt!" Burry threw up his hands in disgust. "You can go back to Amiens, Monsieur l'Échevin. The Englishmen are all mine." And, with the bitterest of grunts, he spun around and stomped to where poor Litcott lay — only sparing the time to shove Citolini out of his way.

As de Briet took off, sergents and all, with every sign of relief at having foisted this particular trouble on someone else, and Madame Mirault grudgingly sent the crowd on their way, Tom thought he'd see what Maître Burry was up to. He'd need to talk with Citolini, at some time — but not where the archer — or Jack Dennis, for that matter — could hear.

So he would have passed by his travelling companions with no more than a nod, but Skeres, of course, was undeterred, and caught him by the sleeve.

"I'd 'ave wagered you the soldier one'd win out," the lad said, nodding wisely towards the crouching Burry's back.

Tom had to huff in laughter. "I very much doubt that's how he sees it."

"Still." Skeres shrugged. "Better him than the other weasel, eh?"

Of this, too, Tom had his doubts. Sir Francis had schooled him, if in passing, on provincial courts, describing City magistrates as a very slow pain, and the Maréchaussée as a roughshod nuisance — both best avoided as far as a man could. Now if this particular Maître des Archers took it into his head to blame one of their party... A first thought of yet more delay was swallowed by another, much worse, one: not only had Tom lost Mr. Secretary's letter — but now Monsieur's glover had been murdered under his nose. All it lacked now was for him or Citolini to end up in Amiens gaol — although perhaps that would be easier than having to explain...

Tom shook his head hard, and went to join the archer. *There's seldom undoing disaster once it's occurred,* Sir Francis liked to say. *Thus, rather than gnaw on it, apply yourself to preventing worse.*

Let him apply himself, then. "Maître Burry, what have you found there?"

It was no great surprise when the man grunted in answer. Tom had once known a Scot like that, who could converse at length, if not at large, with nothing but a variety of grunts. This one, for instance, was a considering grunt, as Burry poked at poor Litcott.

"Not been dead long. See how he's gone stiff at the neck and jaw — but..." Burry raised Litcott's wrist, and dropped it. It flopped on the cobbled mud. "See? A few hours, I'd say. Who found him?"

"My servantman..." Tom started to say — and stopped short. Had he really? "I think."

"You think?" Burry never looked up from the body. He was lifting the bloodstained shirt, bunching it away from the wound, which looked small, jagged, and black. "Cannions unlaced, see?" He pointed, sniffing. "Maybe he came out for a piss…"

Tom's stomach churned a little — and to cover it, he turned to where the others stood in a small gaggle. Jeannot had joined them, and was talking low and earnest with Citolini — no doubt asking to be sent back to Amiens — while Madame Mirault watched them all from the kitchen door, a coiffed and kirtled Argos.

"Nick Skeres," Tom called, and gestured impatiently when the lad just raised his eyebrows at him. Whoever was going to make this one into a servant, had their work cut out for them.

The lad ambled over, giving a very black scowl to Burry, who rose to inspect him.

"This one?" the Prévôt's man asked, and, on Tom's affirmative, he barked directly at the lad. "Did you find him?"

Skeres's scowl blackened tenfold — a sight to see, what with the purple bruises and the swollen eye — and Burry didn't look pleased, either.

"He has no French," Tom explained, before translating the question in English for the lad.

Skeres never took his glower off the Frenchman. "What business 'as 'e asking?"

"You just answer him!" Tom snapped. "He's like a constable at home."

Skeres jutted his lower lip in a way that made Tom wonder just how Skeres stood with the law at home — but, thankfully, he answered. "Woke up, and 'e wasn't there, so I came down to the yard, and…" A shrug.

Tom translated.

"And he roused the house?"

"'Ouse was all roused," was the sullen answer. "The 'ag there was all a-squawking." A jerk of the chin towards the hovering innkeeper — which went to explain the prompt appearance of both Burry and de Briet. "So I went to tell you."

Tom translated.

Burry grunted and squinted at the lad's colourful face. "Was it him did that?" he asked, cocking his head at the body.

"No," Tom said. "Those rogues, yesterday —"

"Ask *him*!" barked Burry.

Tom did, through gritted teeth, and when Nick answered just as Tom had said — only he had worse names to call the soldiers — Burry eyed them both very suspiciously.

"Look, Maître Burry, I don't know how to prove to you…" But no, in fact he did. Tom beckoned to Jeannot, and the guide trotted over, round-eyed with preoccupation and eagerness in equal parts. "He has some English," Tom explained. "And he was there. He can tell you what happened, and also whether I'm twisting the lad's answers."

This last was said in some sharpness, but Burry accepted it as a good notion, and after that things went a little smoother.

Jeannot confirmed the previous day's misadventures, and then stood there, nodding solemnly at every word that Nick Skeres said, and Tom translated.

Thus it was ascertained that the lad had slept like a log all night, heard nothing, only found Litcott gone in the morning, nearly stumbled into the body when walking out in the yard but not otherwise touched it, and had no notion whether anyone else had.

"'Ow the devil should I know, you lousy Papist toad?" was Skeres's corollary to that last — which Tom thought it diplomatic not to translate.

After which Skeres and a grinning Jeannot were dismissed, and Burry brought his attention back to the corpse and the wound. He knelt down again and, unclasping a knife from his girdle, he began to work at the wound.

Surely not his eating knife, Tom wondered queasily.

"Madame Mirault will have a table where I can work better," Burry muttered. "You said he was a glover?"

"Travelling to join the Queen of Navarre's Court." And so fussily proud of it, poor fellow. "A present from your Duke of Anjou to his sister."

Oh, the look on Burry's face! Tom had had more than his fill of this story — of telling it, and of being thought a Bedlamite for it — as though he were to blame somehow for the caprices of queens and princes…

"Did you see? I think his neck is bruised." He pointed to the corpse, and winced at the clumsiness of it. He could imagine only too well the wryness in Sir Francis's eyes. *When I taught you to distract your opponent, Thomas…*

The wonder was, it worked. Burry, either easy to distract or unbothered by far-off princes and their gloves, reached to move Litcott's collar out of the way. There were bruises indeed across the man's throat, a large band, almost black by now.

Somehow, it seemed unduly cruel. "Why stab a man and strangle him?" Tom wondered aloud, thinking of the murderer with his hands around his bleeding victim's throat, squeezing…

Burry shook his head. "Not quite strangled. Look." He had to raise a stiffening shoulder to show the side and back of the neck. "No marks of hand or string, see? This here, instead…" He laid back the thin shoulder, and fingered the blackened throat, pushing at the Adam's apple. "Ah, see? Crushed his windpipe, so he'd make no noise. Like this, I'd say…" He leant down to lay a forearm across Litcott's throat, and pushed. "See?"

Something crunched under Burry's arm — and Tom's stomach surged. "I see…" he choked out.

"And with the other hand…" Burry, Lord smite him, made an upward stabbing motion with his knife, and jerked it sideways. "Hard enough to break the blade." He braced himself upright, and sheathed his knife. "Doesn't look like he left the hilt around — not that it'd help that much, unless it was one of you, eh? Anyone missing a dagger, that you know?"

Even with his eyes lowered on a patch of muddy, trodden straw on the ground a few feet away — staring at anything but Citolini — Tom could tell Burry was looking at him, waiting for an answer. He looked up. "I … what?" He stammered, and could have kicked himself. *See to it that you always seem in command — of yourself and the matter at hand, Thomas. Especially when you are not…*

Burty gave him a narrow-eyed look. "You look a little green to me, Monsieur," he said. Amused, for a mercy, rather than suspicious. Yet. "Cheer up, Monsieur — this is nothing! Pray you never come across a gutting. Spilt bowels are no sight to do a man's heart any good — and, Saints preserve us, the stench! Or drowned bodies, either. Let them be in the water long enough, and they bloat like bladders, and the fish eat bits away, like eyes, and lips. But take them out early — and the froth! All that froth at mouth and nose… And, however they die, pray that you find them before they begin to rot…"

Tom swallowed hard, and took as steady a breath as he could through his nose — not that rain, blood, and urine combined were much help — and he crossed his arms so he wouldn't dab at the cold sweat he felt gathering on his forehead. "I'll keep it all in mind, Maître Burry," he said, trying hard to look unbothered. "Now what?"

This Burry acknowledged with an amused grunt. "Now we take out the blade — not that you'll like to be around, I'll wager?" He looked up, frowned at something past Tom's shoulder, and called, "Madame Mirault!"

All the time the innkeeper had been hovering about, trying to eavesdrop, and didn't even look much flustered at being caught at it. She fussed close, twisting her hands, and asking what, oh *what* was a poor widow to do now that rogues, brigands and murderers made themselves at home under her roof...

"You can begin by clearing me a table by a window with good light, and have this poor man laid upon it. And send for the priest, maybe."

The priest! It struck Tom for the first time that Litcott must now be buried here in Halcourt, among Catholics, because there was no way they could bring him to Paris... At least the man had not sounded like a Puritan.

Madame Mirault was not happy, either. Not at having a heretic buried in their graveyard, much less at having him cut and stitched on her table.

"Come, come — he won't be the first!" Burry cut through the woman's lamentations.

Not the first Protestant to be buried in Halcourt, Tom wondered idly — *or not the first murdered man at the Trois Poissons?*

Whichever it was, it didn't please Madame Mirault, who whirled around, throwing up her hands and calling Burry names, for all the world like a bacchante of Picardy, but the archer called her back in his whip-crack voice.

"I also want the dead man's things, Madame. And these men's, too. The possessions of every Englishman that you have here."

The old lady flounced away and disappeared inside the inn, followed by Luchette and the stableboy, never stopping when Tom called out to her — because, truly...

He turned on the archer. *Firm, Thomas — not angry. Anger is a weakness.* "I don't think so, Maître Burry," he protested, quite firmly, if he said so himself. "We belong to the English Ambassador's household, and won't be searched like common criminals."

"Well, that one's no Ambassador's man, is he?" Burry pointed at Jack Dennis. "And what about the glover?"

Oh, bless the Law of Nations, and its safe, sound ground! "The glover travels — travelled under my care," Tom said, holding the man's glare with one of his own. "And Master Dennis belongs to the Post. There are laws about that too, and treaties — ones that your Prévôt won't want to break."

"Won't he now!" Hands on hips, head thrown back, Burry would have made a good statue of scornful disgust. "See now, why I wanted to foist the lot of you on that fool de Briet?" He scowled for a while — at Tom first, then at the others, who were striding closer in a tight bunch. Then he huffed in defeat. "All right, *que diable!* Let's carry him in."

Jeannot and Nick Skeres — both grumbling — were ordered to do the carrying proper. As they bent to pick up the body, Burry bent too, quick as an adder, and caught Skeres by the wrist.

"Oy! Let go!" shouted the lad, yanking with all his vigour — to no avail.

"Skeres, be quiet!" ordered Tom, all they lacked now being a brawl with the Maréchaussée — and then, to the archer: "What now, Maître Burry?"

The Frenchman made no answer as he observed closely the lad's cuff, and pushed back the sleeve to check the shirt underneath. He did the same with the other arm, and then gave a momentous snort. "Could have changed shirts — which I'll never know, for Saints forbid we touch the bags of an ambassador's servant's servant!" he groused to all and no one in particular, as Jeannot, bless him, offered up his own wrists for inspection — quite unasked.

Burry gave the guide's cuffs a brisk look, then waved the man away to the body.

"Wasn't even going to check Jeannot, the mangy cur," Skeres muttered under his breath, as he joined in the effort.

Tom glared at him — but, in good conscience, had much the same thought. Burry *had* only wanted to go through the Englishmen's bags — and little as Tom suspected Jeannot... "What is it, Maître Burry?" he asked, and couldn't help the edge. "Are there no French murderers? Or Flemish, for that matter?"

Burry spared him a baleful glance before stalking to the inn, followed by the corpse-bearers.

Tom received another scowl from Citolini.

"You *are* a fool!" the Italian hissed. "Now go and make enemies of the Maréchaussée!"

Which, considering he had been keeping things from the Maréchaussée for Citolini's sake, struck Tom as the blackest ingratitude.

Before he jumped down the man's throat, he took off for the kitchen — but not before catching Jack Dennis's amused glance.

CHAPTER 5

What cheer the common room of the Trois Poissons had had the previous night was all gone in the ashen light of morning. All that remained was the smell of woodsmoke — now cold and stale. In fairness, the soggy corpse laid on the table by the window hardly promoted snugness, nor did the stools and benches pushed out of the way, nor the grim people standing among them.

On another table were piled a dozen bags and bundles, and by that Burry stood, hands on hips and head thrown back, arguing with a none too pleased Ralph Garrard — Madame Mirault making an interested audience.

Tom made his way to them.

"And I tell you, maître or no maître," the merchant was all but shouting. "You'll keep your paws off my truss. I'm an English citizen, pox take you — an honest merchant, up and down these roads these past fifteen years. Lay a hand on what is mine, and you'll hear from the Ambassador…"

Burry raised his eyes to the smoke-black ceiling. "Another one! Ay, go cry to the Ambassador — look, here comes his man." He jerked his chin at the approaching Tom.

Garrard turned with a look of half-relief. "I wasn't even travelling with them. Tell this oaf, Mr. Walsingham!"

"He wasn't," Tom said. A little brusque, perhaps — but he had trouble of his own a-plenty, without borrowing someone else's. Then again, if it hadn't been for Garrard the previous night… "We'd never met Master Garrard before yesterday," he amended — before it occurred to him that he knew that for certain of himself alone.

Instead of calling him out on the blatant fallacy, Burry turned to the innkeeper for confirmation.

The woman gave a glum, grudging nod. "That's as may be," she said. "But they were thick as thieves soon enough. Why, hadn't it been for Monsieur here insisting, I wouldn't have taken in the others at all — and I wish to all the Saints I hadn't!"

Burry turned to Garrard again. "You insisted?"

"I did not!" Garrard had the mottled blush on his big face that put one in mind of apoplexies and calentures. "The lady was going to throw them out in the street." He glared sideways at the widow. "I said they could share my room, is all."

"And they did?"

Tom was beginning to feel a little sorry for Garrard, enough to jump in. "We did — that is, my colleague, Master Dennis and I," he said. "My servant, Master Litcott, and the guides slept in the hayloft."

Burry hummed thoughtfully, rubbing at his grizzled beard and considering the two Englishmen — but mostly Garrard ... until the merchant lost all charity.

"Oh, go ahead, damn you!" he shouted, grabbing a couple of bags from the table and tossing them at the archer. "And the trunk, too. Do what you like, and choke on it! I have nothing to hide."

Burry deftly caught the bags, put them on a bench, emptied them, one after the other, and rifled through the contents with brisk but careful hands, paying most attention to shirts, cuffs, and collars. When he was done, he asked to see Garrard's hands and wrists, much like he had done with Skeres.

But truly, was that the man's one manner of inquiry? It burned on Tom's tongue to point out that even the thriftiest murderer would know to get rid of a bloodied shirt — but he remembered just in time that Burry was not his to assist, much less to keep suspicious of them all.

After that, Burry wanted to inspect the three couriers' passports — which was not made easy by the dried mud on them — and asked each man where he had spent the night, and how he had known the dead glover. Jack Dennis and Citolini both answered the same — the night spent in the room upstairs, and Litcott met the day before, although Citolini, Tom observed, had a manner of glum fretfulness about him. Tom's own answers differed little, to the extent of having been saddled with the glover back in Richmond a week earlier. Of his interlude with the young woman he made no mention — because it most surely had no bearing on the matter, had it? It was an omission he quickly regretted — all the more when Citolini threw him a frowning glance: what if Burry questioned Luchette? What if any of the others mentioned his absence at some point? And besides, didn't this mean he couldn't vouch for the others' presence in the room, any more than they could vouch for his...?

Lying is always a sin, though at times a necessity, Thomas. Lying without necessity, however, besides being a sin, is very foolish.

He would have taken Burry aside, and confessed his foolishness — but before he could, the man turned to the corpse, put aside his gloves, and unsheathed his knife again.

"What do you think you are doing?" asked Citolini, looking as queasy as Tom felt, and even reaching out to grab the archer by the sleeve.

Burry didn't even bother to look at the Italian, just calmly tugged his arm free. "If it makes you ill," he said, "go away." And with that, he lifted Litcott's shirt again, it having slid back as they carried him in, revealing the wound.

Tom made himself stay and observe — all the more because Citolini had gone away in great strides to stand at the room's far end, near the staircase, resting an elbow on the newel post in an attempt at unconcern. Not a very good one, Tom thought — and quenched the little flare of satisfaction. It was hard to grudge the fellow some twitchiness, considering it was his blade inside the body...

Meanwhile Burry, armed by Luchette with rags and a bowl of water, was wiping crusted blood from Litcott's scrawny chest and stomach — with a curious brisk gentleness. The wound, once cleaned, looked small — an inch or so — neat at one end and jagged at the other, and mottled all around with bruises the colour of dark grapes.

Unfortunate simile — now he'd never eat grapes again without remembering... Tom's stomach twisted, and twisted again when Burry began to cut the wound wider, and stuck his fingers inside.

Oh Lord.

Tom looked away — anywhere else would do. Even poor Litcott's face, slack-jawed in death, dulled eyes sinking into his head. The bruised throat... The stained sleeve, the fisted hand...

The hand! The fingers — a forefinger bare and bruised!

"The ring!" Tom blurted out.

Burry looked up from his gruesome work with a puzzled frown.

Tom pointed. "He wore a ring there. A mourning ring, I think."

Burry leant over to observe the bruised hand. "Did he carry money on him?"

"A purse." Tom tried to remember. There was no purse at the body's girdle. "Not much, I think. Travelling money. But perhaps he'd leave it behind if he only went…"

Burry gave an unconvinced grunt, and turned to look over his shoulder at the table with the bags. "I know, I know," he snapped, when Tom opened his mouth. "I'm not to touch a stitch of yours. You do it, then. See whether there's a purse there — or a ring."

Both Tom and Citolini obeyed, which was a good thing — for unlike the rest of them, Litcott had travelled with a good amount of truss. The small bale of dyed leathers they barely rifled through as unlikely. One satchel held the glover's tools — long needles, threads, a variety of shears, a few wicked-looking awls, and other things Tom had no name for. Then there were clothes, some workaday, some finery for a new life at Court, shoes (even a pair of dancing slippers, poor Litcott!), brushes and combs, a small Bible, a wooden box packed with herbs and remedies wrapped in twists of paper, a wooden pomander… No purse — and, which was no great surprise, no ring.

"*Et bien*, so he was robbed," said Burry on hearing that. And then, with a horrible, sucking sound, he slid the broken blade from the wound and held it glistening to the light.

At Tom's elbow, Citolini swallowed hard. Tom took great, great care not to look at him.

After that, Burry grudgingly allowed Garrard to leave, and Tom went to the courtyard to see the merchant on his way. It was raining again, although not half as heartily as it had been, and they waited under the arched gateway as the stableboy saddled the horses.

"I'm in your debt for this," Garrard said. "If you hadn't noticed the ring gone, I'd be still kicking my heels at that archer's pleasure."

Tom found it in himself to smile a little. "Well, as we were all in your debt for a roof over our heads last night…"

"Still, you have my thanks, Mr. Walsingham." Garrard shook his head. "When I see Dover again, it won't be soon enough."

Something in that snagged at Tom's straying thoughts. "Won't you stay in Amiens for the fair?" he asked.

"Thank the Lord, no," said Garrard with a shudder. "I have a man there, minding my business. A day and a night to see he doesn't rob me blind, and then it's Calais and home for me."

Calais and home… Suddenly, Tom found himself wishing for Calais and home too — wishing for them very much. The bustle at Scadbury, Father and Edmund hunting all day, guests coming and going, the children's antics, Mother ruling over it all… Or Barn Elms, with Cousin Ursula and little Frances making much of him…

"I'm sorry about your fellow." Garrard's words — not soft, for the man seemed one of those who hadn't it in them to speak softly — cut through Tom's thoughts. Tom found him watching, the bird-like stare holding some sympathy — perhaps mistaking his wistfulness for something else. Something that should have been there, by right — because a man lay murdered on the table of a slatternly inn in Picardy, and all Tom Walsingham could think was to be homesick. He sighed, half over the glover, half at his own hard heart. "Ay, poor Simon Litcott, rest his soul. What a thing, to come all the way here to die like that!"

Garrard nodded in that purse-lipped, ponderous way one takes at funerals — just as his man came from the stables, leading the horses. "Well, Mr. Walsingham, I'll be on my way. I wish you…" The merchant shook his head, absently rubbing his horse's nose. "I wish you better times and better luck, eh?" He looked up at the sky as he said it, one hand outstretched, palm up, like some ancient auspex reading omens.

Better times indeed… "And to you a safe journey home," Tom answered.

And with that Garrard was mounted and gone, and Tom was left alone to contemplate the untidy stable-yard of the Trois Poissons under the rain. Someone had thrown a bucketful of sawdust where Litcott's blood had pooled. Simon Litcott, lying dead in the common room, and waiting for Tom to do something. See to the burial, first, and then go on to Paris to explain the man's death to Cobham — not to mention the loss of the letter — and perhaps, somewhere between the two, try to find out who had made it his business to stab to death a silly and quite harmless glove-maker.

The clouds above had settled into a bruise-hued lid, and the rain was starting to thicken. Better go back inside. There would be time enough to get soaked again once they were on their way — supposing Burry let them… With a last look at the reddened sawdust, Tom took a sprinting step — and then stopped where he was, his eye caught on something.

There was a paler mark on the wall, not far from where the body had been, looking … new? Tom ran his fingers over it — as large as his hand, roughly rounded upwards and shallow, barely a scuffing, and paler than the age-grey daub.

Could it be… Could it be from a man's boot — a man who had let himself in over the roof…?

The building was low enough on that side of the yard — likely a pigsty at some time, with two boarded-up arched doors. And up above between those, right where the mark was — or nearly … was that a…? Tom stepped back to better see — and yes: right at the edge of the roof a couple of tiles were displaced, showing a brighter patch underneath.

Tom let himself out of the gate, and turned left into what had to be the inn's cramped back alley. It was no tidier than the inside, a runnel of waste and filth in the rainy day. Tom squelched in carefully. There were footprints in the mud — a good deal of them, of varying size and depth, all filled with turbid water. Who knew who had walked there — and when…? But against the inn's wall leant a jumble of broken barrels, rotten timber and who knew what else, stacked high enough that a man could make his way to wall's top, and jump down to the pigsty roof from there. All of it black with rain and mud, and Tom could see no paler marks on the outer wall — but still…

He went back to the yard, and found Burry standing just where he had been, hands on hips, hat pushed back as he squinted up at the disturbed tiles.

"So this is it, eh?" he said, without so much as looking back.

"It could be, yes," Tom said carefully. In truth, there wasn't much to show anyone had been in the alley, nor was there any clear proof to the contrary… But this thought he kept to himself.

"*Et bien, alors!*" Burry abandoned his study of the eaves to narrow his eyes at Tom. "Common thieves, I'd say — and your man just chose the wrong moment to take a piss."

Which could well be — if not that… "But was anything stolen?" Tom asked.

"Madame Mirault says not." Burry rubbed at his beard. "I'd say the thief nearly fell on your man, and went to silence him, then things turned ugly…"

"And the thief lost his nerve?" Try as he might, Tom couldn't keep the doubt out of his voice.

He wasn't surprised when Burry grunted. "What, are all thieves smart-witted in England? It wouldn't be the first time at the Trois Poissons — and, if you ask me, it's likelier than your forest rogues coming back." With a shrug, the archer turned on his heel and made for the kitchen door — a good notion, if only because it was raining hard by then.

Likelier, ay — if not for a certain broken hilt under the body... But, even if he'd been minded to share that with the archer, there was something... *Madame Mirault says not.* Fuming, Tom trotted after the Frenchman and plunged into the kitchen behind him — a small, black, smoky Tartarus, too dim, and too warm after the damp chill outside. "But you knew that already, didn't you?" He gestured back at the door, the yard, the mark on the wall. "You'd noticed before, or why would you ask Madame Mirault if she'd been robbed? Only, you'd much rather have an English culprit! Is that how you do by foreigners here?"

Burry stopped, and blew his cheeks out. "Ah, but you mistake me very much, Monsieur," he said. "I like the common thieves much better, see... If it was common thieves, I doubt it is our business at all. Have your Ambassador send to the Mayeur in Amiens — or the Bailli, if he likes."

And that might not be half a bad notion. Let Sir Henry deal with it. Still... "That's all you have to say? What about the assault, yesterday? We were robbed and misused. Soldiers or adventurers — that *is* the Maréchaussée's jurisdiction."

"Yes — and we'll try to root them out of the woods of Dury — but in all truth..." Burry stretched his lips, as if to say, *wish us joy of it.* "Have your Ambassador send to the Prévôt."

Of course.

"And, you know…" Burry sucked his teeth. "You always have the right to kill and maim those ruffians, if you bump into them again. It's the law."

Tom snorted. "Ay — perhaps when they're not three to one of us! And now, if you're quite done with us, we'll leave." He turned to go, stopping on the threshold when Burry called after him.

"I don't know that you can, Monsieur. There will be the inquest."

The man's impudence! But this time, Tom had a good answer. "Truly, Maître Burry?" he snapped. "And just what court will hold it? Yours? The Bailli's?"

"Well now, that…" For once and for a wonder, the fellow seemed a little discomposed.

Tom raised a hand, palm up like one concluding an argument. "Well then — whoever wins us, can send to the Ambassador."

And off he strode, leaving Maître Regnauld Burry to give his attention to the Flemings, for a change — although, in these parts, being Flemish might not have been half the sin being English was — and he went to find his fellows, trying to think how on earth Sir Francis would sort this tangle in his place.

CHAPTER 6

Paris, Quai des Bernardins, the residence of the English Ambassador

"And so I left behind Nick Skeres to see that the poor man was buried decently in Halcourt," Tom explained. That he'd paid for it all from his own purse, he swallowed. This would go in his expenses later — and surely Sir Henry would see to it that the Embassy paid for it.

Sir Henry Cobham, Her Majesty the Queen of England's Ambassador in Paris, nodded his long head, pale eyes fixed on the fire that roared in the ornate fireplace. "Yes, I suppose that is the best that could be done," he said to the flames. "And we'll write to all those gentlemen your Maître d'Archers mentioned, no doubt. Not that I hold much hope."

He still had to look Tom in the face — as sharp a sign of disapproval as this smooth-mannered man was likely to give. Tom, cold, tired and sore after the long day in the saddle, stood rigidly before the Ambassador's desk, and felt very much a fire-less Prometheus, chained to the boulder and having his liver chewed out.

Sir Henry, this mildest-seeming of eagles, hummed. "But this is for the best, perhaps. We don't want the Maréchaussée — much less the King's Bailli — poking their noses into this, do we? Not if..." He looked up, frowning at some point between Tom's shoulder and Paolo Citolini. "Are we certain those soldiers have Mr. Secretary's letter?"

"Yes, Sir, quite certain," said the Italian — who knew how to look smug and grim at once.

Sir Henry looked at Tom, then, in silent enquiry — and Tom wanted to object that they didn't know for certain, that the rogues might not have known — but...

"They knew of Monsieur's packet after it was shown to them." And leave it to Paolo Citolini to take every advantage there was to take.

"And *that* they didn't take," Tom snapped.

"And *that*," Sir Henry cut in reproachfully, to show just what he thought of his couriers squabbling, "should tell us where their interest lay." He turned to the Italian. "Nothing you carried was taken or touched, was it, Paolo?"

Citolini shook his head. "Nothing but my dagger. Then again, I did not wave my letters in their faces..."

Tom took a breath to retort, but was quelled with a look — and so, he noted with some satisfaction, was Citolini.

"Nor were Walsingham's taken," Sir Henry pointed out. "Not the ones he carried openly."

Tom's brief satisfaction drained away. He'd given that particular circumstance a good deal of thought, all the dreary, soggy way to Paris through morning and afternoon. "They took the one we couldn't — *wouldn't* — lay a claim to..." he murmured, eyes lowered on the hem of the tapestry that covered the desk.

"Indeed. Although..." Sir Henry tapped at his chin, turning to the fire again. "I'll say I'm at a loss: how would they know about it — and where it was?"

Tom sighed. "Litcott —"

"*Corbellerie!*" Citolini spoke over him, palms up in appeal to the Ambassador to witness that Thomas Walsingham had lost his wits. "How could that one possibly know...?"

"He did." Tom looked up from the tapestry, quite miserably. "The last night in London..." He cleared his throat. "The night before we left, I … I tore my doublet's hem on a nail. Litcott said he'd mend it, and…" He glowered at the Italian before he could speak. "I didn't tell him of the letter, of course I didn't — but he must have felt it as he worked…"

Citolini huffed, eyes raised to the painted caissons of the ceiling. The things the Italian got away with, just because he'd been with Sir Henry many years!

But perhaps Sir Henry had other things on his mind, things more pressing than his Italian's manners. "So he was the Duke's man, after all," he murmured, looking at his two couriers in turn over steepled fingers. "He *must* have been."

"He looked such a dullard!" Tom groaned. "But now he's dead — and by the hand of the same men who held us up, nothing else makes sense. In fact, he went missing for a while, that morning in Amiens, and never explained where he'd been. Laying plans with those rogues, I'll wager."

"Oh yes — when you lost him." Citolini, of course — the arrant weasel!

Would he be this spiteful in the Italian's place? Tom had barely the time to wonder, before…

"Ah, well." Sir Henry rose to his feet — clear dismissal. "It matters little, Paolo, does it? At least we know for certain that he was wilfully helping the French — and that the French are not above foul play when it comes to this Royal marriage." He turned to Tom. "Do you know what was in the letter?"

"No, Sir!" Tom answered, a little shocked — for in truth he did know, the gist at least, Sir Francis believing in practical training — but that was a matter between the cousins, and for Cobham to ask such a question…

However he took Tom's startled answer, Sir Henry let it pass. "There is little hope it was not about this wretched courtship, I fear," he said. "Mr. Secretary will have to be apprised."

"I can leave in the morning," Tom offered — half out of zeal, half thinking of home. "I am to blame for this, and it is only fair —"

"We'll see, Walsingham, we'll see." Sir Henry reached to pat his arm, much in the way he'd pat a dim-witted hound. "Now go and have some rest. And you as well, Paolo. We'll see tomorrow."

And Tom walked out of the Ambassador's study, so sore of heart and bones, as though he'd hauled Sisyphus's stone up and down every hill in France.

It was a short walk from the Quai des Bernardins to Tom's lodgings in Rue des Anglais, short even in the rainiest, greyest, weariest November twilight — only made longer by a whirl of furious black thoughts of Citolini, Cobham, poor dead Litcott, and Sir Francis back at home, and ruined prospects…

Once he'd paid the link-boy with the light, Tom had to knock and call a while, and wait in the deepening gloom, before the bookseller who kept shop downstairs deigned to come and let him in.

"But you are back, Monsieur Walsn'am!" The man squinted near-sightedly in the scant glow of his one candle, as though Tom appearing on his own doorstep was a matter for great wonder.

Too weary for retort, Tom gave the landlord all the smile he could muster, and pushed past, picking his way through the darkened shop from bookshelf to table, and to the staircase in the back. On the first landing stood a woman, and a man on the second — each holding a candle, like so many statues of Philosophy.

"But you're back, Monsieur Walsn'am," said the female Philosophy, just as surprised as her husband had been — even as her male counterpart cheerfully boomed from above: "Is that you, Tityrus? *Ave atque vale!*"

Tom waved upwards at Thomas Watson, his fellow-lodger and fellow-courier, and stumbled upstairs, mumbling bonsoir to Madame Rouet, and hastening past as she sniffed at his muddied, sodden state. That the bookseller's wife was not too fond of having three gentlemen from the English Embassy under her roof — and never spoke of her foreign lodgers without much head-shaking — was more than Tom could bring himself to consider at the moment.

Oh, but it was good, at last, to sink onto his own carved stool at his own fireplace, and to say "*Ave,* Corydon" to Watson, and to let Levieux, the Huguenot they kept to take joint care of them, help him out of his cloak, jerkin, gamashes and buskins. Home, at last — or as much of home as there was in Paris.

And there came the Third Thomas — Phelippes, small mouse that he was, pale-eyed, pale-haired, and narrow, clerk to Sir Henry, the best of decipherers — and the bearer of a cup of mulled wine for weary travellers.

"Oh, Saint Philippus!" Tom exclaimed, taking the cup, and the man scrunched his pock-marked face and solemnly saluted the Thomases reunited.

Tom toasted back, and they sat around the fire, with Levieux hovering about. Watson presided, as usual, and as he would have, Tom suspected, even if he hadn't been the oldest among them at six and twenty, for he was tall, big-shouldered and big-voiced, and swarthy, and vivid, and used to drawing attention.

He was not best pleased at the moment, gnawing at a knuckle as he took stock of his returned friend.

"Tityrus, you are bedraggled," he pronounced at last. "What have you done with yourself?"

All the warmth and cheer drained out of Tom at that, and he laughed bitterly. "Where shall I begin?"

"Senex, begone," Watson had the wit to order before the dam broke. "A warming pan in our prodigal's bed — and then to sleep yourself."

And when Levieux, who was resigned to all sorts of Latin and Greek names but balked at having his work explained to him, had grumbled himself off, Tom took breath, and told the Thomases the catalogue of his woes, starting with Richmond, and ending in Quai des Bernardins.

"And thanks be that I didn't stay behind myself," he moaned at the end, leaning forward to rub at his face. "The tales Citolini would have told!"

"Upstart braggart," Watson exclaimed. "And you saving his hoity-toity hide from rogues and Maréchaux alike!"

Phelippes hummed. "*Him* you should have left behind."

And Tom, who had thought about it — and done nothing lest the Italian should refuse, groaned again. "To bury *my* slaughtered charge? And in truth, there's little he could tell to make it uglier. Why, I'll count it a great fortune if they don't kick me out of the Service!" He rubbed harder at tired eyes. "But what I still cannot credit, is Simon Litcott. That silly dullard, rest his soul, an agent of the French!" He shook his head at the raised eyebrows and tilted heads of his friends, who were thinking, no doubt, of parts played and lies told (and, perhaps, of fools employed) — but then they hadn't travelled for days in the company of that lack-wit…

"Still, you say that he went missing," Phelippes said.

Tom nodded. "Twice."

"Item." Watson held up one long forefinger. "In London, you say, the night before you left…"

"To take instructions?" Tom wondered. "Later found in a tavern with a wench, though."

"Not the unlikeliest of excuses," Phelippes, a bit of a Puritan, mused glumly. "Nor the most unusual."

"And, item —" Watson again, with a second finger. "Yesterday morning in Amiens."

"Giving no account of himself," said Tom. "Off hiring the adventurers?"

"Who, you say, did not rob or even much harass him…" Phelippes frowned. "*I* would have had them harry me a little, though. *Verisimilius.*"

"Nobody noticed… I, for one, never gave it a thought." Tom sighed. "And then, later that night, one of those rogues came to meet Litcott at the Trois Poissons — to deliver the letter and take his fee."

Watson held up a hand. "Wait, though — *quaestio*: if so, where is the letter?"

Oh, Tom knew that — knew it with the bleakest clarity. "It never changed hands that night. Litcott fell foul of the Frenchman somehow — money, most likely, considering the theft of his purse and ring. And after that…"

For the briefest while, there was only the low clicking of the fire in the hearth.

"You saw those fellows, Tityrus." Phelippes carefully leant down to poke at the embers. "Would they have the wits to sell the letter?"

Tom thought of the pack-leader's sharp, assessing manner. The cold eyes under the ragged hat. "Even with Litcott dead, the Duke may well have had his wish," he murmured wretchedly. "For there's no doubt that Monsieur le Duc sent him, is there?"

Another short silence.

"*Ergo*…" said Watson — and let it trail.

"*Ergo*, O Thomases…" Tom climbed stiffly to his feet. Oh Lord — but he was sore! "*Ergo*, I've been well and truly conned for the gudgeon that I am. How I'll explain it to Sir Francis, I don't know."

And then, there being nothing for it until the morrow, he went to bed, and turned, and tossed, and dreamed of Burry making Litcott's windpipe crunch under his forearm — a very alive Simon Litcott, grinning, and laughing his high-pitched laugh.

CHAPTER 7

Morning came most swiftly — though with no rosy-fingered Aurora for a messenger. It was Levieux instead, shaking Tom anxiously, and whispering that there was some uncouth lad downstairs, wanting to see Monsieur Walsn'am.

Tom sat up, squinting in the grey light. The bells of Notre-Dame across the Seine were booming, with the nearer chimes of Saint Yves, and Saint Julien, and Saint Jean, and Les Carmes in counterpoint, and watermen peddling in the street.

"Seven," Levieux supplied without having to be asked.

So, who was it, uncouth or otherwise, coming to bother him at this ungodly hour? In his nightgown and slippers, Tom went off to find out, trying not to wake his room-mates. Even before he reached the landing, with Levieux on his heels, he knew the English voice. A most uncouth lad — of course.

Armed with Levieux's candle, he leant from the banister to see the top of Nick Skeres's curly head, as the boy shouted at the bookseller's wife and surly apprentice. They all were shouting at each other, not understanding a mutual word, no doubt — though the tone of the conversation was hard to mistake.

"Madame Rouet," Tom called. Three faces looked up — none of them filled with joy.

"Oy, Master!" Skeres bellowed, and Tom waved him silent.

"Madame Rouet, I am most sorry," he said in French. "Please, let him up. He is my servant — and I crave your pardon for his manners. I haven't had him long."

Which wasn't quite the truth — but easier than explaining.

"And are you keeping him?" the landlady asked, scowling upwards in a most tempestuous manner.

Tom made the vaguest of gestures for all answer, and devoutly hoped not, as he watched the lad charge up the stairs, elbows out and chin jutting — a minotaur in a huff.

"When Senex announced some sort of ruffian, I should have known it was you," Tom said in greeting, shepherding them all inside. "What are you doing here?"

"That archer of yours," Skeres shrugged — not without throwing a narrow-eyed look at poor Levieux, who hovered at Tom's shoulder. "'E gave me a paper to ride with the Stranger Merchant's man."

"I know," Tom said. "I asked him to. Have you taken Litcott's things to the Ambassador's?"

"I went there —" Skeres looked around as he talked, with a thief's guarded curiosity. "And they said I 'ad to wait, and see that Italian when 'e 'ad the time, and I don't like that one, so I asked where you was, and…" Another shrug, as though that explained everything.

Which it mostly explained — but didn't make right. "Ay — well, they'll still want to see you. Send you back to England, I reckon. You're not truly my servant, you know that."

Skeres glared in betrayed outrage. "Nor that Italian's, either. I don't take orders from a Papist, I. I … I … I was a-thinking that you'd keep me…" And he looked down, scuffing a boot against the floor, looking for all the world like a beaten mastiff pup.

Oh Lord. Tom blew out his cheeks. "Senex," he ordered. "Breakfast for Master Skeres." And to the lad: "Some bread and cheese, before —"

But the mastiff pup was in a sulk, and shook his head, eyes on his boots. "'Ave to go back," he mumbled. "'Afore the Italian stirs. Wanted to give you this, is all."

He took out of his sleeve a folded piece of paper, dirty and creased, and stained with water, and tightly written on the inside, once prised open.

"What is this?" Tom asked, squinting at the cramped writing. "Where did you…?"

"Inside the glover's doublet." Skeres looked up, truculent again. "They made me 'elp with sorting 'im, they did. And there was this rip, like…" He gestured vaguely at a sleeve. "From when 'e fought, I reckon. And there was this inside, and no one saw me take it, and maybe 'twas important, and damned if I give it to Master Chit-o-lean-y."

"So you give it to me?"

The lad nodded fiercely, quite pleased with himself — and well he might be. Tom scanned the paper. Part of the writing had washed out, no doubt from the water, as Litcott had lain in the rain — but what remained… *To dye skins the colour of Azure … seethe it in water, wherein roche alum was dissolved …* hardly something one would carry in secret — and yet it had been. *Ergo…* "Cipher…?" Tom murmured under his breath, and right then Watson appeared on the threshold, half dressed and scratching at his Spanish beard.

"What in thunder is all this nattering —" He stopped as he took in the stranger. "And who, equally in thunder, is that?"

"This is Nick Skeres — but never mind him now." Tom held up the paper. "Look…"

"Ah, *the* Nick Skeres — the loyal Dolius. You wouldn't have six sons, perchance?" Watson laughed — earning himself a glower from the lad.

"Don't turn his head for him." Tom pushed Watson away. "Go drag Philippus out of bed."

Skeres glared suspiciously after the departing man. "What did 'e call me?"

"Oh, that was praise, Nick Skeres." Tom turned Litcott's paper in his hand, and smiled as he steered the lad towards the door. "And not too undeserved, either. Now go back before they miss you. And not a word, mind you. And be civil to all, if you can."

And with that he pushed the door closed behind Nick Skeres, and turned to lean his back against it, facing his befuddled friends.

Tom held up the paper again. "Unless I'm very wrong, O Thomases, we are going to find out about Simon Litcott."

No time at all, and they were all a-whirl. Phelippes at the table, with paper and quill and inkhorn and candle, grumbling at times that *he* was no kin to Mr. Secretary, to blithely keep things from the Ambassador... And yet he pored, and squinted, and jotted notes, with Tom and Watson going about as they dressed, and ate bread and cheese provided by Levieux, and watched over the decipherer's shoulder, offering suggestions that the man mostly waved away.

In truth, Tom wasn't sure how he would explain the ciphered paper — if truly it was that — in his possession, not without getting Nick Skeres in trouble.

"You'll say the lad forgot," Watson suggested, as he speared another piece of cheese on his knife. "Or that he misliked to keep the thing on him more than he had already."

Tom was about to say that Skeres forgetful seemed a likelier notion than Skeres timid, when Phelippes clicked his tongue, and reached behind his back to wave for attention.

The Thomases were on either side of him in a heartbeat.

"So the thing is…" The little decipherer nibbled at the end of his quill. "There isn't enough left to tell much. Two recipes for dyeing leather on the face of it — hiding not a message but the key to a code."

"God damn the rain!" Tom swore — and winced at Phelippes's reproachful glance. "I'm penitent, Philippus — but … nothing, then?"

"I wouldn't say nothing, no." Phelippes tapped a little jig on the stained paper with his forefinger. "Two things I can tell you: what few words I can find are French…"

"*Ut erat demonstrandum*," chanted Watson.

"Ay — but the cipher itself…" Phelippes looked glumly at Tom. "The cipher looks English to me."

English. Twice, in the new silence, Tom followed that tidbit, back and forth to its obvious meaning, seeking along the way for alternatives — but none presented — unless… "Are you sure?" he asked — a foolish question, for he had yet to see Phelippes mistaken on a matter of ciphers. Thus, more to the point: "Could the French be using it? Couldn't the Duke…?"

Phelippes pursed his lips in thought. "But why would he? It is an oldish thing, besides, not much used these days."

Again the stunned silence, as the unlikelihood sank in.

"You eat more of that, masters?" Levieux asked through it, pointing at the trencher at Phelippes's elbow.

"Begone, Senex," Watson ordered distractedly.

The man grabbed what he'd come to fetch and scuttled away, as the three Thomases traded gapes.

"Then … not the French," Tom breathed at last. "Not the French — but someone at home, trying to make it look like that!"

The streets were full by the time they made their way to the Quai des Bernardins, and they had to elbow through the early morning bustle of peddlers, handcarts, apprentices, bourgeois riding mules, watercarriers, beggars, monks, young blades on horseback, begowned students, and women in high pattens.

The rain had stopped, and half of Paris seemed to be abroad, arguing, laughing, peddling chestnuts, and ballads, and combs, and lids, and whatnot.

There was no talking in that din, and Tom grimly led the way past the Place Maubert and to the River, reckoning possibilities in his head — the same ones, if he was honest, that they had already gone through as they trotted down the bookseller's stairs. Some agent of King Philip, perhaps — Spain having much to lose by an alliance of France and England — or some adherent or other of the Scottish Queen... One'd think they might like the prospect of a Catholic prince in London — but Tom shared Sir Francis's opinion that those fellows hardly knew their own minds at times. Though in truth, England had no lack of factions averse to the French match, even inside the Privy Council. Not just the more Puritan-minded, but Hatton and, even more, Leicester — no matter what he said these days. The Puritans and the Favourites, the jest went...

"Ay, well — we ourselves..." had murmured Phelippes, with a sideways glance at Tom.

And Tom had to agree — for he knew only too well his cousin's deep — if guarded — dislike of the notion. Hadn't Sir Francis carefully observed opposition to the Match between Queen Elizabeth and the Duke during his French mission last summer? Hadn't Tom himself been carrying — and lost — instructions for Sir Henry to covertly hinder the marriage negotiations?

Watson's exclamations that Sir Frank would never do that — *that* being to endanger his own kinsman's life in such a caper — heartened Tom somewhat. And indeed, the caper itself seemed far clumsier than Mr. Secretary liked.

For all that, if Nick Skeres hadn't found the ciphered paper, they'd still be thinking that the French were to blame…

"*Mais voyez, alors, bricon!*"

Tom jolted out of his gyrating thoughts as he ran into a fishwife with her basket and a saucy tongue on her, just a few strides from the Ambassador's side door. He threw an apology at the cursing woman, ran up the steps, and knocked.

He had time to catch his breath and order his thoughts somewhat, before a servant let the three of them in — without raising an eyebrow, for all at the Embassy knew the Thomases went around in a trine.

The moment he was inside the chequer-floored hall, Tom took a breath of relief. Now let Sir Henry have the whole garboil … and at once he was ashamed of it — until…

Until the servant said that the Ambassador was gone, and he could see Mr. Middlemore if he liked.

Tom's heart sank again.

Sir Henry was at the Louvre, Mr. Middlemore announced, standing by the Ambassador's table, wearing pea-green silks and a ruff so large, and so deep, and starched so stiff, he had trouble moving his head. The nithing. Sir Henry was at the Louvre, lodging tactful complaints about the assault on Her Majesty's men.

"Yes," Tom said, with less patience than was politic. "And he must be stopped. There are things he needs to know…"

Middlemore carefully turned his pomaded head to look at him askance — for all the world like a lamb pie on a platter.

"You will be received when Sir Henry returns — if he's of a mind to see you."

Tom inhaled deeply, trying not to wonder how much Middlemore knew of his disaster. "No, Sir Henry must hear what I have to say before he does anything at Court. Things may not be the way he thinks they are."

Middlemore bent sideways to prop both fists on the desk — likely the only way that he could stare directly at Tom. "And you never thought to tell him last night?"

Explaining to Cobham would be one thing — but to this pompous fool? Tom tried for that stone-like finality that sometimes signalled the nearing end of Sir Francis's patience. "That's part of what Sir Henry must hear, Mr. Middlemore — and you are wasting time. The Ambassador must be apprised, and Mr. Secretary as well."

"Oh, Mr. Secretary is being apprised, have no worry," Middlemore said, smiling in all importance. "Citolini is on his way to London."

"What? No!" So Sir Henry *was* punishing Tom, after all. To send another home, behind his back — and the Italian of all men! And, most of all, carrying mistaken news. "I must … I need a passport to go after him."

"Sir Henry said nothing about you going."

Tom breathed deeply again. *Rule your soul — because, unless it obeys, it rules…* But surely Horace never had to deal with such obdurate idiocy? "Because he didn't know, you bootless atomy!" Tom exploded. "He's off acting on wrong premises — and so will be Sir Francis — Mr. Secretary — unless —"

Tom stopped short. Fool — fool! Cursing Middlemore couldn't have helped his case — but the mistake had been another, that familiar appellation…

On that *Sir Francis*, Middlemore's gaze filled with resentment first, and then malice. "Yes, well, it is a matter you'll discuss with the Ambassador," he announced, drawing himself straight like Hades passing judgment. "When he comes back — tomorrow. Give you a good day."

And thus dismissed, Tom stormed out to the hall, where the Thomases waited.

"No good, I take it?" Watson asked.

"Lord smite Harry Middlemore!" Tom fumed, never breaking stride — and he let himself out, leaving his friends to follow.

The tavern of the Poulet Noir was cramped, and less than clean, and of a dubious enough character to have poor Phelippes a-twitch — but it lay next door to a livery stable, and so it had to do.

"You could have waited to have your expenses settled, before you went and called Middlemore names," Watson grumbled good-naturedly, trying to be inconspicuous with his purse.

The Thomases were putting together their money — an unchancy occupation in such a place, but going back to the Rue des Anglais would mean yet more time squandered. So they hunched together around a corner table, whispering, and looking very much like three thieves splitting their booty.

Tom reckoned sums, discovering of a sudden how much costlier life could be without the Service to rely on. "Horses — with feed and water, two ferries, passage to Dover, bribes and such-like… No, that's enough." He stopped Watson when he would have added two more coins.

Watson waved him away. "You'll have to eat, between here and London, won't you? And sleep, and besides, you never know what can happen —"

"Never know!" Phelippes snorted under his breath. "He knows all too well what will happen if they catch him without papers!"

Not that he was wrong... Tom swallowed his doubts and patted the little cipherer's arm. "A little faith, Philippus! I can pass myself off as a merchant, a student, or —"

"Ay — a student with the Queen's licence to travel on her own confidential business — because that's all you have to show when they stop you — not that it would work, mind you, because all the world and his wife will know you as a Queen's man between here and Calais..." Phelippes leant across the table to whisper fiercely. "And when they catch you without a courier's passport — then what of your credentials?"

Tom's stomach churned. Credentials lost, career wrecked, Sir Francis... Oh Lord — Sir Francis! And yet, if he didn't go... "I'll stay off the highway," he murmured. As watery a plan as could be — no, worse: a foolish one, because foreign couriers were forbidden to travel by any other route than the Royal road.

Even Watson — ever bright, impish, daring Corydon — only had a glum pursing of lips to offer, and a suggestion that those rogues must have hit Tom on the head — quite hard.

"Oh, let me..." With his fiercest scowl, Phelippes twisted around on his stool, and called for ink and paper.

"No!" Tom caught him by the sleeve. "Don't! If I'm — if anything happens, forged papers will only make it worse!" For Phelippes more than anyone... Tom squared his shoulders, and looked from one Thomas to the other, as stern as he knew. "There's nothing for it — Sir Francis must hear this right. And Sir Henry, too." He nodded at Watson. "Off you go to the Louvre, Corydon. *Dum loquimur…*"

Watson rose, looking none too happy. "I know, I know. As we speak, time flies! I'll see you soon, Tityrus."

Unless they caught him with no papers, and threw him in some French prison to rot — from which neither Cobham nor Mr. Secretary would be in any haste to rescue him, seeing what a muddle he'd made.

Tom managed a tight smile for Watson, who clasped his shoulder and said his *Vale*, and right then…

"Oy, Master!" came from the door, loud enough for all Paris to hear. "Master Walsingham — ho!"

Oh yes — and there was that. Tom closed his eyes, and wondered once more, dear Lord, what had he done…

Elbows wide and chin jutting, Nick Skeres plodded his way to the Thomases, scowling when Phelippes would have waved him silent.

"What are you doing here, Nick Skeres?" Tom asked — and, perhaps more to the point, "How did you find me?"

As was to be expected, the lad shrugged. "That old Papist you 'ave," he began — in his thundering whisper.

"Be quiet," Tom snapped. "And if you mean Levieux, he is no —"

"Ay, well — 'e makes out 'e 'as no English — but…" A tap to the side of the nose. "But I tell you: 'e 'as."

The departing Watson burst out laughing. "We know, Dolius — we know — but I've a notion that anyone would begin to speak in tongues, just to be rid of you!" And, with one last wave, he was gone.

Tom sighed. How true. "And didn't Levieux tell you that I'd gone to the Ambassador's?" he asked.

"Ay — but I can't go there again — or they will see that I'm not on my way back 'ome. But there was this servant-lad coming out of a small door, and I asked, and 'e —"

"What do you mean?" Tom frowned. "Why should you be on your way home?"

For once, instead of shrugging, the lad snorted. "When I went back, earlier, they sent me to see this fop — wouldn't credit 'is ruffle, you wouldn't — all in a dudgeon, and where 'ad I been, and now I 'ad to catch up with Mastro Paolo and the other by myself…"

"What other?" Tom asked.

"Same as the other day — that Dennis."

"The Merchant Strangers' man?" Phelippes blinked short-sighted eyes at Skeres. "Why does he ride with Citolini still?"

"'Ow do I know? Maybe 'e's shy."

And indeed, he'd asked for company in Dury, hadn't he? And even then Tom had wondered… "Well, never mind him. You must go after them?"

Another snort. "Ay — so the fop, Mr. Middling or the like, 'e 'ad them give me an 'orse — ugliest jade they 'ad — and money, and a paper. But I'm not going with that one, I'm not —"

"Nick Skeres — you have a passport?" Tom cut in. "They gave you a paper so that you can travel?"

"Why not?" the lad asked, as though Tom had suggested he was not baptised — and he rummaged in his sleeve for the passport, and triumphantly held it out.

Tom took it, nodding to himself as he read the familiar French wording. *Let pass Nicholas Skeres, English citizen, of the English Ambassador's household — travelling to join Monsieur Paul Citolini…* "Do you think, Philippus…?"

103

"No!" Phelippes elbowed him in the ribs. "And no, and no. They'll still know you at Post stations —"

"No post horses, then," Tom said, rising to his feet. "And no highway, and —"

"*And* if they catch you outside the highway, it won't matter what papers you have."

"True, true." Tom was beginning to despair — damn the mistrustful hearts of the French, putting all sorts of strictures on foreign travellers, and couriers most of all. He watched, chewing at his lip, as a well-bosomed tavern maid brought paper and inkhorn, leaning against Phelippes to set the things on the table. And Phelippes, bless his innocence, coloured and looked away.

"I guess we're back to…" Phelippes began, and had the sense not to say it aloud in front of Skeres.

Tom shook his head, and handed back the passport. "You'd better be on your way, Nick Skeres," he said. "If I give you a letter, will you —?"

"Or else you come with me, and carry it yourself."

Tom frowned at the lad. What was he about now? "I just told you…"

Skeres took the air of one explaining to the slow-witted. "I came all the way to Whatyoucallit with no paper of mine, didn't I? Yours did for me, and the glover."

"Yes, but…" Tom stopped, and took a sharp breath. Indeed, his own passport had served for the three of them — with Skeres himself described as… "A servant!" He snatched back the paper, scanned it, and turned to Phelippes. "*And a servant!*"

Phelippes was already rummaging in his satchel for quills, and Tom grinned at his ad interim man. Or rather… "Well, well, Nick Skeres. I think you've just acquired a servant of your own."

CHAPTER 8

"And must we stop 'ere, of all places?" Nick Skeres groused, as they dismounted in the stableyard of the Trois Poissons.

"I told you, I have questions to ask." Without rain, they'd made good time to Halcourt — not that Tom meant to change horses here — and he hoped the Trois Poissons would be a less unchancy place than most. As long as they didn't stumble into Maître Burry again, no one was likely to want their papers.

"Couldn't you ask yesterday?" Skeres grumbled, squinting over each hunched shoulder, for all the world like a cut-throat in a play.

"Ah, but that was before you gave me that paper." Someone, someday, would have to explain silence and submission to the lad. "Now act a tad less ruffianly, will you, and I doubt a soul will bother with us."

The lad's effort at innocence was nothing to set a man's heart at ease. A good thing that, at that time in the afternoon, there was no one in the yard to see it. Tom left Skeres with the horses, and entered the stables. As he had hoped, the stableboy was there, lazily brushing a small chestnut cob.

He knew Tom at a glance, and stiffened in suspicion. He must have been about fifteen, raw-boned, and ragged-haired, and, for a surprise — not well-disposed to foreigners.

To Tom's enquiries he only shrugged and shook his head. Even when offered a silver maille, he eyed it greedily, but went back to brushing the horse.

"*La patronne* says we've had enough of you," he muttered, sullen-eyed, not even looking when Tom fished a second coin from his purse.

"And I'll be on my way, if only you tell me —"

"Oh, look who's there!"

Tom turned — and lo! the maid — Luchette — stood on the threshold, one hand on the doorjamb, the other on her hip.

"Come back to see me, have you, Monsieur?" she teased.

Grey daylight did her no favours, and she looked a good deal less creamy than she had at night, with the rough hands and the mottled flush of one who had been hard at work in the kitchen. But her eyes still twinkled when she smiled, and there was a dimple on her cheek that Tom hadn't noticed before.

"I … er…" he murmured. Such dazzling eloquence! And before he could think of something better, the stableboy cut in.

"Nosing about, that's what he is," he said sullenly.

And Tom, who'd been doing just that but wasn't going to be told off by an ostler, snapped: "Asking questions, that's what I am — and getting no answers."

Luchette clicked her tongue, and stepped in. "What do you want to know?"

"*Non, sotte!*" The stableboy grabbed the maid by the elbow, and hissed to her, too fast, too low, and too thick with Picard speech for Tom to understand well.

Luchette freed herself with a shrug and a little shove. "*La patronne* barks worse than she bites," she said, and turned back to Tom.

Tom hoped, for her sake, that she was right, as the widow had struck him as rather the biting kind — but there were things he had to know. "This boy sleeps up there?" he asked, tipping his head to the ladder that led to the hayloft.

Luchette nodded. "He has his own place, though, not where your men stayed."

She pointed to a spot that would have been nearly above the gate. Almost too good. Tom threw a glance at the boy's suspicious scowl, and bit down the obvious question. *You must pick it out of them by piecemeal, Thomas…*

He hummed to himself, looking up and nodding. "A sort of keeper, then. He'd hear all that happens. If the gate opens…"

Luchette chortled. "Who, him?" She elbowed the boy in the ribs. "Sleeps like a log, he does!"

The boy scowled, like one who did not like to be dismissed. Now, if Tom were to take a guess…

"A pity, then. I thought he slept up there for a reason…"

It was almost too easy.

"I do, too!" the boy protested, suddenly looking younger than Tom had first thought. "And I don't grease the hinges on purpose, so I can hear if the gate opens. Only it rained too hard the other night, so I didn't hear."

Tom looked at the roof overhead, thinking how the rain would have drummed on the tiles. "A good deal of noise," he said. "And you wouldn't hear who might go up or down the ladder, either?"

At this, the boy shrugged. "Men go up and down at night, you know," he said. "That's one thing. Thieves's another."

"Not that you heard either!" scoffed Luchette. "Or when they climbed in!"

So that had been Burry's explanation — thieves climbing in from the alley? As the Ambassador had said, just as well… Still, the stableboy was unconvinced.

"Well, if it hadn't rained, I'd have heard — the climbing, *and* the gate!" He turned to Tom. "They did open it. Found it open in the morning."

"Open wide?"

A shake of the ragged head. "Just pulled to, with the bolt drawn."

"Maître Burry says that's how the thieves went out," Luchette explained gravely. The archer's words carried weight here — no matter how faulty his reasoning.

But then, he couldn't have known... Tom walked to the door to peer out. The gate stood wide open now, but it was easy to imagine Litcott slipping out of the stables, waiting for some preordained signal, opening the gate for the adventurers, and then...

"Oy, Master!" Skeres tiptoed close, head low between his shoulders, to whisper thunderously. "Are we going or not?"

Anyone, seeing him, would have thought he must be the murderer.

"In a minute," Tom said, and beckoned for the lad to follow as he went back to the pair in the stables. There was an exchange of unfriendly glances. "So, who found that poor fellow?" Tom asked.

There was some shuffling of feet, some looking askance.

"Gilles here did," said Luchette at last, a little grudgingly.

Young Gilles straightened up, and nodded in solemn assent.

So finding a murdered man must be a matter of some standing among the population of the inn — perhaps of the whole village?

"You found him — and...?" Tom prodded.

"And nothing. There in a heap, he was. Odd place to sleep off his wine — and in the rain too ... that's what I thought — only ... he had his eyes open."

"Did you move him?" Tom asked.

"*Mais non!*" The boy blinked, swallowed, and crossed himself.

"He ran into the kitchen like a scared rabbit, calling for *la patronne*." Luchette scowled at the boy. "Made me spill a pail of water."

"Got my ears boxed for my troubles." Gilles scowled back.

"You earned it. And by the time *la patronne* had heard it all, that one came in." The maid pointed at Skeres.

Skeres didn't like it. "What? What does she say? What does she want with me?"

Tom was going to explain, when he heard young Gilles mutter something so very unlikely that… "What did you say?" he asked, turning on the boy.

Gilles seemed to think better of it, and shook his head, and made as though to go back to the chestnut horse, and squirmed when Tom grabbed him by the shoulder. He threw a wary look at the lowering, grumbling Skeres — and little wonder, if he thought…

"What is it that you said?" Tom insisted.

Luchette shoved the boy in the shoulder. "Tell him, *sot!*"

Gilles directed another glare at Skeres over Tom's shoulder, and then ducked his head. "Maybe *he* did it," he mumbled, scuffing at the straw on the floor, "seeing as they had words, him and that man."

Tom turned to frown at his manservant. Not that he believed Nick Skeres the sort to crush windpipes — but… "Did you have words with Litcott the other night?"

It was no great wonder when the lad glowered with all the might of Jupiter throwing bolts. "Did they say so?" he blustered, reaching to grab the boy, if Tom hadn't stepped between. "Lying through their teeth, that's what they are! Not that I didn't 'ave plenty to say to 'im — but I was dog-weary, and you said —"

"Yes, yes — be quiet!" Tom shushed, and turned back to Gilles, who had backed half behind a sneering Luchette. "Why do you say it was Skeres?" he asked. "Did you see him?"

Gilles chewed his lip, and eyed Skeres. Then either fear or honesty won out, and he shook his head. "Heard them. But it was English that they spoke. So there."

So there, indeed — although what this truly meant… Tom counted the Englishmen at the Trois Poissons that night. Himself, Skeres, Litcott, Jack Dennis, Garrard and his servant — and there was Citolini, who would surely pass for English to the boy. And in fact… "Are you sure it was English? How would you know English from, say, Flemish?"

The boy shook his head in grim refusal. "One was him as died, all shrilly-voice, that one. And he was English, wasn't he?"

And until this morning, Tom himself would have thought Litcott spoke nothing but English. Now, though… And besides, why couldn't the Flemings speak English — or perhaps even Garrard's bed-fellow? He'd hardly spoken a word, that one, and certainly not English — but still…

For all we know, the Échevin had said, *it could have been any of you*… And Tom had deemed him a fool playing at slyness. But now… It was a disturbing thought, and one Tom kept to himself.

"When was that?" he asked instead. "Late in the night? Did they wake you?"

"No, that was earlier. I'd just gone up…" Young Gilles was in the process of shaking his head, when Madame Mirault began to shout for Luchette from across the yard.

"*La patronne!*" The young woman clicked her tongue, and rushed to the door. On the threshold, she stopped and turned to give Tom one of those twinkling smiles. "Don't let her catch you here, Monsieur. But if you ride this way again, you'll come and see Luchette, won't you?" She threw him a kiss, and fled.

Tom watched her go, clogs picking a way among the puddles, willing himself not to colour, not to imagine Skeres's knowing look, and most of all not to think of Sir Francis.

CHAPTER 9

Because the sky, while lowering the colour of pewter, kept its water to itself, and because Tom drove them as though the Furies were on their heels, they made good time. They hired horses in places that were not Tom's used stations, sending ahead Skeres, for good measure, with his paper and his complete ignorance of French. They lost themselves in the Fair-day bustle around Amiens. They slept in a flea-ridden hovel, in straw so filthy and alive with vermin that even Skeres was content to be up well before dawn, and snatched hasty, cold meals, and on they went, speaking hardly a word to anyone — until, the next day by mid-afternoon, they came in sight of Montreuil on its stubbed hill, and the river Canche.

It was beginning to rain again, and Skeres eyed the walls and the towers, looming in the grey drizzle. Wooden scaffolds clung at the ramparts, with men scurrying up and down them.

"Do we stop there?" the lad asked.

Tom shook his head. "No one stops in Montreuil," he said — wisdom gathered from other travellers, for he'd never entered the town himself. And besides, Citolini most surely hadn't — never one to lose time, or to renounce even half an hour of daylight...

So they rode around the town at the foot of the hillock, through terrain that, marshy on the brightest summer day, had been churned by the rains to a quagmire of peat and tawny-coloured clay. One would have thought it enough to make a fellow wary — but not Nick Skeres. Oh no. The fool must keep urging his horse, a disgruntled-looking hob with a narrow, stubborn head — and when the beast stumbled yet again, Tom lost his patience.

"Will you stop that, you lack-wit!" he snapped, turning in the saddle to glare over his shoulder. "Just let the poor beast pick its way. It knows better than you do."

Skeres looked rebellious, but in the end he just sat deeper in the saddle and let the horse do as it pleased, all the time grumbling of heads bitten off and rank injustice.

Tom swallowed a sharp retort. Hardly the lad's fault, was it, that he'd learnt precious little at the Trois Poissons, and that he was risking his career because Middlemore was a fool... Not that he was going to admit that — but Skeres either smelt it or, more likely, had no qualms at all.

"Worse than a bandog all day — and what 'ave you to bark about, I'll never know," he groused. "We've been going like 'ares, and never an 'itch, and not a soul as knew you..."

"Yes, well." Tom rose in the stirrups and squinted ahead, where the dull curve of the Canche spilled past its fringe of bare poplars and willows, drowning the marshy banks all the way to lap at the edge of the village of Attin. "You can avoid Post stations — but the ferry, now..."

The ferry at Attin had been on Tom's mind. The only way across the Canche, and manned by people who may well remember him from a dozen passages. And therefore, *quaestio*: would they remember him well enough to let him pass unchallenged?

Thus it was rather warily that Tom approached the ferry house at the village's edge, and dismounted, motioning for Skeres to do the same. The ferry — one of those flat-bottomed affairs that are punted across along a rope, was on the nearest bank, in the process of taking passengers. A dray-cart was boarding, among much shouting from carter and ferrymen. A pair of women with baskets fussing with their hoods, a horseman leading his mount, a stodgy figure with a mule, and half a dozen men on foot in muddy labourers' clothes awaited their turns — the men calling cheerful insults at the carter, whose horses seemed to have small liking for the ferry and the big ferryman's efforts.

A grey-bearded man was taking fees on the bank — and Tom's heart lifted at the sight. "Charon!" he whispered to himself. Perhaps Skeres was right, and there was no great cause to grumble.

"What?" the lad asked, craning his neck to give his master a suspicious frown. "What carrion?"

Tom very nearly laughed. "Charon, Nick Skeres. *Charon*: the ferryman of the dead — and, though you wouldn't believe it to see him, a blessed stroke of luck. Half blind, and never asks for papers. As long as his son is busy with that cart… Now wait here."

Leaving the reins to the servantman, and fishing two sols from his purse, Tom made his way through the small crowd, and reached the old ferryman.

"Two men and two horses," he said in his best French accent — the one that, as long as he confined himself to a few words, didn't give him away as an Englishman. He was quite proud of it, truth be told — and all the more when it worked. With no worse than a squint of his milky eyes and a nod, old Charon took the coins. Now let the draught horses be restive enough to keep the son at the ferry's other end a little longer… Tom was walking away in some satisfaction, when he felt a tap on his shoulder.

"But look, now. Look if it isn't you!" a cheery voice exclaimed.

Oh Lord! Tom's heart sank. Gritting his teeth, he turned to find the beaming, anxious face of the man with the mule. A face he knew, too…

"Firmin Basot!" the man said, thumping himself on the chest. "The other night — in Halcourt, eh?"

Of course. Tom swallowed a groan. Garrard's bedfellow — definitely not a foreigner, then. And here, of all men, of all places — here to know the English travellers! Just when Tom was beginning to think… Ah, well. One should never tempt the Fates.

"Monsieur Basot, yes." With the best smile he could fake, Tom caught the man's elbow, to steer him away from the old ferryman. "I never thought to see you here." And wasn't that the truth!

Basot chuckled. "Ah well, I've finished what business I had in Halcourt, and thank la Sainte Vièrge for that! I didn't like to stay there at the inn — not after…" He shook his head, flabby cheeks quivering. "Poor fellow — one is never safe with those rogues, not even under a roof. A shame, I call it. A black shame!"

Tom murmured assent, and would have extricated himself — but Basot now had a firm grip on his sleeve.

"And I'm going home, now, you see — and look who must be there, but the English gentleman again!" The man had this wondering air, as though meeting again were some portent, rather than a confounded nuisance. "And look, Basot, I told myself, you never spoke to an Englishman in all your life, and now you meet no one else — and meet them twice! But yes — twice that thin-faced little fellow, first — and now twice you…"

That thin-faced little fellow… Could it be that Tom's quarries were just ahead? "You met Jack Dennis? He's never here, is he?"

Basot looked about, round-eyed, as though the Merchant Strangers' man should appear from thin air. "Dennis? Is that his name? Oh yes. But no — not here. I saw him first in Amiens, when I was travelling to Halcourt — and then two days later, lo! He comes to the Trois Poissons with you. And now, two days after that, it's you again —"

"*Allez, Messieurs! Allez!*"

The ferryman's holler broke through Basot's ramblings — and Tom's frowning surprise. From the bank, Charon beckoned with much milling of arms. Most of the other passengers had boarded already, and a boy was coaxing Basot's mule onto the wooden planks.

"Oh, Saints help! Now she'll get all neckstiff…" Basot yelped, and rushed to his mount's rescue.

Let them not miss the passage, now… Tom called to Skeres, who had been waiting at some distance with the horses — and they were hurrying to the ferry when Tom heard Basot, no doubt in answer to some question of the ferryman, say: "No, just the English couriers!"

Tom's heart sank again. *Lord smite all blabbering dunces…!*

And sometimes, Thomas, there is no recourse — but to brazen your way through catastrophe.

"Give me the passport, Skeres," Tom ordered under his breath, and the lad patted all over himself for the damn papers, and couldn't have been more obvious if he tried, and by the time they were in the presence of Charon, the sharp-eyed son had been summoned.

Now let him only not remember too well…

Charon *fils* perused the paper, following word by word with a bony forefinger — with his father and Basot each peering over a shoulder, and Skeres glaring from Frenchman to Frenchman.

"You are Nicolas Skères?" the ferryman asked at last, pronouncing the name French-wise.

"Yes," said Tom — brazen indeed!

"*Mais non!*" said Basot at the same time, and pointed at the servantman. "That one's the lad Skères, the one with the black eye!"

Tom gritted his teeth, and thought of wilful murder, and elbowed the grumbling Skeres quiet, and surely — surely Sir Francis had never had to brazen his way through a catastrophe of such stupidity...?

"Oh — there must be... The Ambassador's clerk..." he tried — without the least hope.

And indeed, Charon *père* and *fils* exchanged frowns, then the son sniffed, and jerked his chin at Skeres: "And you'd be this one's servant, eh?"

"*Mais non!*" Whatever excitement Basot may have felt at dealing with Englishmen, had turned to mistrust, and he jabbed a ferocious finger at Tom. "The lad there is the servant, and this one's the master!"

The ferrymen, Basot, and the boy with the mule, all closed in. There were calls of "what happens?" from the barge, where the passengers crowded at the nearest rail to watch, as though at a play... Tom's muscles bunched, and he had wild thoughts of his rapier, and of leaping in the saddle, and rushing home somehow to warn Sir Francis...

And most of all, Thomas, aequam memento servare mentem. Whatever else you do — keep your head.

And Tom kept his head, and kept quiet, and kept Skeres quiet — as Charon *fils* sequestered the passport, took away their weapons, and had one of the passengers stay behind to help get the Englishmen to Montreuil.

Basot, curse him, scurried onto the ferry, mule in tow, much pleased with himself, and full of tales to tell, no doubt… And then the ferry was sent on its way.

Tom watched the ferry lurch, by punt and rope, across the grey, swollen water. It was raining again.

"Look, master!" Nick Skeres leant in to whisper. "I take the ferryman, you the other — and we run, eh?"

"Why — yes, Nick Skeres!" Tom snapped — and never mind that he'd just had the same thought himself. "And how will you like to run for our lives, then, with the archers on our heels?"

The lad shrugged, craning his head this way and that, to give considering looks at one Frenchman, then at the other — as though Tom had truly asked his opinion in debate, and he were considering…

"No," Tom said, as quellingly as he knew. "You take no one."

And then Charon the Younger, having armed himself with a stout cudgel, started them all back on the muddy road.

It seemed that they would stop in Montreuil, after all.

They had to retrace all the way around Montreuil — the town curling up the hillside like a wet dog, with its two rings of walls and the sluggish river meandering at the foot. Seen from this side, Montreuil lost all stateliness. The outer walls weren't much to see, the squat, round towers battered and overgrown with tangles of creepers, the dry moat filled with debris in places… Besieged at some time, Tom seemed to recall. A pity the besiegers, whoever they were, hadn't made a more thorough work!

Not a soul they met, and the ferryman hurried them ahead, never answering Tom's questions but with glares and scowls.

"Where do you take us?"

Nothing.

"Who is in charge of such things here?"

Nothing.

"The Mayor? The Échevins? You don't have a Bailli here, do you?"

Nothing.

At the Town gate, Charon the Younger seemed quite relieved to hand his prisoners to a bored Town Sergent. The Sergent gave the two Englishmen an unimpressed scrutiny, took possession of papers and weapons, dismissed the captors, and yelled over his shoulder. Two guards appeared from the guardhouse and, on receiving an order, one took the two horses by the bridle, and the other, a fat, greasy fellow, motioned for the two Englishmen to follow. He did so with a good deal of pantomime, and gaped when Tom protested in French.

"*Voyez donc!*" the man marvelled. "You speak French! Him, too?" he asked, turning to better inspect Skeres — and Skeres, of course, bristled.

"No," said Tom. "But look, if you could tell me…"

The guard nodded, with the cheeriest of smiles. "So you're a spy of your Queen, and he's not?"

"No," Tom said again. "We are no spies at all. I can explain. If only I knew who it is I must address…"

The guards exchanged shrugs, and then the fat one said the Échevins, or M. Le Mayeur himself, if they liked. "But that's for tomorrow, eh? Now we go to the Rue de la Chaîne."

Chain Street. It sounded ominous enough that Tom dug in his heels.

"Now look, my good men." He raised his voice for the Sergent's benefit. "I ride for the Queen of England. I can't wait for tomorrow."

The retreating Sergent waved a hand without so much as bothering to turn back, and the fat soldier grinned as though to a fine jest, and nodded, and said that yes, yes, tomorrow — and prodded Tom in the ribs with his truncheon — not sharply, but enough to make him move.

Tom shook his head at Skeres when the lad looked rebellious. No sense in brawling with the Town guards. Perhaps there would be someone in Rue de la Chaîne — someone who would listen to reason...?

The gate opened on a huge square, a market place, by the look of it — but for the most part deserted. A handful of stalls huddled together at one side of the muddy expanse, half of them already shuttered for the day, and a man was dragging away a reluctant donkey laden with covered baskets.

"Filthy little hole," Skeres muttered vindictively, as the guards led them along a row of run-down wooden houses — and he wasn't wrong, although, with its large square and double walls, Montreuil must have looked better, before Leaguers and Loyalists tore Picardy to rags between them.

They marched past a well and a sputtering fountain where cabbage leaves floated, and climbed up an empty, unpaved incline to a second wall. This inner ring looked newer, made of quarried stones, although the gate was more scantily guarded. The Englishmen and their escort were let through with no more than a jesting exchange — jesting and not flattering to the English. Tom scowled, just so they knew he understood and took objection. The fat soldier smiled, and shrugged, and nudged him past.

This upper Montreuil proved to be a place of narrow, none-too-clean alleys, and houses crowding on each other, a jumble of framed wattle and cheap stone. The streets were not paved, not even the one square Tom saw, when they almost tumbled into it from yet another dim alley. A cramped thing, and sudden as a crevice, dwarfed by a looming church, whose buttressed front seemed to weep in the rainy twilight.

Just as they passed by, the bells began to roar above them in the belfry, and others answered all across the town. The *Ave*, Tom assumed, watching the guards cross themselves — and he turned to hiss Skeres silent just in time before the lad gave them his mind about Popish devilry and what not...

They were led along a crumbling, waist-high wall, beyond which lay a bare space... Could it be a field? There were mounds here and there...

"The strangers' graveyard, Monsieur!" the fat guard said, grinning from ear to ear — which made his glum fellow laugh, and the uncomprehending Skeres glower.

Then again, Tom's own patience was very much fraying by then, and he stopped where he was. "Well, that's enough," he said, drawing as tall as he could. *Firm, not angry.* "I demand to know where you are taking us."

The fat guard raised a disbelieving eyebrow. "But there, Monsieur." He gestured at something behind Tom's back. "The gaol of the Échevinage, what did you think?"

Tom snorted, thinking of Burry and de Briet at the Trois Poissons, trying to foist the Englishmen on each other... Was the Town of Montreuil of a simpler mind than Amiens? Was there ever any understanding of the French?

The Échevinage — likely the back of it, if the gaol was there — was a tall thing of stone, with a row of narrow barred openings on either part of a nail-studded gate, where the guard

121

went to knock. Upstairs, the windows became larger, leaving no doubt on the use of the lower ground.

After knocking a second time, the guard turned to Tom, as cheery as though he'd brought him to the best inn in town. "Count yourself lucky, Monsieur," he laughed. "Had it been the Bailli's fellows instead of us, they'd be throwing you in the oubliette up at the old Château, eh?" And he held out a hopeful hand.

Of course.

You never know what can happen, Watson had said, pressing more money on him — good Corydon! Tom took a sol from his purse, and then another, when the guard threw a meaningful glance his fellow's way. Two sols for being brought to the gaol — not a measly fee! And, thinking of that, would he ever see again the two more he'd paid for the ferry they never took?

No time for more than a passing thought of that, before bolts screeched, and a postern in the heavy gate was inched open. A man with a mop of yellow hair peered out, with a lantern and an ill-humoured question of what the cursed matter was now...

There were explanations, and more talk of English spies, and Tom tried to say that he needed to see the Mayor at once, or an Échevin, and what were they doing with his horses — and nobody paid the least mind.

Then again, what would there be to say to the Mayor, at once or, for that matter, in the morning?

You know what will happen if they catch you without papers...

The postern slammed shut, and the gaoler drew the bolts again — as final, as hopeless a rasp as Tom had ever heard.

"Never been in gaol, 'ave you?" Skeres asked in one of his thunder-like whispers — and Tom had the briefest time to wonder what gave that away, before the gaoler drew close, holding the lantern high to peer at his new guests.

He chewed at his lip, and made a great show of turning to look first at a stairway that yawned black across the hall, and then at a bolted door on the other side.

"River's been up and rising this last fortnight," he muttered, as though musing to himself. "Will be half a foot of water, down there, I'll wager..." And again he turned to the bolted door, and then back to the Englishmen.

"What's 'e say?" Skeres asked, and Tom waved him quiet.

They'd climbed up the hill enough that he doubted there would be river water in the cells. Not that he fancied spending the night underground — but, if they were held for any amount of time, and if French gaols were anything like their English counterparts, they would need every penny of what little money remained, for food and drink and candles.

He ignored Skeres's question, and just looked at the gaoler until the man's face twisted in disappointment. With a shrug and a mutter of fine gentlemen and tight fists, he led the way down the stairwell, and to the first in a row of narrow doors, which he unbolted and dragged open.

"In here," he ordered, with a jerk of his yellow head.

In there was a small, squat cell with a bench against the long side, and no window. Tom had been right, and there was no water on the straw-covered floor, but the black walls gleamed slick with moistness, and the air hung heavy and dank.

It was more than Tom could help to turn back, and grab the gaoler by the arm.

"But I must see your Mayor in the morning!" It was a struggle to keep his voice even. "First thing in the morning, you understand? And I must have back my papers..." For all the good they were going to do.

"But yes, yes." The gaoler tugged free. "Tomorrow, eh?" He stepped out backwards and pushed the door shut, leaving the cell in complete darkness.

Tom hit an open palm against the wood. "Wait!" he called, pitching his voice over the scrape of bolts. "We'll want some supper. And a candle…"

"But yes, yes…" came from outside, and then the man's retreating steps, and the whistling of a jig.

A jig — while Citolini pranced away to Calais, ready to cross to England, and give Sir Francis a half story … a jig!

"Curse it!" Tom swore. "Curse Firmin Basot! Curse all ferrymen. Curse the whole of France to hell!"

"Amen," grunted Skeres somewhere in the gloom, with such truculent fervency that Tom could not help a huff of laughter.

"My mother, when I tell her, will say that I bring these things on my head by swearing like a heathen."

"Then don't tell 'er," said Skeres, which struck Tom as very good advice. With a sigh, he felt his way along the cold, slick wall and to the bench. It creaked a good deal when he sat down, elbows on knees.

"Let's hope it's still raining," he said. "Let's hope it stops Citolini, too. Perhaps even the crossings…?"

"Ay!" Skeres was moving about, banging, by the sound of it, into every wall and corner. "And maybe it will tip over that lousy barge, and drown the little turd with the mule…"

"Basot?"

"What's it that 'e said? Where did 'e know you from?"

Tom snorted. "How come you didn't even notice him, and he remembered you by name? One of my room-fellows the other night. Quiet as a mouse, he was — and found his tongue right in time!"

"See? If you'd let me trounce 'im…"

Oh yes — of course. The lad's one recourse in dealing with his fellow-men, apparently. Tom twisted on the bench, in the general direction of the oh, so reasonable voice. "Nick Skeres, listen to me, for once: you don't go about trouncing men at the drop of a hat. Besides being a sin, it's bound to land you in gaol, sooner or later."

The lad sniffed. "Ay, well. Not trouncing them works just as fine."

And just what did one answer to that? Tom let himself plop on his back, grimacing at the stench of rotting straw and mildew. Perhaps he should have let Skeres trounce the lack-wit Basot, with all his foolish talk of meeting Englishmen twice...

Twice!

Tom jolted to sit up, to more creaking of the bench. "He saw Dennis in Amiens!"

"Eh? Who?" Skeres asked from across the cell.

"Basot saw Jack Dennis in Amiens, two days before we met him in Dury. What was he doing there all that time?"

Skeres hummed. "Waiting for company? Said 'e didn't like to ride alone..."

"So he waited two days, and then thought he'd find company in Dury, rather than Amiens?"

"Ay, well..." A yawn and the unmistakeable sound of head-scratching came from the gloom. "Maybe 'e wanted Englishmen for company..."

"Tilly-vally! Unless..." Tom jumped to his feet, and would have paced, if not for the darkness. "Unless... What if he wanted these particular Englishmen? What if he'd been waiting for us?"

"Ay, well — what then?"

What then, indeed. Why would Jack Dennis…? Tom sat down again, and tried to think like a pupil of Sir Francis's, rather than a cursed fool…

You must always observe, Thomas, the joints and flexures of affairs.

And where did Dennis's sojourn in Amiens join with Litcott's death? Because join they must, surely? Jack Dennis had lied — or at least misled them — and why would he do so, unless…

"Suppose … suppose Litcott had an accomplice, or… No, better still! Suppose he was never a spy — just conveniently there to be killed, and found in the morning, stabbed with a dagger those soldiers had stolen, and carrying your paper…"

"Ay, but why do 'im in?"

"Because…" Tom smiled to himself in the dark at the well-loved sense of pieces falling into place… "Because, Nick Skeres, we must be made to believe that the French had him in their pay, and a corpse will answer no questions, tell no tales, and dispute no accusations. And it was Dennis who brought up the matter of the soldiers with Burry when no one else would. And besides, there is that argument that Litcott had in the stables —"

"Ay — and that wasn't me!"

And trust Nick Skeres to be still gnawing on the stableboy's accusation…

"No, I don't think it was," Tom said. "Still, it must have been an Englishman — because Flemings and Wallons aren't all that rare in these parts, and young Gilles may well know what they sound like, if nothing else."

"And Flemings don't speak English?"

"True — but now we know that Dennis lied. And if it was him arguing in the stables… Perhaps Litcott had seen him in Amiens, too, or … or…"

"Never liked that Jack Dennis," Skeres said. "An Englishman as works for foreigners!"

Tom thought of the counterfeit French ciphering... Not that he doubted Phelippes in the least — but ... was it perhaps a little too obvious? "We don't know that," he said, half to himself. "Well, he *is* a man of the Merchant Strangers, but someone else might have set him up to this."

Skeres grumbled — as unwilling to relinquish the notion of a foreign culprit, as Maître Burry had been eager to have an English one. True enough, a match between England and France was not just an English concern, and the Merchant Strangers, with their own post, would be better placed than most to poke their noses. Still...

Apply mistrust, Thomas — yet don't let it cloud your judgement.

Tom pounded a fist on the bench. "What we do know is that now Dennis is travelling with Citolini — and according to Middlemore, he went out of this way to do so — and we are kept here for who knows how long..."

Suddenly there was whistling in the passage, and a faint yellow line under the door ... at last! Tom jumped to his feet, felt his way to the door, and began to knock and call.

It was the gaoler again. He carried a trencher with bread and slabs of cheese, tankards, and a burning tallow candle.

"There, there," the man soothed. "Supper, eh?" And he balanced the trencher on a hip as he held out a hand.

Tom dug in his purse again. "If not the Mayor, I need to see an Échevin," he said, his try at imperiousness a little ruined by the impatience he could not swallow. "Even a clerk will do."

The gaoler squinted at the sol thrust in his palm. "Yes, yes — you'll see the King, for all I care. In the morning."

Tom added a second coin. "I must see someone now!"

With a sniff, the gaoler pocketed his money, and laid the trencher on the bench. One piece of cheese teetered, and fell to the filthy floor. The man picked it up, blew on it, and dropped it on the trencher again. "You think they're sitting about, burning candles just to wait on you? Tomorrow, tomorrow."

"But I —"

"But you — tomorrow, eh?"

The gaoler retreated and pushed the door closed in Tom's face.

"Tomorrow," he called again, as he drew the bolts.

Tom kicked the door. Had he been a little younger, had he not been Mr. Secretary's kinsman and pupil, had he been alone or at least in the dark, he might have wept.

"Ay, well, you know…" Nick Skeres came to sit on the bench, picked up a piece of cheese (the one that had dropped to the dirty ground), and shoved it in his mouth. "We 'ad to stop, soon or late. Do they eat something else, these 'eathens, beside cheese?"

"Oh, curse the cheese! Can't you see those two will be in Calais by now?"

Skeres shrugged, and eyed the trencher. "Are you minded to eat?" he asked through a mouthful. "Because if you're not minded to eat…"

Tom threw himself on the bench, and wished for morning.

CHAPTER 10

And morning came, at long last. Not that they would have known, down in that lightless cave — but a gaoler, a different one, came to fetch the prisoners (not without exacting his own vail for it), and brought them to the tall, draughty hallway from the night before, where three men stood waiting. They didn't look much pleased with each other. Their mutual grimness, and the fact that two wore swords, and royal lilies over soldier-like buff attire, while the third had a sash of blue and gold, made this some repetition of the tussle at the Trois Poissons, most likely.

The moment Tom was before him, the gaunt fellow in blue and gold threw his hands in the air. "All yours, Sergent," he cried, shaking a finger at the bigger of the two guardsmen. "All yours. But mind, you tell your master that the Échevins wash their hands of the whole matter — the whole of it!" And with that he stalked away, and it became clear that the Town had, none too happily, lost the Englishmen to … to whom, exactly? The Bailli's fellows? The one who threw prisoners in oubliettes?

"Where do you bring me?" Tom asked, as the gaoler opened the postern, and the two sergents had him and Skeres file out in the street, and in the cold, damp, blessedly clean morning.

"To see the Lieutenant," the smaller sergent said. "Lieutenant to the Bailli of Amiens, that is — and you should thank all the Saints… Well no, you won't, seeing as you are a heretic — but you should. Monsieur the Wacogne isn't like the Mayeur, who'd hang all foreigners on sight!"

Which amused the Frenchmen enough that they shared a laugh, before herding their prisoners up the street — Tom looking about, and Skeres blinking owl-like, still half asleep.

Uphill they climbed, past the graveyard and the church, along a largish street, lined on both sides with stone-built houses, for the most part, that looked newish. In fact, a few still had empty windows, and at one point a cart laden with planks of fresh-sawn wood trundled past, swaying this way and that in the yellow mud. Up the street rose another ring of walls, and a jumble of towers and turrets, some with scaffolds around them, and a belfry...

"What's that?" Skeres asked around a yawn.

"The old castle, it would seem." Tom squinted up at the looming huddle of grey piles. "They must be making it into a citadel." And surely it made sense to keep the place well-fortified, with the way it overlooked both road and river...

"Why do we go there?"

And this Tom rather wondered himself. The men at the gate had been Town guards: how had the Lieutenant even known of the captured Englishmen so quickly? And why did he want them for himself? And, now he had them, would he throw them in the oubliette?

Well, not at first, at least. Their destination was a round, squat tower built over and around a large passageway. Through it, men could be seen, working on more walls, perhaps a bulwark, and sawing at planks. There one sergent stopped with Skeres, while the other led Tom up a narrow curving staircase, and to a gloomy, cold, round room that smelt of wet stone and stale smoke and beeswax.

It was hard to tell whether it was greased paper or alabaster screening the square slits in the arm-thick walls — but, whatever it was, smoke and time had stained it the darkest brown, so that all the light came from two fat candles on a table across the room. At that table, entrenched behind tall piles of papers, the Bailli's man sat huddled in a fur robe.

The Seigneur de Wacogne, Lieutenant to the Bailli of Amiens, looked up from whatever he'd been studying. "*Et bien*," he said, squinting at the newcomer. "We have ourselves a brace of English spies?"

Tom bristled at his tone and words, and just in time it occurred to him that perhaps he'd better not make enemies in the Bailliage — much less this particular enemy, right now... It occurred in the unwelcome shape of Citolini scolding him for doing just that with Burry — nothing to help a fellow's temper — but still...

"I'm no such thing, Monsieur le Lieutenant," he said in his best French, and with an evenness that was quite commendable, if he thought so himself.

Wacogne leant forward, peering at Tom over his steepled hands, with a gleam in his deep-set gaze. "I'll confess, Monsieur, that I would greatly prefer it if you were. Because, to be quite frank with you, it would spare me — for the day at least — the discontented bourgeois of Montreuil wanting the old gate here opened again, and our esteemed Mayeur taking it into his head that the Bailli is the right man to pester on the subject. And let me not even start on the Guilds. Did you know that Montreuil has, by charter, the most bothersome Guilds in the realm?"

Well this, now... Was the man horn-mad? But no. Not mad — just fed up with Montreuil — a feeling with which one had to agree. And eager for a chance at earning himself a better post — perhaps by capturing English spies? Tom's heart sank a little. "But, Monsieur, what has this all to do with me?"

Wacogne shook a rather leonine mane of greying hair. "Oh, just that perhaps you'll understand how much I hope that you are not, after all…" He picked up an unfolded paper, and held it to one candle's light. "Nicolas Skères? Our ferryman, you see, says that you are not."

Tom had had the whole of a sleepless night to debate the matter with himself, and to cast for an explanation that wouldn't have him locked in that oubliette while enquiries were made of the Ambassador in Paris… He was beginning to fear that a suspect spy would be too much for the Lieutenant to pass on… But what of a dim-witted courier? Would the man chance bothering his betters over that…?

"Ah, yes — that now…" He tried his best to look flustered, and innocent, and a little dull — for which, Watson sometimes said, he had a most uncanny talent. "Skeres is my man, the one travelling with me — I haven't had him long, you see — but it was all arranged in haste, and surely the Ambassador's clerk must have mistaken things, and I was never more surprised in my life as when the ferryman asked if I was Skeres…"

Wacogne raised a hand to stem the babbling. "And you didn't know that you were travelling with the wrong name on your papers?" he asked in incredulity.

"No one questioned me until Attin, and…" Tom aimed for Middlemore's empty-headed haughtiness. "And I'm not in the habit of studying my own passport, Monsieur."

The Lieutenant pursed his lips — very possibly thinking that such a dunce might benefit from such study, now and then… "But if you are not the servant Skères — then, who are you?"

Tom offered his name, and his travelling licence to prove it — after all it did fit the story of a mistaken name, wobbly as it was…

Wacogne hummed to himself, lowering his eyes to study the licence, worded in English and in Latin. "And just how do you propose to secure passage to England, with this?"

And was that ever a good question! "I am well known to several ships' captains, and the Ambassador's man, the one I'm joining in Calais, will vouch for me." Which Tom could only hope was true — but then again, a Middlemore would have no doubt in spouting his convictions, no matter how doubtfully founded.

The Lieutenant raised thick black eyebrows at that, eyes still fastened on the papers. "Still…" he murmured. "Wal-sing-ham. Is that not the name of your Queen's minister?"

"Mr. Secretary, yes. I am his cousin's son." It was a little harder to maintain the witless arrogance when it came to Sir Francis. Would this Frenchman believe that Mr. Secretary counted such a dimwit among his kin?

"*Et bien.*" Wacogne folded the licence, and piled it together with Skeres's passport, turning both between his fingers. "You'll admit, it's still a rather extraordinary tale. I'm sure your *Sécretaire* will forgive me for keeping you here while we send to Paris." He set the papers aside, and unfolded a long-shanked frame from the high-backed seat, walking around the table to loom over Tom. "Perhaps, though, we'll show you some better hospitality, eh?"

Oh Lord. Oh Lord. "Monsieur!" Two days at best, three more likely — and meanwhile… Tom caught the Lieutenant by a fur-trimmed sleeve. "Monsieur, apart from the name on it, the passport is correct: I must join my colleague in Calais. He wasn't far ahead of me, until yesterday — but I must join him before he reaches England, Monsieur."

And damn the sudden pleading in his voice — but it earned a sharp gaze from Wacogne.

"Well, but you must see, this is just what a spy might say…"

And at this, Tom's patience slipped very badly. "And *you* must see," he snapped, "that if I were a spy, I'd have much better papers — and a better tale to tell!"

Blood rushed up Tom's neck and face. What would Sir Francis think? And, of more immediate importance, what did Wacogne think?

The Frenchman was nodding to himself. "You know, young man…" he murmured, slow as molasses. "You know, somehow I doubt your head is as empty as you'd have me think."

There. There. This was where Tom was thrown in the oubliette for a spy — a dark place full of rats, whence they'd take him only to put him to the question — because they would, wouldn't they? — while Citolini galloped merrily to London, with false news fit to spark a war, and quite possibly with a murderer in tow… Tom closed his eyes and took a deep, deep breath.

"Monsieur de Wacogne, the full truth is…" He hesitated, covering it under colour of watching over his shoulder if anyone might be listening. Could he invoke the interest of France as well as that of England? Could he hint at the danger to the peace between their kingdoms? Could he risk…? Brazening one's way through catastrophe was not the same as spilling secrets of State to a provincial magistrate of the French King — but perhaps there was something he could offer to this dissatisfied man instead of an English spy… "The full truth is, I ride at the personal behest of Mr. Secretary." Far from the full truth — and Tom managed not to wince with the thought. "Matters of great import hang in the balance. Of great import, Monsieur — and not just to my Queen."

Now let the Lieutenant of Montreuil be neither too unversed in the affairs of kingdoms nor too averse to the cursed Match. Let him remember that Sir Francis had travelled to France last summer to negotiate a treaty *and* a marriage...

"You wouldn't mean..." The man leant forward and lowered his voice. "Surely you don't mean the matter of his Grace the Duke?"

Of course, of course he knew! The whole of Europe knew — why not the Seigneur of Wacogne? Tom covered his relief. Instead, there was this manner Sir Francis had, when he wanted to lead a man without committing to speech: a tilt of head and eyebrow, an inscrutable gaze — and, most of all, silence. Not that Tom had ever had much chance to try it on anyone, except himself in a looking glass, and he was finding it rather hard to keep both gaze and silence. Out of the door, he could hear the Sergent shuffling his feet, and the saws and hammers of the men working outside, and he was about to give up in desperation, when...

"I see," Wacogne murmured. He looked down, nodding to himself, and studying the signet ring he wore on his middle finger. "Now, if I let you go, Monsieur Wal-sing-ham — *if* I let you go ... it is much to take on myself."

Tom held the man's gaze, and lowered his voice to a whisper. "That's as may be, Monsieur — but would you take it upon yourself to keep me here because a fool of a clerk mistook a name?"

For a moment the Lieutenant just stood there, the reckoning of risks and stakes plain on his face as he frowned at Tom.

And Tom waited, trying not to fidget. Had he gone too far...?

When it came, it was sudden. With the look of a man deciding the fate of thousands, Wacogne stepped around Tom

— fur-lined robe swishing around his legs — and went to open the door, calling for Tom's horses to be saddled, and something to break fast.

And thanks be! "Monsieur le Lieutenant…" Tom began.

The Frenchman closed the door on the sudden scurrying and calling outside, and turned around, grim-faced and thin-lipped.

And Tom knew, as clear as printed words, what was on the man's mind, what he was struggling to put into words — and what was required of him.

"It is a matter of more than just my gratitude, Monsieur," he said, with his gravest half-bow. "What you have done will be known." Finely weighed words that, he was rather sure, Mother would count as a lie — and not a white one, either…

After that, it was as though the Bailli's men in Montreuil had espoused Tom's cause in full — all a-flutter with bread and cold meat, and saddling horses, and Skeres found again, and even an escort to Attin. And if it seemed that being let out of gaol was no cheap thing in France — more coins having to be handed out at every step — and if the ferry's fee had to be disbursed again, leaving Tom's purse as nearly empty as made no difference, that one worry paled against the relief of being free to go again. Much worse was the conversation with the Seigneur de Wacogne…

Ah well, off to Calais, now — and he'd find a way to cross — but just how he was going to explain Wacogne to Sir Francis, Tom didn't want to think.

CHAPTER 11

Always, as he travelled to London, Tom began to feel almost at home the moment he entered Calais by the old Prince Gate. For all that Calais had been French these past fifteen years and more, you could still call things and places by their English names, and few would bat an eyelid.

But that day the relief at seeing the huge sandstone ramparts of Calais, the colour of ochre against the expanse of sky and sea, was short lived.

"We still have to find Citolini," he glumly said more to himself than Skeres, as they made their way along the busy streets. "Supposing he's not halfway to England already…"

In truth, he rather hoped not. It had rained hard all through the night, and then the wind had picked up. Even in the walled shelter of the town streets, it snatched at cloaks and hats, taut, and cold, and salty. Tom didn't want to hope for any luck, but perhaps…

He took Lantern Street, just off Market Place, and stopped right across from the door of the Dauphin d'Or — the Dolphin to the English couriers who always put up there. "And when we find him," he murmured, looking up at the painted sign that resembled no sea creature Tom had ever seen — golden or otherwise — and thinking of his lack of papers, and the unsanctioned news he brought, "When we find him, he's going to bite like a bandog."

"Ay, well — mayhap Dennis 'as done 'im in," said Skeres, with a look of hopeful cheer to give a man pause.

Tom shook his head, and entered the inn.

The half-English landlord was very happy to see Monsieur Wals'nam again so soon — and why, but yes: Monsieur Paul was still at the Dolphin. Like a hornet in a jug, that one was: raring to go across, and grumbling about it, and never mind that the weather heeds no man— but look, right there he was...

"Monsieur Paul!" The innkeeper waved, a cheery smile creasing his horse-like face. "Look who's been asking after you, Monsieur!"

Paolo Citolini stopped halfway down the stairs, looking as pleased as the innkeeper's hornet and Tom's bandog combined.

"What the devil are you doing here?" was his salutation, which irked Tom a good deal — because, never mind the intelligence he carried, wasn't he a courier too, whose comings and goings were the Queen's business?

Tom moved to join Citolini at the foot of the stairs, and lowered his voice to answer: "I've come to warn you."

For once and for a wonder, Citolini listened. Or at least had the wit to see that no good would come of arguing where half of Calais could hear them. "Come," he said, and led the way to a small parlour behind the common room.

Tom waved for Skeres to stay where he was, and followed.

The room was narrow and dim, and the casement rattled in the wind. Citolini placed himself standing against the wall, crossing arms and ankles, and raised an eyebrow. "So let us have it, this warning that you bring," he said.

And Tom, who had been riding like one pursued by the Furies for two days and a half, with half-false papers and all manners of trouble dogging him, sat down and took a deep breath, and began his tale. He had scarcely come to explain the matter of the cipher, and the English hand that must be behind it all, when Citolini threw up his hands.

"And this, of course, had to be told to you — never to me!" he exclaimed.

Tom had expected this, and had his answer ready. "You'd been long gone by the time Phelippes found fault with the letter," he said — which was both true and vague enough. "And so was Sir Henry, so Watson went after him — and I after you."

Tom was moderately proud of his careful telling — until Citolini sneered.

"You, Watson, Phelippes," he said. "The Thomases at work!" And then he pushed himself off the wall. "*Bene*, you have warned me. You can go back to Paris."

"But —"

Citolini held out a hand. "Let me have that paper," he commanded. "I will tell Mr. Secretary what you suspect — for what it is worth." He eyed the rumpled page as he took it. "How do we know what cipher the French use or would not use?"

"Phelippes says —" Tom tried.

"Phelippes!" the Italian snorted. "Phelippes is a clerk. You clear the French of all suspicion on his word?"

"Yes..." Tom wavered. Not that he doubted his friend — but what had seemed steel-clad logic for more than two days, felt suddenly flimsy under the Italian's purse-lipped scrutiny. "His word, and Litcott himself. Oh, come — you've met him: that dunce, a spy! What about Dennis, instead?"

"Jack Dennis?" Citolini frowned. "What of him?"

"You've travelled here with him, haven't you?"

"Yes. What of him?"

And Tom told of Basot — if not of Montreuil — and of the argument at the Trois Poissons…

At this, the Italian made a great show of exclaiming in disbelief. "You were to reach me in all haste — and yet found time to stop in Halcourt! That young woman must have addled your wits!"

Oh, damn the furious blush creeping up to his ears… "Well, I found out about that argument, didn't I?" Tom snapped. "That can be no chance, that Litcott has words with an Englishman — and a few hours later he dies?"

"Oh, that!" Citolini shrugged. "That could have been anything — and anyone. There were plenty of Englishmen in that hayloft … that servantman of yours, for one."

"Nick Skeres, truly!" Skeres a sharp-minded, subtle spy, weaving manifold deceptions?

"He was there." Citolini spread both hands, palms up. "At hand to argue and to kill. Dennis would have to stalk about the inn like a villain at the play."

And this was true enough — but then there had been the door to the bedroom, opening and closing at some point through the night… Had Tom really heard that, more than half asleep?

"Still, that is neither here nor there," the Italian said, grimly triumphant. "You forget the soldiers. Who else could have used my dagger to do murder?"

Tom looked up, smiling a little as more pieces fell into place inside his head. "The man who hired the soldiers! To convince us that he might never have done it!"

Citolini hummed and tilted his head as one conceding a point — and it occurred to Tom that the man must have done and enjoyed disputations in some Italian university, at some time…

"What if the whole affair with the dagger was a bit of playacting?" Tom pursued his advantage. "What if they gave the thing back to Dennis? He must have known that we'd know it — that at least *you* would. And it was Dennis who brought up the soldiers in front of Burry."

For a few heartbeats there was only the angry wind down the chimney, as Citolini considered Tom's notion. Then the Italian shook his head. "But even if you were right about Litcott — and I much misdoubt that — how did Dennis know what you carried and who travelled with you?"

Tom opened his mouth to say that Dennis didn't need to know that — that anyone would have done: Citolini himself, Skeres... But he could see the fallacy in the argument: Dennis must have known for a certainty that Sir Francis's own courier wasn't travelling alone... "He must have been in London — Richmond, even."

"And how would he be in Amiens two days before you, then?"

"A better crossing, riding at night, alone, with no packhorse, no clumsy glover..." The idea struck Tom as he said it: "Why, the way *you* did. You gained a full day on us."

Citolini huffed. "And that half by chance," he said — and then, as though the admission had escaped him unbidden, he crossed his arms again, shaking his head. "Is it not easier for the glover to have been in the pay of the French? After all, Monsieur sent him."

"Or he could have been working for someone in England. This Lord of his that he always spoke about." Tom had to shake his head, wishing that he'd paid mind to Litcott's monologues...

"And would he always speak about his spymaster?" the Italian asked triumphantly, as one routing rampant stupidity — all sense of a disputation between equals gone.

Too triumphantly by far, in fact, because… "No — no, indeed!" Tom exclaimed. "He wouldn't, and by the same token he wouldn't be Monsieur's man. He could be no spy at all —"

He stopped when there was knocking at the door. It was the innkeeper, come to say that Maître Benabic had sent word with a boy. Benabic — a sour-hearted Breton shipmaster, who loathed all the Queen's men with a will. There must be no English ship crossing, for Citolini to resort to him…

"He reckons to catch the midnight tide, if it's all the same to you," the innkeeper said.

"At last!" Citolini exclaimed, and made to go, slipping Litcott's cipher into the purse at his belt.

"Wait," Tom called after him. "Dennis might have been in Amiens all the time, and someone from London might have sent orders —"

"Enough of this." The Italian stopped on the threshold, hand on the doorjamb, to glare at Tom. "I will apprise Mr. Secretary. Send your Skegg, or whatever he calls himself, to the harbour in good time. He must ask for the *Meance*."

And with that he was gone, and when Tom followed him to the door to ask where was Dennis, he only paused long enough to throw over his shoulder: "How would I know?"

Tom kicked at the doorjamb. Oh curse Paolo Citolini — and curse himself for thinking that the Italian would heed him! Now, if only…

The innkeeper was hovering at a discreet distance, curious, but knowing enough to keep his nose out of the couriers' business. Good man, Dessay — for the most part.

Tom beckoned him close. "Is there no English ship crossing tonight, Dessay? There must be one!"

The man shook his head, slow and ponderous. "Nary a one tonight, master. Nary a one. And not many crossing at all — not with this gale. Why do you think Mastro Paolo goes with that Breton dog? He likes the English like the plague, that one!"

Indeed. Benabic, who liked to say he'd rather drown an Englishman than take him on board — let alone one with few papers and less money…

So deep was Tom in his musings, that he nearly walked into Nick Skeres where he leant against the newel post of the staircase.

"So, did 'e bite you?" the lad asked.

"Well and true. I'm to go back to Paris."

"What, because 'e tells you?"

Tom could not help a bitter laugh. "Had I a passport, I could have argued more," he said.

Skeres gave one of his more mulish grunts. "Ay, well, I'm not going 'ome with 'im."

And because by then Tom had no patience left, he snapped, "You are. You are, Nick Skeres, and you will carry a letter for me — to Sir Francis. Now, while I write it, go find Jack Dennis. Ask the innkeeper. Go to the harbour, if you have to."

It was a very small balm to Tom's bruised pride to see the lad jump to obey for once. A fool, he was — and prideful to boot — and how he'd travel back to Paris with no papers and with as good as no money, he would much like to know.

Because the words kept taking the shape of a child's recitation, rather than a courier's clear-minded account of facts, Tom had long been at his letter — and with little to show for it, when there was a bellow of "Oy, Master," from the common room, and Nick Skeres barged into the Dolphin's little parlour.

Tom looked up in irritation, ready to tongue-lash the lad — and stopped short. Nick Skeres stood there, puffing and red-faced, waving a hand as he caught his breath.

"Next time you want someone fetched, you go yourself," the lad gasped. "See if you find 'em alive!"

"Have you dropped your wits in the harbour, Nick Skeres?" Tom asked, halfway between stern and disbelieving.

And Skeres, of course, had to shake his head — most Minotaurish — as though the question had been in earnest. "Not I, I didn't," he said. "'Tis Dennis as dropped 'imself, wits and all."

"Jack Dennis!" This could not be, could it? The chair screeched on the scrubbed floor and the rushlight danced madly when Tom rose to his feet, quill still in hand. This could not be…

"They fished 'im out, drowned like a cat." The lad swallowed hard. "Mas-tro Pa-o-lo's fit for the Bedlam."

This jolted Tom's mind into a run. "Citolini is there? Did he send for me?"

Skeres snorted. "My eyeballs on an Italian fork, that's what 'e'll send for. 'E didn't want you around, that one."

How very much like Citolini! "Good lad, Dolius." Tom slapped Nick Skeres on the shoulder, and only paused to pick up his unfinished letter, shaking it to dry the ink as he went… Oh, what did it matter! He folded it carelessly, and thrust it into his sleeve. If half of what Nick Skeres blathered was true, he'd have a whole different letter to write — or perhaps none at all.

CHAPTER 12

It was a short walk from the Dolphin, through the old Lantern Gate and to the Port Master's quarters — so what had put Skeres so out of breath, Tom didn't know.

Not until they were pointed to a storeroom, and the lad shuffled and dithered on the threshold, fingering his collar. So this was what it took to shake Nick Skeres?

He scowled at the body where it lay on a table, among the staked barrels and bales of sail-cloth, with candles at feet and head... He scowled, and swallowed hard, and Tom remembered him rather green around the gills on the crossing to France. He'd thought of a bad stomach then, but perhaps it was a fear of drowning...

There were four men around the body, and they all looked up and around at the newcomers — sallow-faced and grim in the light of a lantern, huddled around the slack, waxen corpse like a death scene at the play.

One was a youngish man in the red and blue livery of a Town Sergent, and the brusque fellow with the white-streaked beard had to be a man of the Port Master's. Third, shrinking away from the others, came a spare man in seaman's baggy cannions — the one who had found the corpse, perhaps? — and then there was Citolini.

Citolini, who had been speaking, fell quiet when Tom entered, and opened his mouth to scold, and then thought better of it.

"Mr. Walsingham," he announced, glaring at Tom, and at Skeres behind him, with a promise of words to come. "Also in the service of the English Ambassador."

The Sergent and the bearded man nodded in greeting, and the seaman snatched a knit cap from his head, as Tom stepped closer.

"You know this man, Monsieur?" the Sergent asked — either zealous or suspicious — earning himself a sharp look from Citolini.

"Jack Dennis, of the Merchant Strangers' Post," Tom said. And perhaps a spy and murderer — although… "What happened to him?"

The Port man raised one eyebrow, as though at a very foolish question. "He fell in the harbour and drowned. Benoît here found him caught in a boat's moorings when the tide went down."

The little seaman looked up and then down again. "Down the Tollhouse quay a bit," he muttered, like one repeating himself. "Wouldn't have seen him, but for the bag."

The Sergent nodded at a saddlebag heaped at the body's feet. "It was left on the quay. He must have dropped it when he fell."

Tom frowned, thinking of falling, slipping, flailing his arms — and what he held in his hands… But then perhaps Dennis had carried the bag slung over his shoulder. "And no one saw? From the Tollhouse, or the quay…?"

"If they did, no one said." By the Port man's demeanour, one would think people fell to their deaths in Calais harbour every day — too many of them to bother noticing.

"Wouldn't he call for help, struggle…?" Tom tried.

The Sergent reached to turn Dennis's head. "It looks like he hit his head falling. He was stunned for sure, and the water cold."

Tom did his best not to shudder as he leant over the body to see the dark swelling at the base of Dennis's skull. The daze of pain, the cold grey brine pushing into mouth and nose and throat and lungs... Tom shook his head a little. He tried to take a deep breath — but it choked in his throat.

You look a little green to me, Monsieur... Burry's mocking voice echoed in his mind — and to be truthful, two dead bodies in three days felt like rather more than his fair share. And rather more than chance allowed, surely?

He willed his fingers steady as he reached for the wet doublet. No blood — but that would have been washed away, surely? — no tears in the fabric, nothing to show that Dennis had been stabbed, and under the limp collar, no bruises on the throat — although a few showed almost black at temple and cheekbone... From where he'd fallen, and slipped in the water? For sure, not much of a struggle was left to see in the fellow's dead face, the sunken eyes, the slack mouth. If anything, Jack Dennis looked more peaceful than poor Litcott had in death. Drowning, it would seem, was a quieter business than being stabbed, for all that...

Take them out early — and the froth! Burry had said. *All that froth at mouth and nose...*

"The froth!"

Four pairs of eyes — five if one counted Skeres — fastened on Tom as he exclaimed. He shook his head, and made himself observe the body as coldly as he could, from the sandy hair plastered to the skull, to the sodden clothes and livid hands, down to the one remaining boot — and most of all the bloodless face, the grey-lipped mouth, open and empty.

"Where's the froth, if he drowned?" he blurted. "Shouldn't there be froth at mouth and nose? He isn't bloated, yet…"

Citolini clicked his tongue, the way he'd chastise an unruly horse. "What would you know of it?"

And Tom stopped short — because, indeed, what would he know, but for a French archer's words, spoken as likely as not in jest?

Few things pose greater danger, Thomas, than presuming to know more than you do.

Relief came from unsuspected quarters, though — in the form of the Sergent humming assent. "There's that," he said, rubbing at his chin. "I've been telling myself: this one doesn't look drowned."

"They don't all froth." The Port man waved both hands. "And besides, if he's been in the water long enough…"

"But he hasn't." The Sergent raised his voice, turning to face the other. "You've seen enough of them that you should know."

"What are you saying, Sergent?"

"I'm saying, what if he was dead when he fell?"

"And what killed him? A small knock on the head?"

Two fighting cocks facing each other, and the seaman looking on, eyes amused and keen…

"*Messieurs!*" Citolini's voice cracked through the argument. The Italian stood tall, arms crossed, face stern. "It matters little enough if Master Dennis drowned or not."

Tom opened his mouth to object, and closed it. It did matter very much — but if what he thought was true — and in fact, if it wasn't — it was nothing to discuss before these three. He would have nodded to the Italian, if Citolini had bothered to look at him.

He didn't, of course. "Now let us arrange for burial, and I will see to it that his papers are delivered to his masters."

And *he* would see to it! Leave it to Citolini to be sensible and practical in the midst of it all.

The Frenchmen looked at each other glumly, not liking to be taken to task by this high-horsed foreigner…

The Sergent recovered first — and perhaps the matter was his to worry about. "The Échevins will have something to say to that. And I must see his papers," he said, drawing up straight. "His passport, if he truly was a courier."

Oh, curse all officious Gauls! One saw quite well why the Romans would want them all undone and conquered… "He was," Tom said. "And carrying post. You know that you can't touch that." Not that he'd liked Jack Dennis — but it might have been any Queen's man lying on that table, and his papers in the bag…

The Sergent sighed, and scratched his head under his hat. "*C'est bien alors, Monsieur.*" He motioned to the bag. "You'll watch what I do."

Never glancing Citolini's way, lest the Italian think he was seeking permission, Tom reached for Dennis's saddlebag and handed it to the Frenchman, who made a great show of opening it and emptying the contents on the table, by the body's shoulder. A shirt, two dirty collars, comb, sponge and brush, and a hefty, sealed packet that the Sergent turned in his hands.

"The post," Tom said pointedly.

The Sergent threw him an unfriendly glance, and set the packet aside. "Is there no passport?" he asked.

"Perhaps he carried it on himself," Tom said, because that was his own habit — when he had a passport to carry — but if that was the case, there would be little left to read… He looked at the wet corpse long enough to see Citolini fussing with Dennis's purse, under the interested gaze of the Port man and Benoît.

"Ah, here it is." The Sergent had found the passport in the bag, after all, and was reading it under his breath. "*Jacques Denis … de Londres … les Marchands Étrangers…*"

"Jack Dennis," Tom corrected, out of habit. "John, more likely."

The Sergent shook his head, and pointed to the first line on the paper.

Jacques Denis, indeed. Had the man been no Englishman, after all? How did this change things…?

A soft exclamation made Tom look up to meet Citolini's quick frown.

"Is that a ring?" the Port man asked, reaching to touch something in Citolini's palm — but Citolini snatched it away.

"I'm sure it is a ring," the Frenchman insisted.

"A ring, yes — and it will go to the man's kin. Here, though…" The Italian poured a handful of coins back into the dead man's purse. He stepped around the table to hand it to the Sergent. "About half a livre, in French and English coin," he said, slow and loud, for everyone to hear. "Surely it is more than enough for a decent burial." *And a bribe if you want one*, he didn't say.

The Sergent twisted his mouth at the implication — not that it stopped him from taking the purse — and then he nodded to the packet, set aside from the pitiful heap of the dead traveller's possessions. "So that is for you to take," he said — and, after some thought, he folded the passport and slid it into his belt. "And this is for the Échevins to see. Anything else you want, you'll take it up with them at Town Hall."

And with that he marched away, beckoning for the seaman to follow. When the Port man hurried after them, loudly demanding to know what the devil was he to do with the body, the three Englishmen were left to themselves in the half-dark storeroom. Skeres, still keeping a wary rear-guard, shuffled somewhere in the shadows.

Tom took a deep breath of the cold, damp air, the smell of brine, and wet rope, and burnt fat from the tallow candles, and...

And however they died, pray that you find them before they begin to rot, Burry had said, over Litcott's corpse... Tom swallowed hard. Litcott, indeed. What if...?

"The ring," he said, making his voice steady. "The one you found in the purse."

Citolini narrowed his eyes. "It will go to this man's kin."

Patience, patience! "You don't think that I want it for myself, do you?" Tom snapped. "Don't you see that Litcott's ring is missing, and if I'm right about Dennis..." Or Denis, or whoever he was. Tom held out his hand, only to have the Italian scoff.

"Even death is not enough to assuage your suspicions, is it?"

"He was alive the other night." Tom forged through a sense of being callous. "Let's have a look."

Citolini stood there, in the flickering, smoky light, face bunched in some sort of angry calculation, that had likely little to do with the ring itself. Skeres shuffled behind Tom's back (hopefully not in threat), and at length the Italian shook his head.

"*Al diavolo!*" he muttered under his breath, and dug something small out of his purse. "Here, have it then."

Tom took the ring. An ugly, hefty silver ring, a little tarnished where two hands were carved to clasp a tiny skull… He hissed between his teeth. "Litcott's."

Citolini pursed his lips. "I cannot say that I have paid much mind to the man's ring," he said.

Tom studied the thing, trying to remember. The bulge under the glove, the restless fingers turning it round and round, the dull gleam of old silver, the skull… "It looks very much like it. What are the odds that they would each have a ring like this?"

The Italian nodded, and looked away. "It seems that you were not wrong."

Now, wasn't this a day to mark with a whither pebble! Tom swallowed a grin, and strove for graciousness instead — saved from having to answer when Skeres came to peer over his shoulder, and poked a stubby finger at the ring.

"All the fuss 'e made of it, and it's just the sort they give out at funerals!"

"A mourning ring, yes. Surely there will be…" Tom went to hold the thing to the lantern's glow, turning it this way and that — and sure enough, something caught the light: carved words ran all around it, a little worn, but legible. "*Memento. 1578. Temper…?*" He squinted at the unlikely word, because who spoke of a dead one's temper…? "*Temperance Dudley!*"

For a few heartbeats, all there was to hear was the wind outside.

"This can never be…" Citolini took the ring, peered at it, making sure for himself.

"Lord Leicester's sister," Tom murmured. Of course. Again, pieces fell into place inside his head. "His Lordship, the one who only travels in fair weather."

"It does not follow —"

"Yes, it does!" Tom began to pace. "When Dennis killed Litcott, he took away the ring: why would he, unless it was because it would reveal the tie to Leicester?"

"*Corbellerie*! Certainly Sir Francis knows who was Litcott's old master."

And that was true — but ... but... Tom ran a hand through his hair, thinking furiously. "Or he may find out — but what of the Ambassador? He'd gone to Court before it occurred to anyone to wonder. And in truth, if not for the cipher and the ring, would you have thought past Litcott being sent by the Duke?"

Citolini shook his head, for all the world like a horse shaking a fly. "I do not know that I do now," he said. "Truly, that Lord Leicester would... Besides, he speaks for the Match these days. Why would he...?"

But to that Tom had an answer. "Ay — that he does. He *speaks* — courting the Queen's favour. But all London knows his heart's not in it!" Or perhaps only those did who had a cousin in the Privy Council? How much was Paolo Citolini allowed to know? "Why, perhaps..." Tom felt his sleeve, before recalling that the paper wasn't there. "The cipher! Perhaps, now that we know what to look for, there will be something..." Oh curse Robert Dudley, Lord Leicester for a Janus-faced fool, scheming to ingratiate himself with the Queen — all the more desperately, now that his Countess had borne him a son and heir — and yet still loath to see Her Grace married to the Duke of Anjou! Unlike the Italian, Tom had no great trouble believing it. *Danger lies with men who think themselves more cunning than they are, Thomas.* And Robert Dudley, to Tom's thinking, was one of them.

Citolini's hand went for his purse, but just to push the ring back in. "Oh, *basta*!" he exclaimed. "You've gone through it a hundred times, and found nothing. The decipherers at Seething Lane will know what to make of it."

"But now that we know what to look for…"

"On this one thing you are right — that Mr. Secretary must see this, and the ring. He will know and decide. Now —" And it must be handed to Paolo Citolini: he had a knack for dismissing a man just with the way he turned from him to another, as he now did by bringing his glare on Skeres. "I want your papers, Skegg."

The lad shifted his weight, and looked at Tom askance. "Skeres, it is. Nick Skeres," he muttered.

"Skeres, then." Citolini held out an impatient hand. "Mr. Ambassador said that you are to go back with me."

It did not please him, the way Skeres waited for Tom's nod to obey.

It didn't much please Tom, either, to give that nod. Oh, the garboil the Italian was sure to make of this! Then again, he'd known, hadn't he? Tampering with the papers…

"What is this? What servant?"

Tom looked up to see Nick Skeres match Citolini scowl for scowl.

"I added it," he hastened to say — and wished it sounded less hurried. "The Ambassador was away, and there was no time if I were to catch up, and you know how Middlemore is —"

"You added it!" One might have thought Citolini seething in outrage — and perhaps he was, but he surely liked being outraged at Tom. "You have no passport of your own? You did a forgery?"

Tom made to protest — and stopped short, because what had he to say to that? What he'd done was no better than

154

forging a whole passport, except perhaps to keep Phelippes out of harm's way. "I did," was all he said.

"You did!" Citolini threw up his arms. "You did! And you a Queen's courier — Mr. Secretary's kinsman! What if they had stopped you? What if they...?" He turned away with an exclamation of disgust, and just in the nick of time Tom managed to elbow Skeres quiet, before he blurted out that they had indeed stopped him ...

"Have you no wit to see the damage if you — *you* of all men — were caught with unlawful papers, taken as a spy?"

That much of the Italian's ire was play — or else he would forget himself enough to raise his voice, wouldn't he? — was no consolation. Forged papers, the Walsingham name, Tom's career, and most of all, Sir Francis. Oh Lord, Sir Francis — eyebrows raised, lips twisted in disappointment as he heard the sorry, foolish tale...

"And all because you fancy who knows what plots and conspirations!"

Ah that now! That was too much. "Fancy!" Tom snapped, and swept an arm towards the body on the table. "Did I fancy that?"

Citolini turned a frown on poor dead Dennis, absently jingling his purse, where he had put the ring together with the cipher. "We will never know now. He may have found the ring somehow. He may have slipped in the harbour. Or else he may have worked for the French."

"The French!" Tom almost laughed at that. "Then why would he..." Again he stopped short as the pieces in his head tumbled into disarray. What if Dennis was a French agent, indeed? What if Litcott had surprised him with the adventurers? Why take the ring then — but perhaps he'd tried to make it pass as the work of thieves? And most of all there

was the fact that Jack Dennis had not been Jack Dennis…
"There's that he might not have been English," he said
reluctantly, and told of the passport, and of Jacques Denis.

A satisfied grunt came from Skeres. "I knew I didn't like
'im!"

Tom shrugged. "Perhaps he was a Huguenot, perhaps he
came over back in seventy-two, perhaps…"

"Perhaps he was just born a foreigner." There was a bitter
edge to Citolini's voice, to his tight smile. Bitter and weary.
"And therefore he must have been a scoundrel and a rogue.
Certo!" He shook his head and went to the door, only pausing
to call over his shoulder, "Walsingham, you will stay behind,
see to the burial — and send to Paris for papers. We will see
what Sir Henry has to say. And you come with me, Skeres. I
have work for you."

And with that, he was gone.

Skeres didn't budge from Tom's side. "Arrant Papist
bugger!" he groused. "And you with no money… 'Ere!"

Tom almost smiled when, with a grunt, the lad perched
himself on a barrel, yanked off a boot, and shook a few coins
out of it.

"'Ere, take it!" he insisted, when Tom hesitated. "I'll charge
you a pittance. Friend's interest — 'onest."

Why did this come as no surprise? With a huff of laughter,
Tom accepted a handful of French sols. "Thank you, Dolius,"
he said. "Now go with Mastro Paolo — and be civil, if you
can."

The lad's snort did not bode well, as he crammed his hat on
his head and marched to the door. Just as Citolini had, he
stopped on the threshold, door in hand, holding it tight against
the gale outside. "You're never going back, are you?" he asked,

nodding his chin in the direction of the corpse. "You know 'e didn't go down by 'imself."

Did he truly? Tom shook his head. It was hard to believe in such a chance — and yet, if the man had been the spy, then who had killed him, and why? "I'm not sure what I know, Nick Skeres. I'm not sure anymore."

Tom stepped out of the storeroom, into the blustery gloom. The last dredges of the day lingered like a gleam on dull pewter, and the gale had tautened, snagging at cloak and hat. Tom held on to both, and dragged his steps towards the gate, watching the torches move here and there on the quays, and the yellow glow of windows among the fishermen's houses across the harbour.

How was he going to explain it to Sir Francis? The string of mishaps, his own boundless stupidity, and France — good Lord have mercy — *France*! And now he was stranded in Calais, with a plot afoot and no means of crossing to England. He snatched at wild thoughts of taking Dennis's place on the ship, of laying hands on the dead man's passport … but he'd hardly bribe it out of the Échevins' hands with Skeres's few sols, and even if he could… The *Meance*, and Guion Benabic, of all the shipmasters in Christendom! Benabic, mistrustful Breton that he was, who knew Tom well from previous crossings, and likely had known Dennis too…

There was no way. No way, and Paolo Citolini would see Sir Francis, and tell the tale — a tale that he would strive to make as ugly as he could … but no, this was unfair: no rancorous telling could make things uglier than they were. The trouble was the way the Italian refused to understand beyond what seemed to be, and Tom had cornered himself beyond putting a remedy to it… If this was not failing Sir Francis's trust, he didn't know what was.

Ne cede malis… Don't yield to misfortunes — but for once even Virgil held no consolation. How could he not yield when —

A sudden flurry of calls and orders and a loud slam dragged him out of these black thoughts, and he spun around to stare at the Lantern Gate being shut…

Curse it to Hell! Tom broke into a run, calling that they wait, flailing his arms… Not that they paid any mind — and why would they? Oh, curse it all — was there no bottom to his foolishness? There he stood, gasping like a beached gudgeon, shut out of Calais until morning, gnawing on disaster and, whatever his great cousin might think, with no way on God's earth to prevent worse from happening! Although, in truth, was there much worse that could happen? *Ne cede malis*, indeed!

"Is that you, Mr. Walsingham?"

And now what? From the last clutch of men to come from the town, someone was waving to him — a tall, huge fellow with a link-boy and a servant lugging trusses at his heels.

Tom knew the booming voice, and when the little procession of three made its way to him, he knew the big, red face and round stare in the link-boy's greasy light.

"Master Garrard!" he called.

"Well, well, save and preserve us!" The merchant reached to grasp Tom's shoulder with Herculean heartiness. "At the Gate House they're all agog with rumours of an English courier drowned. I'm glad it isn't you."

And he did look glad, Tom thought, a little heartened. "Jack Dennis, the Merchant Strangers' man," he explained. "You met him in Halcourt."

158

"The one that travelled with you?" Garrard's round stare never wavered. "God's feet! It seems that we were an ill-fated flock, under Madame Mirault's roof…" He sighed, shook his head. "And fated to meet again, too. A little more fair weather, a little less bad tempers at the Customs, and I'd be in Dover by now. And instead… Are you for home with the *Meance?*"

"Not I, no."

Tom would have sworn he'd made a tolerable business of keeping to himself all the day's bitter misery — but something must have seeped into the three small syllables, because Ralph Garrard's mouth crooked in sympathy in the jowly face.

Did blushing show by torchlight?

The merchant grabbed Tom's shoulder again, and turned him around, towards the harbour. "It's a wretched night," he said. "Let's go talk by a fire, eh?" And, with a nod at link-man and servant, he steered them all towards the fishing houses of the Courgain.

Very soon, Tom was sitting by a peat fire, with a pot of mulled wine between his hands — half reckoning how many of Skeres's sols would be left to him after he'd returned the favour, half listening to Garrard's fulminations against the greediness of the French Customs-men.

"I'll lay a wager a good many of them are drowned," the merchant groused. "But that's neither here nor there. Tell me of that poor fellow — Dennis, you say? What happened to him?"

"I think…" Tom stopped short, and reined in his thoughts. *A habit of secrecy, Thomas, is both policy and virtue.* What was with him, that a sip of wine and a liking for the man before him made him want to loosen his tongue? His prospects in the Service may be scant, at this point — but, until Sir Francis kicked him out, he was still his cousin's man! "I think that he must have been careless," he said instead. "I think that he slipped off the quay."

Garrard clicked his tongue. "Another who won't be going home, poor soul," he murmured. "And that other fellow of yours, in Halcourt… It's fearsome how little it takes! A misstep on a quay, a careless servant doesn't shut a gate — and lo! Two men dead, one after the other. An ill-fated flock, in truth. You'd almost think…" A pursing of mouth, a sip of the warm wine, a look askance…

Tom swallowed his snort, eyes lowered on his steaming wine. You'd think indeed! He was no fool, this Garrard, and he seemed much taken with the whole mischance.

"And a courier will expect some trouble, I'll wager — what with all the comings and goings, and the roads being what they are — but a glover…" The merchant shook his head — a slow, purse-lipped shake. "Murdered in foreign parts, poor soul! Must have regretted he ever left Lord Leicester's service."

Tom's very bones drew taut. What did this one know…? How? Slowly, slowly he made himself look up, an eyebrow raised in question.

"You didn't know?" asked Garrard, half amused. "He spoke of little else!"

True enough — but naming names, and to Ralph Garrard? "His Lordship this, His Lordship that…" Tom offered cautiously, and Garrard took the bait.

"Ay, rest his soul!" Another shake of the head, a sad half-smile. "Did he ever show you that ring he wore?"

And the ring, too! Tom shook his head. "I never paid much mind to his ramblings, poor fellow…"

It might have been a soft laugh with another man; Garrard's guffaw boomed loud enough to make his servantman look up from where he sat, drowsing by the hearth.

"Ay, well — that hardly kept him from showing me and Dennis. Funeral ring of some Dudley or other... Fair proud of it, he was."

"Was that at the Trois Poissons?" Tom asked lightly. A stupid question if ever there was one — for where else could it have been? — but it kept the merchant going.

"I walked to the stables after supper, needing to say a word to Best here." He nodded sideways towards the servant. "And Dennis came along for company's sake. And your glover was there, rest his soul, and we got a-talking. And at one point, he takes off this ring and shows us. Dennis was all taken with it."

So! "Was he now?"

"Wanted to see it, bless him — turned it this way and that to the light... Lord knows why! As ugly a trinket as ever was. Teased your glover for it, poor fellow, and he'd have none of it..." Garrard shook his head again, and went back to his wine.

"Poor Simon Litcott," Tom said — and surely it was a sin that so little of his heart or mind was in it — but the merchant's tale needed sifting... The three men in the stables were easy to picture. This would have been, Tom decided, while he was busying himself with Luchette — fool that he was. And had young Gilles, from his hayloft, mistaken the teasing for an argument, missing Dennis's softer voice between the glover's shrill protests and Garrard's noise? Jack Dennis — or Jacques Denis — much taken with the ring...

He was jolted from his conjecturing when another question came.

"Did he have kin at home?" Garrard peered over the rim of his cup. "You'll take back his things, surely — and Dennis's too? There's a task I don't envy you... But no — you said that you are not crossing on the *Meance*."

"Not I, no." Tom worked hard, and it came out quite even this time. "Master Citolini took that upon himself."

"Chee-to-leeny? ah, yes." Garrard hummed. "That's your Italian friend."

"He's not…" After Citolini's parting shot, Tom's conscience felt stung and most busy. "He's English, not Italian." Nor was he a friend, by any measure — going out of his way to leave Tom behind, rushing off with ring, and cipher, to tell his own tale…

Oh Lord!

Oh Good Lord, what if…? To the low hiss of the fire, the sucking, hungry murmur of the rising tide outside, the pieces rearranged themselves inside Tom's head.

"Citolini…" he breathed.

Citolini, so high-handed in dismissing Lord Leicester, so eager to throw blame on the French! And his dagger inside poor Simon Litcott — seemingly stolen and then given back — so that, whatever else happened, those French hounds, and not Paolo Citolini would be blamed for the glover's death! And then, today, taking the cipher, stalking away from the Dolphin right after learning Tom's suspicions of Jack Dennis — and so coy about the ring in the dead man's purse…

"Walsingham, lad! What is it? Are you well?"

When Garrard shook him by the arm, Tom looked up into the round, steady stare, and nodded without thought.

Once he got rid of the ring, Citolini only needed Sir Henry Cobham's misinformed letter to Sir Francis, and an hour with Lord Leicester, and after that it was a matter for the Council, for the Queen herself… How much damage could be done, before things were set straight? Oh, damn Lord Leicester!

"Master Garrard!" Tom pushed to his feet, schooling voice and face to as calm a demeanour as he could muster. *No one will credit a wild-eyed schoolboy, Thomas.* "Master Garrard, I must cross tonight. I need your help."

Ralph Garrard's face went from worry to wonderment, and then he raised half-amused eyebrows — and Tom's heart sank under all the lack of weight of his nineteen years... But he was a Queen's man, by God, and a gentleman's son and, failing that, a kinsman to the all-powerful Mr. Secretary — who, had he been in that tavern, would have been dignified and inscrutable, and never felt the slightest turmoil before this wool merchant.

Thomas Walsingham drew up tall, and looked soberly at the man before him.

"You know that I ride for Her Majesty the Queen," he said, slow and soft. "And I am not allowed to tell you more — but much hangs on my reaching England tomorrow."

Garrard blinked twice before recovering. "I will assist, Mr. Walsingham. In any manner I can. Do you need passage bought for you?"

"Yes — yes, but..." It was a good deal harder to keep dignified and inscrutable while begging ... no, not begging: commandeering. "For reasons that I'm not at liberty to explain, I find myself not only in want of money but of papers."

"No papers!" Garrard frowned. "But Benabic — curse his eyes! — Will he let you on the *Meance* without —?"

Tom shook his head. "He knows me for an English courier. He'll make trouble if he can. But on the other hand..." Tom let his gaze slide past Garrard, to the corner where the merchant's servant dozed by the fire.

Garrard looked over his shoulder, and a smile creased his red face. "Best!" he called, making the youth startle, and he beckoned him close. "Best, I think you'd better find yourself a bed here for tonight."

CHAPTER 13

On consideration, they left it to the very last moment. It was near midnight, when Tom clambered from a rowing boat up an unsteady rope ladder, and set foot on the *Meance*'s windswept deck, hauling Ralph Garrard's truss with him. The merchant was on board already, squabbling with the shipmaster and Citolini at the mainmast's foot, by the light of a lantern that swung in the wind, with much waving of hands and calling of names.

Nobody paid much mind to the servantman who, after stowing his master's possessions in a corner of the lower deck, curled by them, his back to the world, as though sick or afraid — or both.

And thanks be for a piece of good fortune! Tom much doubted that the ruse would have worked in daylight — but at last the anchor was hauled, and the released *Meance* bucked to the wind, and was underway, and so was Tom, to England, for a miracle and the good will of Garrard! When he felt the ship list — leaving the shelter of the harbour, surely — and heard the big, wet snap of sails drawing taut, he took a gulp of air. He rather regretted it — as the *Meance* carried cheap wine and a score of hands, beside master and passengers, and stank with the spilling of it all.

As a rule, Tom would have spent much of the crossing up on the open deck, breathing the sharp sea air rather than the vapours of wine gone bad and bilge water — but this time…

When Garrard's voice called for Best in the gloom, Tom propped himself on an elbow. "Here," he called — and it belatedly occurred to him to tack a "Master" to his reply.

The merchant lurched his way among crates, coils of rope, and a snoring seaman or two. Once he hissed and cursed under his breath — bruising his shins on something sharp? — and then came to crouch by Tom, hulking black against the greenish gloom.

"We're out in the Channel," he rumbled in what passed for a whisper with him. "You can show yourself. They won't have you tossed out at sea now."

Tom checked a huff of laughter. "With Master Benabic, I wouldn't swear…" he began — and let it trail, for it wasn't the Breton that gave him pause. If Citolini was Lord Leicester's man — or anyone's man, in fact — he may well have done murder twice. What was to keep him, if he saw his plot threatened, from killing again? And on this thought… "Have you seen that foolish fellow of mine?" he asked.

Garrard was quiet at first, and there was no mistaking the quality of his silence: considering how easy it would be to push a man overboard at night.

"He's in the quarterdeck," he said at last. "A little green in the face, and grumbling to one and all — never mind that they don't understand a word… You'll have to teach him French, one of these days." And then, hands on knees, he pushed himself upright with a grunt.

Tom watched the merchant pick his uncertain way towards the lighter square of the open port, wobbling when the *Meance* tilted, creaking under them. Hades stalking Tartarus… With a sigh, he settled on his back as the *Meance* bucked again — was this what they called tacking? — and wished himself in England, on the highway, with a good horse under him, or even a middling one. That he didn't suffer as others did on shipboard, didn't mean that he liked travelling by sea.

Other crossings he'd spent busy tallying his expenses. This time, he doubted he'd ever have to worry about his courier's expenses again — and he couldn't even bring himself to worry about that … well, not very much, at least — not when all he could see in his mind's eye was the Queen's wrath, the French Match undone, Monsieur dispatched home in disgrace, all of it in an uncontrolled torrent, escaping perhaps even Sir Francis's hand…

Even those things that you most desire, Thomas, are always better attained through your own reasoned doing than by chance.

And here, whatever one may think of the French Match, any reasoned doing was rolling downhill like Sisyphus's stone — and Tom's own prospects with it, and Sir Francis's trust … not that it would greatly matter if Citolini murdered him too … though, while the Italian didn't know that Tom was on the *Meance*, time would be better spent in devising a manner to outrun the man to London, rather than dwelling on murder … supposing that Paolo Citolini was the murderer and the spy … but what if he wasn't? And if not the Italian, who else…?

Oh, nothing ran round and round with such befuddling vigour as torturous thoughts — and it felt like hours and hours of this inner Morris-dance, inside the stifling, creaking, tossing confines of the lower deck, before a change came from the deck, with cries, and curses, and loud thumping…

"What is it?" Tom asked of the sailors, who were stirring at the commotion — but, before they could answer, the port was slammed open, and the roiling night rushed inside.

"Get to the pump, you *pautonniers!*" someone yelled, and the sailors scrambled out in great haste.

Bracing himself against the hull, Tom followed. He could feel a change in the ship's going — a dragging stutter as though of a restive horse… Wind and spray slapped him in the face when he stepped on the deck, and he flattened back against the bulkhead, gasping and gaping in the tumult of swarming shadows, and seafoam, and madly swaying ruddy light, and voices howling over the wind… This was Tartarus, surely — or Hell in that Italian poem Watson was so fond of quoting… And Benabic, like a great devil, was everywhere, shouting, swinging a lantern, pushing men down the port to the hold… "Heave-ho!" he yelled. "Heave-ho, *bricons*!"

Now we sink, Tom thought — in a gush of relief. Breathless, unreasoning relief, of all things, that Citolini's scheme would be thwarted if they went to the bottom, that he shouldn't face Sir Francis…

"Ho, lad!" a sailor slapped him on the arm as he hurried by, pausing long enough to give him a mad, toothless grin, eyes aglitter in the quivering light. "It's nothing, eh? A little pumping, some caulk — Saint Malo help! By daylight you won't even know, eh?" And he was gone.

I won't know because I'll be drowned? Tom wanted to ask, but the wind threw the words back in his throat. Just as well. Foolish words, they were. Water leaked in a ship's hold all the time — what were pumps for, otherwise? — and precious few ships were wrecked for it, were they?

"Go away, plague take you! Go back inside, what are you staring for?"

Tom startled at Benabic's shout. The Breton milled an arm his way, swearing … but not at him. Someone else had earned the shipmaster's displeasure, someone standing somewhere above and back… Tom turned to look up. Citolini leant out of the quarterdeck's port, holding a lantern of his own — and paying no mind to the swearing Breton. Citolini was scowling downwards, scowling at Tom.

Their eyes met across the wet, swirling, red-stained darkness, amid the shouting, creaking, and snapping of sails — and in the uncertain light, the Italian's face was a mask of rage in black and copper. Rage — and, perhaps, disbelief?

Ah, well. Now he knew.

It was no surprise that the old sailor was right enough. Near daylight, when the *Meance* sat at anchor just out of Dover Harbour, Tom would have hardly known of all the night's ado — if not for a taste of having fallen short. Relieved at the thought of sinking — for shame! Let Sir Francis never know what a dim-witted, weak-hearted fellow he had for a cousin… The only consolation was, he had gone back to the lower deck afterwards and slept, for all of the mayhem above and beneath, and for all of Citolini's scowling rage. He'd slept soundly enough, and long enough, that by the time he'd stirred they were in sight of England — and thanks be for that!

So now he was making his way out of the lower deck, and rather wishing to break his fast. Ah, but it was a boon to step on deck in the sharp, grey, clean morning air, and see Dover nestled at the foot of its ghost-white cliffs, and stretch his cramped back until it popped, and —

"*Homme à la mer! Homme à la mer!*"

The shrill cry tore through the air, and more shouting answered in French, Breton and English, and running feet, and calls, and bustle. By the time Tom rushed at the ship's side, a small crowd milled there, all pushing to lean over and calling. One man was holding by the belt a boy of no more than twelve — he of the shrill cry — and another was throwing a rope ladder down the curved flank of the *Meance*, and a third shouldered his way through the press carrying a long pole with a hook at one end.

This was Benabic himself, red-faced and wild-eyed, and swearing fiercely.

"Here, damn his eyes, take this!" he shouted, thrusting the pole to the man on the ladder.

Once at the shipmaster's side, Tom tugged at a thick woollen sleeve. "What's this?" he asked. "What happens?"

Guion Benabic turned on him like the Lernaean Hydra. "What happens?" he ranted, shrugging off Tom's hand. "That I'll be damned before I take another Englishman on my ship — that's what happens!"

Tom's heart clenched, and he leant over the ship's side to see, only to be yanked away with little ceremony, to stumble into the mainmast.

"Stand back, *la peste* take you!" The shipmaster's glass-blue eyes had a savage glint under the low, grey-black brows. "Another drowning's all I lack!"

A drowning! "What do you mean? Who —"

"Master — oy!"

Tom found himself hauled to his feet by a very round-eyed Nick Skeres.

"What the devil are you doing 'ere —?"

But the lad's enquiries were cut short by more shouting from the sailors, as a black form was hauled over the side, to roll on the deck.

"Citolini!" Tom exclaimed.

White as chalk, clothes torn and dripping, a cut on his cheekbone, the Italian lay curled on his side in a puddle of brine, retching and writhing.

The sailors lifted him from the rough planks until he was on his hands and knees, thumping his back as the poor fellow coughed up Channel water.

Calling for blankets, Tom went down on one knee, gripped one cold, heaving shoulder. "How did you fall?" he asked.

"Like a thrice-damned dunce, that's how!"

Tom looked up at Benabic's red face. "How do you mean?"

"Who falls at sea in this weather?"

Of that Tom had his doubts. The night's wind was somewhat becalmed, but it seemed still quite sharp to him, and the *Meance* pitched and rolled at her anchor. Was it enough to unfoot an unwary man?

Benabic was contemptuously sure. "Drunk, as like as not."

"I was thrown," Citolini gasped, hoarse with saltwater and hacking.

Tom winced in remembrance. He had pitched into the moat once, at Scadbury, and drunk half of it before his brothers fished him out. He remembered the burning lungs, the raw throat for days afterwards… But thrown!

It could be that they kept no blankets on the *Meance*, or else blankets were not to be wasted on English passengers. The ship's boy brought a piece of sail-cloth, and threw it about Citolini's shoulders. The Italian tried once to rise, and thought better of it, huddling against the boardside.

"Someone threw me out of the ship, down into the sea," he insisted — in English — though, even through chattering teeth, he sounded more Italian than was his wont. When he repeated his claim in French, the sailors exclaimed and swore, and crossed themselves, and one or two laughed.

Benabic swore the loudest, with much throwing up of hands. "The English!" he spat, and turned on Tom. "A servant, are you? And now this one was pushed overboard… Should have done it myself — thrown the lot of you out at sea! A servant! *Tchah*! Pack of liars! Strike me blind if I ever let another

Englishman on the deck of the *Meance* — papers or no papers!"

"Yes, yes, Master Benabic," Tom cut through the protestations, as stern as he knew. "Let the boats come to row us ashore, and we'll be out of your hair. You've been well paid — papers or no papers — and that's all that concerns you."

He was rather pleased — although he took great care that no one should see it — when the Breton, with a last scowl and waving of hands, walked away, grumbling to himself.

All the time, Tom felt Citolini's gaze on him.

"*Mi hanno gettato in mare!*"

For all of Watson's tutoring, Tom's Italian was middling — but he had enough of it to know the man was insisting, still, that he'd been thrown out at sea.

"Pushed overboard... Seems hard to believe, doesn't it?"

Finding Ralph Garrard at his shoulder, Tom wondered fleetingly if the merchant had Italian at all, before turning his attention to Citolini again. Had it been anyone else, he might have believed it — eagerly, even. But this was Citolini, the one who, in Tom's reckoning, should have been doing the pushing. Had the man tried to get ashore first, to give Tom the slip and precede him to London? It sounded fantastical — but then Citolini could swim, or so he had boasted a hundred times.

Tom watched the Italian closely — the huddle of shivering limbs, the drenched clothes, the drawn, blue-lipped face...

Faces speak as much as tongues, Thomas. Discern a man's secret heart through his transparent face.

"This man who pushed you," he asked, eyes fastened to eyes. "Do you know who it was?"

Citolini's contemptuous shrug was somewhat ruined when it became a great shudder. "I did not see. There was just a great push from behind. It could have been..." The black eyes shifted from Nick Skeres, who stood glowering, fists on hips, to a much perplexed Garrard, and then, most tellingly, to Tom himself.

"Ay?" Skeres gave a snort of laughter. "Picking on Master Tom, eh? Not that I'd blame 'im, mind you, if —"

"Skeres!" Tom snapped. "That's no way to talk to your betters!"

The lad threw him a look of betrayed mulishness — but, for a wonder, fell to silently watching his own feet.

The insolence, though, seemed to have done Citolini good.

"*Master Tom* should be in Calais, by right," he said, as he clambered to his feet, bracing himself against the boardside. He even had some colour back in his cheeks by the time he was upright. "Another forgery, more lies. The Ambassador will not like it."

No, he most certainly would not — nor would Sir Francis. The whole questionable journey, the half-lies to Wacogne, the forged papers... Oh Lord!

Tom pushed aside the litany of his sins as another sudden thought grabbed him. "The cipher!" He grasped Citolini by the arm, half shook him in his agitation. "What have you done with Litcott's cipher, and the ring?"

The Italian breathed in sharply, hand going to the purse at his belt. It hung, limp and half open, the strings slack...

There — there went what little proof there was... Oh, Tom had seen the ring, no doubt of it — but whatever there had been to find in the false dye recipe, whatever missed tie to Lord Leicester, was gone, washed away past recovery...

"They are gone." Citolini held a small handful of silver coins, English and French, and the upturned purse. He shook his head. "Paper, and ring, and most of my money. Gone."

"Oh, Citolini!" Tom sighed, surprised to find that, for the most part, he was disappointed. Not that he truly liked the Italian — but … one of their own! Because there was no doubting, now, was there? Not with the cipher so conveniently disposed of, and the attempt at either running or diverting suspicions, or both…

Right then, there was much shouting of "Oy, ship!" and "*Ho, la barque!*" The boats arriving, in their own sweet time.

The sun had gone up, meanwhile, and even broken through the clouds. A few golden beams slanted their way through the greyness — the first sunlight in days — raking long, sparkling streaks across Dover Harbour, making the chalk cliffs glow a stark, cold white over the town, amid much keening of seagulls. Tom crossed the deck to see a largish boat bobbing by the *Meance*. Garrard was stepping gingerly down the rope ladder, his truss already piled down in the boat.

Once more, the merchant was to be thanked…

"Oy, master!" Skeres, of course. Skeres coming to stand by him, nudging him with his elbow, grinning as one with no cares in the world … no, as one much pleased with himself.

"What now, Nick Skeres?" Tom asked wearily.

The lad gave a broad wink, and held out a folded, crumpled paper. And a ring!

Now this couldn't possibly… Tom snatched both items. "How do you come to have these?"

Skeres grinned and leant in to whisper in Tom's ear: "Took 'em last night, I did. When there was all that ado with the pump."

Dear Lord in Heaven. Just *where* had they found Nicholas Skeres? "You stole them from his purse…?"

The lad nodded, and tapped his nose. "Put in a pebble and a scrap of paper, so 'e couldn't tell. Seemed to me it was no good that 'e 'ad them, eh? That I 'ad no letter of yourn to give to Mr. Sec't'ry, but maybe, if I 'ad these … eh?"

Tom shook his head in disbelief. "Indeed!" he breathed.

"Ay, well, if I'd known that you was on the ship, maybe I'd 'ave left it alone. Just as well, eh? Though I'll say, Master! Never took you for one to sneak on a ship like that." And, with a well-pleased laugh, he gave Tom's shoulder a hearty slap.

Tom tried to glare at him, and, when the lad was not perturbed in the least, he gave a huff of laughter of his own. "You are a hopeless servant, and a thief to boot — but not half a fool," he said. "Now go find my bags, and mind: between the two of us, we must never let him out of our sight."

And, as Skeres trotted away, Tom sought out the long, black, bedraggled figure of Paolo Citolini, leaning against the mast and grimly looking back.

It was going to be a long journey to London.

Argus of the hundred eyes was no more eager sentinel, it turned out, than Nick Skeres, once he was set onto a fellow.

As they were rowed ashore, and as they made their way through Dover Port, quiet enough on a Sunday, up to Biggin Street and the Greyhound Inn, where the Post was, the lad never budged from Citolini's side, most mastiff-like in his pugnacious zeal.

Ah, but it was good to be in England again, to warm one's hands at a good English fire, to gauge an English sky through the window, to have an English Postmaster assisting the Queen's men as a matter of course.

It would have been a great relief, if not for the black figure hunched by the fire, stiffly pretending that he was not being watched.

"Now be of good cheer, young Mr. Walsingham! A day or two, and you'll be sleeping in your bed, won't you?"

Tom made himself smile at Ralph Garrard, and thought that perhaps he should have gone into the wool trade.

To get his receipt for the cost of Tom's passage, Garrard had seen them to the Greyhound — but had, himself, all the loud heartiness of one who would be at home, come night, and no worse than book-keeping ahead of him. No wrecked prospects, no ill news to carry, no daunting kinsmen to face... Yes, the wool trade sounded quite restful.

And he must have failed to keep his musing to himself, for Garrard frowned a little and fixed his stare on Citolini first, where he sat by the fire with his own scowling guard, then back on Tom.

"You won't be in trouble now, will you?" he asked slowly, and then he seemed to gather himself. "Well, not my place to ask."

Tom shook his head, and it irked him, when the Italian looked up from his study of the flames, to find himself turning half away. Looking at, of all things, the row of Dutch blue and white plates hung above the dark wainscoting ... what a fool!

He blushed a little to find Garrard watching him with intent sympathy, and he shook his head.

"One knows better than to waste trust, Master Garrard. It is a tenet learnt early. Still, to have it thrust in one's face..."

"Ay, well, at times one's well reminded of why it's a tenet at all," said Garrard, and smiled a little.

A tight-lipped smile, it was — half kindly and half mocking — and Tom was awkwardly put in mind of sore lessons learnt in boyhood. Was the merchant going to comment on his young age, and...?

175

Before he could, for a mercy, the Postmaster bustled into the parlour, announcing that the horses were saddled and ready, at the gentlemen's pleasure.

Away, at last!

There were brisk farewells, and the donning of hats and the scraping of chairs. This up and going, the saddled horses lifting their heads, the leaving on the Queen's own business — the thrill of it still stirred Tom at times, just as it had on his first journey. That Paolo Citolini didn't even try to take the lead, that he just sent a moody, ill-used look Tom's way before following him out to the cobbled yard, was enough to dampen it somewhat.

Let this not be his last day as a courier, Tom hoped, as he swung in the saddle. And then, to the pealing of Sunday service bells, he spurred his mount out into the windy street. Away to London.

CHAPTER 14

If that day was to be the last of Tom's career in the service, it wasn't going to be a good one to remember — nor a truly bad one. Glum going it was, if swift enough, as they trotted through a rust-grey Kent that looked to winter, on a highway that, for being English, felt immeasurably better than the roads in France, even if it wasn't — not with all the thick, rutted mud of November between near-naked hedges.

At least it wasn't raining — or not much. No more than a few cold drops as they changed horses in Sittingbourne, although the sky was low and swollen, all promise of sunlight left back in Dover Harbour.

Few words were exchanged all day, unless one counted Nick Skeres's grumblings, which both Tom and Citolini ignored. That Skeres never strayed far from the Italian's elbow — even as they had a hasty dinner of bread, cold ham and ale while their mounts were saddled — was another thing no one chose to comment on.

Tom would have liked a little more subtlety — but had a well-formed opinion, by now, that the lad just didn't have it in him to be subtle.

So they rode in silence, for the most part, and in the early afternoon crossed the angry Medway at Rochester, hooves clattering on the old stone bridge — and after that the road did get better, or so everyone said.

All the way Tom turned black thoughts in his mind, blacker and blacker as they neared London, and tried to put himself inside the Italian's head, tried to fathom the enormity of wilfully betraying Sir Francis's trust, tried to sift apart certain fact, logical supposition and his own fancies...

Item: Better than anyone, Citolini knew what Tom carried and how — if not quite where;

Item: Citolini may have been in Amiens earlier than he said, in time to hire the adventurers;

Item: Citolini's dagger — and his alone — had been apparently filched, to throw the blame on the French rogues...

For the first time since Calais, it occurred to Tom to check what the Italian wore these days ... a broader, shorter blade, serviceable and plain, bought in Paris, likely, because it would be hardly wise to take to the road unarmed. Some wonder twitched in Tom's mind about that dagger ... that beautiful, red-hilted thing that Citolini had worn and cherished for as long as Tom had known him. Old Venetian work, the man called it — so perhaps brought over from Italy in his flight, perhaps his father's memento, and then sacrificed to the ruse...

When, feeling himself watched, Citolini threw an unfriendly gaze over his shoulder — unfriendly, and cold, and calculating — Tom stowed his doubts away and urged his Post sorrel faster. That Paolo Citolini should be a man to lavish sentiment on a dagger, surely must be classed under the name of Fancy? Because, in fact...

Item: Citolini might well have been in the stables at the Trois Poissons, arguing with Litcott — though, what they had to argue about, Heaven knew — while Tom was ... well, was otherwise engaged;

Item: in Halcourt, Citolini might well have been the one slipping out of the bedroom in the dead of night;

Item: in Calais, Citolini had had time to dispose of Jack Dennis after learning Tom's suspicions of the man...

Item: Citolini had been quick to espouse the notion that the French were behind the whole thing. Quick to espouse it, and very slow to relinquish it … in fact, Tom could not say he ever had — while…

Item: Citolini had dismissed, rather high-handedly, Lord Leicester's involvement, even after the ring was found. And in fact…

Item: Citolini had tried to keep the ring to himself — had it not been for the long-nosed Port fellow, and when he could not…

Item: Citolini had also been quick to take hold of the ring, as well as the cipher, and to seize on a pretext to leave Tom behind in Calais…

All of it well and good, but for each scrap of fact a brace of questions remained, gyrating in Tom's mind, cawing loud and black as a murder of crows in the fast fading November light.

It was, on the whole, a welcome distraction when they entered Dartford, so near sunset that the guards were making ready to close the gate, thinking no doubt of home and hearth and supper. Tom filed in last, looking over his shoulder at the shadow-drenched country. Out there, barely a dozen miles to the West, was Scadbury… Would he have to ride back home in disgrace, after this whole tangle was sorted?

The twilight was darker within walls, and the muddy squelch of their mounts' hooves echoed in the narrow streets of Dartford — the last citizens abroad, carrying lanterns and scurrying out of the horsemen's way. A drunk cursed at them as Citolini's gangly mare pushed him into a red-latticed tavern's wall.

"Glass gazers! Murthering ruffians! Rascals! Dogs!"

Once Skeres was dissuaded from taking exception, the man's wobbling howls followed them as they picked their way along High Street.

Tom had to knock long and fiercely, before an ostler dragged himself from his Sunday repose to answer — and he could at last, sore in mind and body, dismount in the yard of the Royal Oak.

As Post inns went, the Royal Oak was a good enough place. The kidney pie had dried plums in it, a roaring fire held the damp night at bay — and, best of all, they had a small room to themselves, where Tom and Citolini shared a two-poster, and Skeres had a clean-looking pallet.

Tom gauged his chances: should they keep watch in earnest, splitting the night hours between himself and Skeres? Surely there was no need for that, was there? What with himself on one side, and Skeres on the floor on the other, where could the Italian go? But then, Citolini had slipped out from between two sleeping men in Halcourt, and out of a crowded room, and come back at his pleasure…

"Victory loves prudence, Dolius," he whispered, answered with a grunt as Skeres dragged off his buskins — and very nearly Tom himself off the bed with them. "You sleep now. I'll call you."

Not that Citolini would do murder now, would he? Not with the three of them in the room, never this close to London, surely? Then again…

Tom propped himself to sit against the painted headboard. Whatever wisdom there may have been in quoting Catullus to Nick Skeres, there was none in lowering one's guard. So he sat there in the darkness, half listening to the lad snore heartily, and let his doubt keep him awake.

Observe the joints and flexures of affairs, Thomas…

And the truth was, if Tom was honest, that this affair's joints had gaps as wide as Cerberus's maw, and its flexures creaked very much…

Why hadn't Citolini made sure the paper was found on Litcott?

Why hadn't he disposed of the ring after killing the glover? But then...

How had the ring found its way to dead Jack Dennis's purse?

Had Dennis been in league with the Italian — both in Lord Leicester's pay, or were there more players to this game?

And, supposing Citolini was Leicester's man, what of Ambassador Cobham?

All the pieces inside Tom's head had grown sharp corners, and they pinched at his temples from within...

He hadn't meant to sigh aloud, or to rub at his eyes, or to move — but he must have, for Citolini stirred.

The bed creaked under him as he turned.

"Walsingham?" he whispered in the darkness. "What is it?"

"Go back to sleep," Tom whispered back — and wondered if the man had been asleep at all. There was a short silence, then Citolini moved again, rolling back, away from Tom.

There was a grunt across the bed, and the sound of scratching.

"Master...?" Skeres's voice asked around a yawn.

Tom decided he'd kept his watch for the night. "Yes, Skeres," he called softly, hoping it was enough of a signal.

A sluggish "Ay...", more grunts, and a protracted wooden keening from the pallet seemed a good sign. Tom lay down and went to sleep.

"Oy, where are you goin'?"

The raised voice and the swinging of the bed roused Tom from a deep slumber.

"Let go, you oaf!" This was Citolini's angry hiss.

"What's this?" Tom sat up, clumsy with sleep.

"Papist ruffian was turning tail, that's what. Cuttin' our throats in our sleep, and turning tail!"

Blinking himself awake, Tom dragged himself to his feet, felt his way to the table, knocked off the rushlight … but he had no tinderbox, anyway… He wrenched open the one window's curtain. There was a lantern burning in the courtyard, and even through the parchment panes, its faint yellow glow was enough to water down the darkness.

"Be quiet, you pair of fools!" Tom snapped under his breath. "Skeres, let go."

Citolini, shirt-clad and wild-haired, stood frozen in the middle of the room, with Skeres clinging to his knee.

"Ay, let go, says 'e!" The lad grumbled, grasping a fistful of Citolini's shirtsleeve for good measure. "So 'e'll do us in like 'e did the others!"

"Skeres!" Tom's reprimand came too late. Most things seemed to come too late, where Nick Skeres was concerned… Tom pinched the bridge of his nose. "Ay, well. Let go all the same."

Skeres grudgingly did, and scuttled back to his pallet, only to retrieve his knife from the tangled blankets.

Citolini never stirred, eyes wide and gleaming in the half-darkness. "*Diavolo!*" he cursed under his breath. "Is this … you think that I… You call me a murderer and a spy?"

There. If the man hadn't believed himself caught out, now he most certainly did…

"I don't," Tom said. "Not yet, at least."

"And yet you and your man keep guard on me."

"Sir Francis will hear us both, and decide."

Citolini threw up his hands and laughed — a harsh and brittle thing in the faint light. "*Certo!* He will hear his nephew and he will hear the foreigner — and choose between them! Or is this all his doing, from the beginning?"

Unease prickled at Tom, and the memory of a breathless walk through the Parisian crowd, and Watson's words... "He'd never do such a thing!"

"Would he not? Your doing, then. How did you come to think that I killed the glover? And Dennis too?"

Tom sat down on the bed, trying to decide what he should say, what he should keep to himself. "You could have done it," was what he settled on — and frightfully weak it sounded, even to his own ears.

Small wonder that Citolini pounced on it. "I could have — yes! And what of you? Where were you when the glover was killed? And Dennis? But no, you are Mr. Secretary's nephew... You can be no murderer, can you?"

Cousin, rose to Tom's lips — and he swallowed it.

"Or what of him?" Citolini swung around, to find himself facing Skeres — little more than a burly shadow.

"What of your man, here? Could he not have done it?"

The lad sputtered in indignation — but, if only for fairness' sake, Tom's mind explored the possibility — and yes: Nick Skeres had been in the hayloft at the Trois Poissons, and out of sight as Dennis took his deadly plunge... Oh Lord. Had it been just this morning, in the Greyhound's parlour? Garrard's crooked smile... *One should know better than to waste trust.* But was one also to suspect one and all?

"I will assume that you wanted to use the pot," Tom said, feeling far too weary and old. "Now let's sleep. We'll be in London tomorrow, and we'll put it to Mr. Secretary. This is his to decide."

And he watched as Skeres, grumbling very blackly, lowered himself out of view beyond the bed, and Citolini stiffly sat back on the bed, eyes glittering, hands clasped in a hard knot in his lap.

So now the Italian was on tenterhooks, perhaps enough to act rashly, and Skeres brooded with betrayal...

Tom didn't draw the curtain and, much as he made a point of lying down and turning his back to the Italian, he did so clutching his dagger under the pillow, and did not go to sleep again.

CHAPTER 15

Morning came at last, dim and sluggish.

They broke their fast in hurried silence — Tom ignoring with much care both Citolini's burning glances and Skeres's sullenly averted ones — and soon they were on the highway again, for the last score of miles.

The road was better, this close to London, and they kept to a goodish canter at first — but, the closer they rode, the more travellers they found. Soon enough — far too soon for Tom's taste — they were slowed down to the smallest trot, wading their way through a stream of dray-carts and handcarts, and women with donkeys and baskets, and still it wasn't much more than two hours before, even in the hazy day, London could be spied — bristling and black, breathing woodsmoke like a dragon asleep.

Had the wind not blown inland-way, Tom fancied he could have smelt the city by the time they were forced to unravel themselves to a single file, winding among the thickened morning bustle... Skeres forged ahead first, trading ill-humour with a sturdy dairy maid as he pushed past her, and Tom held back his mount, making it dance sideways a little, until Citolini had no choice but to pass him.

The Italian threw him a white-rimmed glare as he went, half anger and half fear, if Tom was any judge... He spurred his horse ahead, misliking to let the man out of his reach — or he would have, but a drayman chose that moment to move his cart to the left, a square thing loaded with empty-sounding barrels. It was swerve aside or have his horse skin its knees against the cart, and Tom swerved to a stop just in time. The carter, as square-built as his dray and, to see him, a good deal fuller than his barrels, gave an annoyed look over his shoulder, and muttered of reckless young cockerels.

And what was it with cart-men — were they chosen solely for sour temper…?

"Draw aside!" Tom snapped. "Queen's service!"

The man twisted ponderously on his bench, and began to tell Tom just what he thought of the nuisance that were the Queen's men on a road — and over the man's head Tom caught Citolini's eye again — wild and white-rimmed, and…

"Hold!" Tom bellowed.

Too late.

Citolini, damn his eyes, had already spurred his horse past two peddlers, over the road's edge, through a gap in the hedge and off into the path between two ploughed fields.

There were cries, and curses, and oaths as the loose crowd surged all around.

"Stop that man!" Tom shouted, spurring his own mount out of the tangle. "In the Queen's name — stop him!"

Not that there was anyone to do it… Catching a glimpse of Skeres, half turned in the saddle and chewing his lip, Tom urged his horse through the gap in a spray of mud. In a heartbeat he was tearing after the Italian among fields, meadows, and curving hedges — the noise of the passers-by crying aim fading behind them.

Citolini rode a big bay with a long stride and a stubborn head, but Tom's sorrel was younger, lighter and, it soon proved, blessed with a longer wind. Before long they were galloping nose to rump, and then to saddle, and then Tom did something his father would have whipped him for: he reached for the Italian's reins and yanked. Taking exception, the bay bucked and swung around, and Citolini, leaning from the

186

saddle to backhand his captor out of the way, found of a sudden more thin air than horse under him, and fell. He landed on his back, a boot caught in the stirrup, and would have been battered sorely, had Tom not held on to the bay's reins with all his might as both mounts pranced — and still it was hard work to keep them from trampling the Italian on the ground.

"Skeres!" Tom shouted over his shoulder, in between clicking his tongue at the fretful animals. Not that he was sure...

But Skeres was there, indeed, drawing to a halt, clomping out of the saddle, and taking hold of the bay, cursing the large creature, slapping its heaving neck where another would pat it, until it was, if not soothed, subdued.

By the time Tom had quietened his own horse and dismounted, Citolini lay curled in the coarse, sodden grasses, free of the stirrup, winded, panting and wild-eyed. Nick Skeres loomed over him, fists on hips, with a most smug mien of vindicated innocence.

"See?" he asked. "Turned tail again, 'e did!" *And I didn't and came to help you*, hung unsaid. He wasn't even out of breath.

Tom, who was, took a moment to catch his wind and wonder. Surely Nicholas Skeres knew nothing of Virgil, and of fear betraying base souls? Because there was no mistaking the raging fear that twisted the Italian's ashen, sweat-soaked face...

Tom crouched at the man's side, making himself keep still at the violent flinch — for all that thoughts of daggers and dead glovers came to mind.

"I still hoped it wasn't you, fool that I am," Tom said — finding, of all things, disappointment biting at him. "But what innocent man would run like this?"

And Citolini laughed — a dreadful, choking sound. "An innocent man who is not English-born!" he gasped. "An innocent man who will be so good a scapegoat for the deeds done by the kinsman of Mr. Secretary."

Tom shook his head, startled into half-speechlessness. *His deeds!*

And as he gaped like a carp, of a sudden Citolini uncoiled, gathered his legs under him, and shoved at Tom.

Caught unaware, Tom stumbled backwards, but didn't fall. He recovered quickly enough to lunge for Citolini, grabbed at doublet and sleeve, caught an elbow to the chin — and then was bowled aside as Nick Skeres landed on the Italian.

They all went down together, the three of them in one winded, ungainly heap. Tom unfolded himself, clambered to his feet. People were running up from a scatter of cottages nearby — women, for the most part, but there were also a few old men and small children, all of them with eyes round and glinting.

"In the name of the Queen," Tom called over the magpie-ish chattering, "this man is apprehended."

Not that he had the authority for it — but it was a fact of life that a convincing show of power would mostly go unchallenged, and no one in the gaggle of cottagers seemed willing to dispute him. And if they had, all it would take was to expose the prisoner for a foreigner... Tom swallowed the thought with a guilty start, and looked down to find Citolini flattened on his stomach, with Skeres sitting on him. Still the Italian managed to glare upwards.

"They'll put me to the question," he gasped, squirming under Skeres's weight.

"Come now, the question!" Tom scoffed. Sir Francis was slow to turn to torture — but if there were truly more than Lord Leicester's offended pride at work...

The Italian must have sensed Tom's doubts. "You know that they will. And for all I know, you could have done it all!"

Could he, indeed? Yes — for all that Citolini knew, Tom could have hired the adventurers, stabbed Litcott, feigned finding the cipher, pushed Dennis off the quay at Calais... That is, if Citolini was innocent — but could he truly be? Harder than ever to tell, now... Tom swallowed his unease, and turned to gaze at the spires and roofs of London, mercifully close at last. More mercifully still, because the rain was starting again, in fat, cold drops.

"Tie Mastro Paolo's hands," Tom ordered Skeres. "See what papers he has about him, while you are at it. And then, Fates willing, to London."

CHAPTER 16

"What will become of him?" Tom asked, watching as two of Sir Francis's men escorted Paolo Citolini across the courtyard, to be locked in what could have been a servant's room, had it not been for a barred window and a heavy bolt on the outside of the door.

The Italian dragged his feet on the rain-black cobbles as he was led around a newly arrived waggon, and twisted to throw a glance over his shoulder at the two Walsinghams — bitter, and despairing, and betrayed. *They'll put me to the question*, he had said — and Tom didn't know that he was wrong.

"We'll see, Thomas." Sir Francis fingered his pointed beard, dark grey eyes fixed on the retreating Citolini until the man was out of view. "There are a few questions I'd much like to ask of him — first among them, about Sir Henry Cobham."

The thought had occurred to Tom. Sir Henry owned, supposedly, a loyalty to Mr. Secretary and a shrewd head on his shoulders. Had he missed Leicester's man in his own household, or turned a blind eye, or…

Tom sighed, and wished he hadn't when that made Sir Francis take a good look at him and click his tongue.

"You'll need a fire, something to eat, and dry clothes, no doubt," said Sir Francis. "But first, I must have the whole story. Come."

Thomas followed his great cousin back into the dark, wainscoted passage, squeezing past a servantmaid carrying a pile of folded tablecloths. The house in Seething Lane hummed like a disturbed hive, alive with the master and mistress's return from Barn Elms, and the hall smelt of rain and must and woodsmoke, as the servants bustled about.

But for the weight of failure on his shoulders, Tom would have enjoyed the aliveness of it, and of his own arrival ... after this, would he ever enjoy such things again? He swallowed the thought as he climbed the large staircase of carved oak. Sir Francis was several steps ahead, his robe of black velvet hardly rippling at the hem — but there was never knowing what he might observe...

At last they were in the study, and it was quiet there, and austere with the dark cabinets and the unpatterned tapestry on the desk, and warm with a great fire that a lad was tending in the hearth.

The lad was told to run along, and Sir Francis sat at his desk, motioned Tom to another high-backed chair — the one closest to the fire — and then, with his hands folded in front of him, fixed his dark, deep gaze on his kinsman.

"Now tell me, Thomas."

Tom sat, feeling all the aches of ten days in the saddle and a heavy heart, and the damp clothes clinging like the embrace of some muddy river nymph, and whatever relief he might have found in relinquishing his troubles into more capable hands than his, drained out of him. Ah well — he'd known the moment would come. He had prepared for this.

He took a deep breath, squared his shoulders, and began the litany of his varied and numerous failings.

It seemed to take a very long time, and it was a struggle to keep the whine out of his voice in certain moments. Sir Francis never interrupted — but then he seldom did, watching the speaker's face closely, storing aside all his questions, and then rolling them out, one by one when the fellow had worn himself weary and slack with the telling...

A most effective manner, one Tom admired and lacked the patience for. When, at the end of the sore recitation, Sir Francis nodded and leant a little forward to begin the questioning, Tom shivered hard and saw something flicker in his cousin's gaze.

Two years of close study had taught Tom to *see* those flickers — like a carp swimming up in a pond, a curved flash of light, and then back down to the depths, the surface never broken. To see them, he had learnt — to read their meaning, though, was a horse of another colour. He sat straighter for the questions.

"And of my letter, I gather, there is no trace?" Sir Francis asked.

Tom shook his head. "It wasn't among Citolini's things, nor among Dennis's. I had a look at Litcott's too — but no, no trace of it."

Sir Francis tilted his head a little. "Now the question is how much of a fool his Lordship is. Destroying the letter and having us blame the French would be a very foolish game; letting the French have it, and hoping to lure them into breaking the negotiation…"

This now, this Tom hadn't considered — but surely… "That would be lunacy!"

"Indeed. And also we cannot discount the chance that the French may have got hold of the letter beyond and against his Lordship's intentions."

True enough — but… "That would not change the matter…"

"Hardly at all, when it comes to consequences. Also, the matter remains of this Jack Dennis, or Jacques Denis." Sir Francis frowned at Litcott's ring that lay before him on the desk — the dye recipe being already in William Wade's hands for deciphering — and then raised his eyes back to Tom. "Whose man would you say he was, Thomas? Lord Leicester's, in consort with Citolini?"

Tom blinked, teasing the even-voiced question apart, snatching for the threads of his scattered thoughts... And thoughts to voice on this he had, after nibbling at the question for two days and two nights. "But if he was, why keep the ring? No, I think..." He paused, waiting for the little nod of permission. "I think Dennis must have known what was afoot, somehow — perhaps even had a hand in it. He knew of the ring, that is for sure. That poor fool Litcott showed it to him, so perhaps Dennis took it as a safety against Citolini and his master? Only, when I, like a fool, told Citolini of my suspicions of the man..." Tom shook his head in disgust at his own stupidity. A habit of secrecy, indeed! But another, fire-new thought rode on the tail of this one. "What if... Let's say that Dennis, or Denis, it matters little — let's say he was a ruffian for hire, under colour of the Merchant Strangers' post... Perhaps he played go-between for Citolini and those adventurers? Why, he might well have been the one to kill Litcott — and that would explain the ring..." Tom caught himself, cringed at the eagerness in his voice. "Not that any of it explains what became of the letter," he finished — and show him the fellow who ever drew an argument to a feebler close!

"More questions for Paolo Citolini, I suppose," Sir Francis hummed, and something else flickered in the dark gaze — and was that a twitch of the mouth behind the folded fingers? So now he had Mr. Secretary laughing at him...

Or it must have been something else, because, without the least sign of hilarity, Sir Francis rose, and Tom followed suit in clumsy haste. Lord, but he was tired...

"Meanwhile, I'd better have a word with Lord Leicester," said Sir Francis. "A word or two about the expediency of ruses. Pray that he had the sense to have the letter burned, Thomas — or this will make the King of France very happy.."

Tom was more than ready to pray — but even if the letter was lost or destroyed, even then... "But still, Sir — the moment the Duke asks about his glover...?"

"Indeed," Sir Francis nodded. "Indeed — but, as luck would have it, the Court is moving back to Whitehall today. Always avoid disorder in your own affairs, Thomas — but profit from confusion in those of others. If this move is half as disarrayed and ponderous as usual, we may yet have your murder changed to an accident before Her Highness and the Duke are even in sight of London."

Tom watched his cousin pick up the ring and weigh it in his palm. He didn't seem annoyed, not the manner of annoyance that had secretaries of state dismiss couriers from their service, sending them home in disgrace... He seemed so little annoyed, in fact, that...

"Supposing..." Tom said. "Supposing that Dennis was his own man, and not some other player's agent..."

"Yes, there is that, of course." Sir Francis slipped the ring into the purse at his girdle, and looked up with a little frown, as though considering what manner of kinsman he had. "Perhaps, Thomas, it would be better if it weren't widely known yet that you are back in London."

And here Tom had let himself believe, in some foolish corner of his mind, that he'd attend his cousin at Whitehall, a stern witness to confront Lord Leicester... What a half-witted, presuming coxcomb!

Shoulders sagging, he looked down at his travel-stained boots scattering clumps of mud on Cousin Ursula's neat, matted rushes…

"For the way I conducted myself, Sir…" He had to clear his throat. "I have only regret…"

"Have you, Thomas?"

Tom looked up to find Sir Francis had moved around the desk, and stood there watching him with raised eyebrows.

And all of a sudden it wouldn't be kept inside anymore, and all broke out of him in one plaintive torrent.

"There wasn't a blunder I didn't commit, a foolishness I avoided! I travelled without papers — worse! With forged ones! I let myself be caught, and lied my way out of it. I swallowed whole the story that the glover might be a French spy…"

"Well," murmured Sir Francis, "so did Sir Henry Cobham — and he should know better."

Tom shook his head. "But he'd never met the fellow," he said, quite bitterly — until it struck him that Sir Francis had meant this in a teasing spirit. Cautiously he looked up to find Mr. Secretary's expression a good deal more cousinly.

"And if only I'd travelled faster, if Citolini hadn't caught up…"

On his way to the door, Sir Francis stopped at Tom's side to pat his arm, frowning to find his sleeve still damp. "Now come, before you catch your death."

Tom followed him out into the gallery, where Davies, Sir Francis's big, stolid-looking Welshman, waited as though he'd divined his master's intentions, together with a servant boy, who was bidden to take Master Thomas to Lady Ursula.

"She will know what to do with you," was Sir Francis's salutation. "And I will say, Thomas, that borrowing blame is a very foolish habit, and you'll do well to rid yourself of it."

And with that he was gone, straight and black — and Lord help Robert Dudley, weaver of silly schemes.

Tom watched him descend the stairs with Davies behind him like a huge, lumbering shadow. On his own fate he was still rather unclear — but one thing gave him a good deal of relief: whatever else may happen, Sir Francis had things well in hand.

After some brisk clucking over her husband's abrupt departure, her home's disarray, and Tom's battered state, Lady Ursula herded him to the kitchen, dragging along a bemused Nick Skeres — and installed them both at one end of the long table. At the other, a kitchen-maid was busy with what looked like flour and bits of poultry.

"At least it's warm in here," Lady Ursula said, "And you can have…" She looked around, and her eyes settled on another bustling maid, her arms full of earthen pots. "Bridget, girl — leave that. Manchets, and butter, and some of that cold ham for Master Thomas and his man. And … shall it be mulled cider? Yes — mulled cider, Bridget — well spiced and hot."

Bridget curtsied and scurried away, and Lady Ursula, hands on hips and head tilted, went to stand where she could have a good look at Tom.

Tom couldn't help smiling up at her a little. Unlike Mother, even when she fussed, Lady Ursula did so with a humorous curl of lip and eyebrow.

"Well, did you bait a bear, Tom Walsingham?" was what she said, reaching to tug Tom's collar straight, and tilt his chin aside. When Skeres snorted, she turned narrowed eyes on him. "What did you say you're called?" she asked.

Tom had the satisfaction of seeing the lad colour, scarlet patches blossoming on jaws, ears and knotted brow as he fumbled to his feet. "That'd be Nick Skeres, Mistress," he muttered, and then adjusted it: "Y'r Ladyship."

"Nick Skeres," Lady Ursula acknowledged. "And what manner of beast would you say Master Tom baited?"

One had to hand it to the lad: for all his thick-witted ways, he was quick as the devil to grasp when he wasn't truly in trouble. His short-lived guilty manner melted away, and there was the hint of a cheeky curl to his still swollen lip as he answered: "An Italian one, y'r Ladyship."

Lady Ursula swung back to Tom, an eyebrow raised in question.

"Citolini," Tom said — all amusement gone — and stopped when Bridget came carrying a full trencher and two steaming mugs.

They all kept quiet as the maid fussed with the knives and a small crock of butter, but there was no mistaking Lady Ursula's frown.

"You never had a fight with Mastro Paolo, had you Tom?" she asked, voice low, as soon as the maid curtsied herself away.

"It's rather worse than that." Tom looked away. He looked at the busy, warm kitchen, with the ruddy glow from the fireplace gleaming off the copper pans hung on the whitewashed walls, the yellow-glazed cupboards, the weak sunlight that poured through the latticed window to checker the flagstones, the scent of freshly baked bread, of herbs and onions, the spicy steam from the pot scalding his palms ... and then he looked back at his cousin. Sir Francis, it was known, confided much in his wife — but, cousin or not, what secrets a lowly courier knew were not his to lay before kindly ladies... Was this the way it would always be — as long as he continued in the Service? Oh, but he missed the Thomases! The ones he could have talked to — both of them two half-kingdoms away... He blinked, and saw Lady Ursula waiting. He'd been dim-witted enough already over this whole matter... He squared his shoulders, shook his head and said: "I trusted him, and should not have."

And perhaps his attempt at equanimity fell short, because Lady Ursula clicked her tongue and reached to pat his arm.

"Well, but we all trusted him, Tom," she said — and, being Lady Walsingham, never asked what the man had done. "My husband, Sir Henry ... such a gentlemanly, well-educated creature. A little hot-headed, a little sullen — but that you'd expect of an Italian..."

Hot-headed, sullen. Did Citolini know how Lady Walsingham thought of him? Tom nodded, eyes lowered on his cider. "But I failed to see when the mask cracked — and two men are dead because of it."

Lady Ursula's hand tightened on Tom's arm — just as another snort came from across the table.

Tom looked up to meet Skeres's glance over the cup's rim, then the lad looked down and shrugged. "And 'ow's that your fault, I'll never know," he mumbled. "A stab in the dark, a push off the quay, and gone."

Faithful Dolius to the rescue, for all that Tom had suspected him...

The lad turned to Lady Ursula for support. "'Ow was 'e to stop that Papist ruffian, eh, y'r Ladyship?"

"How, indeed?" Lady Ursula looked from Skeres to Tom and back again, brown eyes smiling.

But they didn't understand — it wasn't that simple. A stab and a push — as though the trouble all were in the two crude acts! But nobody wanted to see ... a push and a stab! Who had said much the same, as though it were nothing but mischance, two stones rolling this way rather than that...? A misstep on a quay, a careless servant doesn't shut a gate... The not-quite hushed voice, the unblinking stare... Ralph Garrard, it had been, sitting in that tavern in Calais. Of course, there was that Garrard couldn't know... *A careless servant...*

Oh Lord in Heaven!

Tom shot to his feet, the cider sloshing hot out of the cup onto his fingers. "How did he know?"

They all stared at him, Lady Ursula doubtful, Skeres wary, the maid at the table's end with raised knife and round eyes.

"He was gone before us, and I never told him. How did he know of the open gate?"

Not that there was anyone to answer. "And he did mention the Earl, too...!" Tom took a last hasty sip of cider, and plunked the cup down on the table. "Come, Skeres!"

"Where?" the lad whined, with a regretful look at his half-empty trencher. "What's bitten you now?"

"Where did you say you found Litcott the night before we left?"

"King's 'Ead," was the answer.

"Let's go, then." Tom turned to Lady Ursula. "Forgive me, Ma'am. I'll be back. If you could send a man after Sir Francis? To..." Not that he quite knew yet what there was to say... "To warn him that things may not be as they seem."

And with that he rushed from the kitchen, a grumbling Skeres trudging after him. Six manners of fool — that's what he was. Taken in again, and again...

A tug on his sleeve stopped him.

"Come now, Nick Skeres, we have no time. You'd know that young woman again, would you? The one who was with Litcott?"

The lad nodded in grim triumph. "Ay — but you don't think I did in those two, now, eh?"

One should be slow to trust, Thomas...

And Tom, whose faith in mankind had just taken another blow, gave the lad a tight smile and a push out of the door into the courtyard. He would make his apologies — if and when the facts called for them.

CHAPTER 17

It was growing to be a familiar thing — to arrive at some manner of public house with questions whirling inside his head, and Nick Skeres grumbling at his elbow…

"'Twas quicker to walk," it was this time, as they dismounted, and the lad beckoned for an urchin to mind the horses.

"And there'd be no brat to pay, if we'd walked…"

In truth, Tom hadn't wanted to walk. Walking allowed for talk, and he'd rather not talk with Skeres. Not yet, at least — not while he couldn't quite decide to his satisfaction whether the lad was to be entirely trusted. He certainly seemed sincere in his protestations, but… *Nullius in verba.* Murder, it seemed, gave one new appreciation of Horace's ancient wisdom: take no one at their word.

Pushing aside thoughts of Gordian knots and Cretan labyrinths, Tom entered the King's Head.

He'd been there a few times for the fine ale, with his brother or with Watson. The place belonged to the better sort of tavern, with pewter vessels hanging from the walls, clean sand on the floor, and two glazed windows, large enough that candles were not sorely missed in the grey light. The Princess Elizabeth was said to have dined there, straight out of the Tower — but, Watson being the source of the story, Tom reserved his judgement.

Right at the moment, no princesses were in sight. Midmorning was hardly the busiest time for drinking places. A handful of men sat scattered among tables and benches — one of them, at least, a prentice playing truant, by the look of him.

A big, pock-marked tapster in a plain russet jerkin was gathering pots from empty tables, with the sour look of one wasting his life on menial tasks. Near the fireplace, a grey-haired and grey-clad lady stood, the very picture of respectability, surveying the goings on.

Because she looked to be in charge, it was to her that Tom turned.

"Good day, Mistress," he began — and went no farther, as Nick Skeres pushed at his side — the charging Minotaur to Tom's labyrinth…

"We want an 'arlot," the lad said, earning them both a disapproving stare from the landlady.

"Skeres!" Tom hissed, and might as well have hissed at the newel post.

"Ay, well, we do want 'er!" Skeres said, undeterred. "One with a red 'ead."

"We have no harlots, here," the landlady said, in a severe manner Tom's mother wouldn't have disliked — and then she ruined it somewhat by adding: "If you would have a young woman's company, come in the evening."

Which was all the joint and flexure that Tom needed. "Not her company, Mistress," he said, drawing himself tall. "And not any woman. I need to talk to one particular young woman who was here some two weeks past."

"With a red 'ead," Nick Skeres insisted, as eager as you please. "And this white skin, all soft-looking…"

Tom elbowed him quiet. "One who that night kept company with a man in a yellow hat," he said.

The landlady had lost some of her stern ways, and was eyeing the stranger — reckoning, no doubt, the travel-stained appearance against the rapier and the gentlemanly carriage…

Before she could come to a decision, though, a soft voice came from behind Tom's back.

"They'd be meaning Nancey, Aunt Bess…"

Tom turned around to see two girls arm in arm. Yellow-haired both, there was no other resemblance between them. One was a wide-hipped creature with a round face and plump arms, and a careless way about her corset laces; the other, no more than thirteen or fourteen, was thin, prim and wide-eyed. This was the one who had spoken, calling the landlady her aunt.

Tom took a step back so that he could have the three women within his sight — none of them looking happy. "Then, if you please," he said, with all the patience he could muster, "I'd be most grateful for a word with Nance."

Stricken glances passed between the two girls, and the alewife sniffed.

"Now that, sir, would be a feat," she said grimly. "Our Nance has been dead these ten days and more, poor soul."

Dead. Litcott's girl of an evening dead — and then Litcott himself… That could be no happenstance, surely?

"How did she die?"

More glances passed between the women, and the younger girl's eyes welled with tears.

"Oh, Sir, it was most horrible!" she gasped, fists pressed to her chest.

"Alice, child…" tutted her aunt, and the other girl put an arm around her, clucking like a hen, but Alice shook her head, and forged on in a tremulous whisper.

"They stabbed her, poor Nancey — and then strangled her too."

"Ay, stabbed and strangled." The older girl shook her head, but she had a breathless, glint-eyed keenness, and a Kentish colour to her speech. "The one or the other, you'd say, well and good — but stabbed *and* strangled? And cruelly, too." She put a hand at her throat. "All bruised black!"

At her side, poor little Alice winced and swallowed hard.

"Malkin, you fool!" The landlady slapped the girl's hand, and then turned to Tom. "But ay, Sir — what manner of man does that to a poor chit of a girl?"

Or to a harmless glover, for that matter … stabbed and not quite strangled, for Tom would wager poor red-headed Nance had died with a crushed windpipe … what manner of man, indeed.

"Oh, we *know* what manner of man!" The irrepressible Malkin nodded, purse-lipped and impervious to the landlady's scowl. A good match for Skeres, this girl. She nodded on, and looked at Tom.

Of course. He fingered his purse, trying to reckon just how much English money he had left, and pressed a penny in Malkin's hand. "What manner, then, Malkin?" he asked.

Malkin threw a glance over her shoulder, where the glum tapster now leant against the counter, arms crossed and brooding — and then she left Alice's side to grab Tom's sleeve, and led him into a snug beyond the fireplace. The landlady, Alice and Skeres trooped behind, and they all huddled in the grey light, like Caesar's murderers conspiring.

"That's Hugh, over there agin the door," she whispered, with another peep over her shoulder.

"He was sweet on Nancey, poor Hugh," said Alice.

"Ay, well, and he found her dead." Malkin lowered her voice further. "Wouldn't want him to know — but Nance…"

And here Skeres snorted. "Well, what did 'e expect?" he asked — the very notion of lowering one's voice foreign to him. "Seeing as she was an 'arlot…"

Innocent, Tom decided, as he glared at him. Innocent on all counts. Innocent of anything that required the scantiest sliver of subtlety ... either that, or he'd missed his calling, and should have been a clown with the Admiral's players. And what was worse, the interruption had given the landlady leisure to grow some qualms.

"I don't see, though, Malkin, that we should tell poor Nance's business to this gentleman..." she said.

"But, Aunt..." A hand on her aunt's arm, young Alice looked Tom in the eye, blushing as she did. "What are you going to do with what we tell you of Nancey?" she asked, suddenly far too grave for a child of her years — no older than Cousin Frances, in fact, and with the same half-shy, half-questioning gaze.

Tom looked back, just as gravely. "Bring her murderer to justice, if I can," he said. "He killed two men besides her — one of them in my charge." That the murderer also meant ill to the Queen and to England he held back, not sure that, to the likes of little Alice, a dead friend didn't weigh more than a threat to the realm...

The girl nodded and, with the briefest sideways glance at her aunt, said: "Tell him, Malkin."

And Malkin told. "There was this man," she said. "Old, mind you, but with a fat purse. He came here sometimes — not that I'd call it often, but Nance..." A shrug. "She liked to make it out as that he was her particular friend."

"Some manner of friend," the landlady sniffed.

"He beat her," whispered Alice, back from a young Justitia to a round-eyed child again.

"Well, just the once, for all we know." Malkin leant forward, eager to take back the telling of her tale. "And she said she was ill until the bruises were gone, so as Hugh wouldn't see them

— she was afraid as he'd go arter that man — for…" Again, the girl checked that Hugh was well out of earshot, at the taproom's far end, dealing with a pair of early drinkers. "For she said as that man would kill him."

Tom cast a dubious glance Hugh's way. Sturdy-boned and heavy, the tapster looked apt to take care of himself — but then… "How so?"

Again, the women traded glances — bless them, and Sir Francis on his way to Whitehall, ready to singe Lord Leicester's ears… In the end it was Alice who answered.

"Nancey said her gentleman doesn't like to be crossed," she said.

Which might still only mean that he was likely to backhand a saucy harlot — but…

"A gentleman?" Tom asked.

"Well…" The landlady pursed her lips. "That's what Nance called him…"

"A gentleman, that one!" snorted Malkin. "Well clothed and well fed, I'll grant you — but … some sort av merchant's more like it."

"A wool-cloth merchant, maybe?" And that was Skeres, of course, thinking himself mightily shrewd, judging by the sly grin he sported, and the wink…

As was to be expected, there were shrugs from the girls.

"He did wear fine wool, well-dyed," the landlady offered, now on her guard about what she might be expected to say — and sink Nick Skeres!

It was fortunate that Malkin was far blunter. "Still, he was no niggard, mind you — though he only came here to drink," she said with a shrug. "Nance went out to meet him. Not that often, either — but the day as she was killed, she went."

"When did you say that was?"

"Now, that was…" Malkin scrunched her round face in thought.

The landlady cut in: "A week before Martinmas, it was. I meant to send her to Fish Key, what with it being Wednesday, and fish day — but she was gone before day-break."

"Ay…" said Malkin. "Wednesday — and all agog, she was. She said as her gentleman was going to buy her a fine cloak."

Of course — Wednesday. The night before, poor foolish Litcott had let something slip while in his cups, and in the morning Nance had run to sell the wares…

"Do you know where she'd meet him?"

One after another, the three women shook their heads. Ah well, that would have been too much to hope for.

"But you saw him," he said instead. "You'd know what he looks like?"

"Old," Malkin said — who looked herself much of an age with Tom.

"Not all that old," protested the landlady. "Mouse-haired."

"Big, tall, with a red face — and loud," said Alice. "A laugh to make the rafters shake. He seemed so jolly…"

"Ay, but you know what always made me think ill of him?" Malkin nodded knowingly. "He never blinks."

"Ha! Hang me if that ain't —"

"Nick Skeres!" Tom snapped. "Go out and get the horses!"

The lad stared back like Innocence misused — and sent on a fool's errand for good measure. "The 'orses are —"

"Get them!"

Had the good Lord given Skeres a tail, it would have been stuck between his legs as, with a mumble of "Ay, Master," he went.

And truly, how was one to unravel murders with that oaf at his elbow, giving voice to whatever came to his mind?

A hand on his sleeve brought Tom back from the realm of abstract questions to the King's Head.

Alice was looking at him with very large, very round eyes. "You know who that man is, then, Sir?"

Just like little Frances, waiting for reassurance… It was the resemblance that made him give her a stiff little bow. "I do, Mistress Alice. And I will see that he pays for what he did."

The girl blushed at being addressed as mistress, but nodded back.

How he was going to do that, now, was another matter — but this he kept to himself, and thanked the women, and took his leave — not without slipping another penny to Malkin. He was at the door when something else occurred to him.

Malkin was still in the snug, weighing Tom's pennies in the palm of her hand.

"You said your tapster found the girl dead," he said. "Do you know where?"

"Not far," was the answer. "You know where Culver Alley is, right by the well in Fenchurch Street? That's where he chanced on her, poor Nance — all the way behind St. Gabriel's graveyard."

Tom thanked her and went his way, thinking hard.

He joined Skeres out in the street, where the lad waited with the horses and none of the contriteness one might expect of a servant just called to task. Instead, he tugged at Tom's sleeve as he set foot to stirrup.

"So Leicester's man, it ain't your Italian. Who'd 'ave said?"

Tom grimaced, thinking of Citolini's unheeded protestations. One more thing to set a-right — if only he could get to Whitehall in time — another being…

"No — not Lord Leicester's, Skeres," he said slowly, mounting, and beckoning for the lad to do the same. "Now we need a wherry."

Tom urged his horse through the throng, into Mark Lane. Down at the Water Gate there would be wherries Westward bound, surely...

As soon as they turned into the larger Hart Street, Skeres pushed his horse to go apace with Tom's, not much caring whom he inconvenienced.

"What do you mean, not Leicester's man?" he asked, voice pitched over the late morning bustle.

With a grimace, Tom looked around. Peddlers, beggars, prentices and servants, mostly, but no one paid the least mind to the two horsemen — except for a curse or two when their horses' hooves splashed enough dirty water from the runnel to drench someone. Nonetheless, he tried to keep his voice as low as the going would allow. "I mean, Nick Skeres, that no man of Leicester's would have gone out of his way to bring his Lordship's name to my attention, would he now?"

Skeres seemed to ponder this, and then had to fall behind when they turned into the narrowish Seething Lane. He was still pondering by the time they dismounted at Sir Francis's gate.

A groom hurried out to take the horses from them. Tom threw him the reins, and would have hurried away on foot — but...

"Master Thomas, wait!" the boy called. "If you're going after the Master, I've a thing for you to take. From Mr. Wade."

It was a slender packet, bound with string and sealed. Tom slipped it inside his sleeve.

"What's that?" Skeres asked as they hurried towards Tower Street.

Tom couldn't help a huff of laughter. "If you want to keep this job, Nick Skeres, one thing you must unlearn is asking what's inside a packet. For just this once, though, I'll lay you a wager: this is the paper you found on Litcott, and Mr. Wade's note that something in it ties to Lord Leicester."

"But you said…"

"Ay — and this —" Tom tapped his sleeve — "is proof that I am right."

He couldn't help a smile at the way the lad's face knotted in perplexity. By the manner he shook his head, one'd think doubt to be a persistent horsefly…

"But if that murdering bastard ain't Leicester's man, then who set 'im to it?"

Who, indeed. Tom turned the question in his mind, as he sought a way through the traffic, across Tower Street. This was no ill-considered act — quite the contrary. Here was the work of someone who wanted Lord Leicester exposed in his feigned new zeal for the French Match. Someone who stood to profit from confusion and distrust among those who would rather see Monsieur shipped back to France a bachelor. Someone in the Privy Council, placed to know of Sir Francis's arrangements — and of Monsieur's whims. Someone who…

"You are from these parts, aren't you, Dolius?" Tom asked. "What's around Fenchurch Street?"

"The King's 'Ead."

Oh patience, patience… "Yes — that I know. What else?"

The lad hummed in thought. "Churches. St. Gabriel, All 'allows, St. Denys, St. Kate, and there's the well, and Leadenhall's not that far away, and then what? The Ironmongers' 'all, and… Oh!" He lit up. "And the Clothweavers!"

But none of it was any help. "What about Culver Alley?"

"What about it?" Skeres shrugged. "No one goes there."

"Not even those who live there?"

"There ain't many as you'd say that *live* there. Runs all around St. Gabriel's graveyard — and the other side's mostly the back of 'ouses... Oy!"

Skeres shouted, grabbing at Tom and dragging him out of harm's way — in the form of a lady's coach that would have run him down where he'd stopped, in the midst of Tower Street.

The lad gave Tom's arm a small shake before releasing him. "I'll swear, Master, at times you lack a sparrow's wits!"

But never mind the coach! All the pieces inside Tom's head were shaking into place — yet again, and for once, the new shape they made, rather than negating the previous one, at last brought it to fine and full completion. One that Sir Francis would, if not like, recognise.

"A sparrow's wits..." Tom grinned at his bemused manservant. "You'll never know how right you are, Nick Skeres. Come on." And he took off at a brisk pace, back where he'd come from.

It took Skeres a dozen puffing strides to come apace, narrowing his eyes at Tom. "You're never going to Culver Alley, are you? Ain't no place for honest folks."

"No, it's not. It's the place where foolish young women are killed — and where no honest man just chances on their bodies."

A surer knowledge of matters, it turned out, shortened the way (something that Watson was sure to make into a Latin couplet, someday) and, even on foot, they were back at the King's Head in a trice. Malkin met them — a dinner-time Malkin, with her hair bound, and a kerchief tied over her cleavage.

When asked for Hugh's whereabouts, she shrugged, looked around, and, spying the tapster across the crowding room, she waved a hand before Tom could stop her, calling loudly: "Hugh!"

The man's eyes went wide at the sight of who was with the girl. He looked around wildly, dropped the jugs he was carrying in the lap of a fat country barleycorn and, amidst a sudden burst of curses and laughter, bounded for the door out to Fenchurch Street.

Tom shoved Skeres out into Mark Lane. "Cut him off, if he goes Tower-way!" he ordered, and plunged through the mayhem after the tapster. He jostled past the ale-doused farmer and a gaggle of his angry friends, and spilled out into the street — right into a peddler of ballads. The man made a great show of going down amidst a whorl of printed sheets, wailing like one maimed…

"A-ruined, that's what I am," he whined most piteously, clinging like a terrier at Tom's arm. "Look, y'all — a-ruined in my livelihood, and a broken leg… A limp to my grave, I'll carry…"

A crowd was gathering, the way it always did in London's streets, some jeering at the peddler, some hissing at Tom… And in the press of heads, baskets and kirtles, a flash of russet was fast disappearing in that strange, half-leaping trot…

Oh, curse it! Tom scrabbled in his near-empty purse, and threw a half-handful of small coins — all that he had left — down at the thrice-cursed man. A few pennies, a groat or two, a few French sols — there was more than the ballads were worth, but it was no surprise that all it did was renew the man's effort, and pox take him!

"A-ruined, look you!" he began anew.

This time Tom wrenched free. "Queen's service!" he snarled at the bystanders, as sternly as he knew — which earned him round-eyed stares, and barely room enough to be on his way. And if there was any way to make his doings more blatant, he couldn't think of one.

There are few greater virtues than discretion, Thomas…

Ah well, this was for later. Gritting his teeth against Sir Francis's certain disfavour, Tom shouldered his way through the midday throng — because, of course, if one had to pursue a man in the streets, it would be at noon…

The only good thing was, the pursued was just as hampered as the pursuer — and it wasn't long before Tom caught sight of his quarry, ducking between an ox-cart and the well as he tried to gain, of all places, Culver Alley.

Skeres's voice echoed in Tom's mind: *No place for honest folks…* Grazing a shin against the well's steps, he plunged into the dim, muddy, stinking lane.

"Halt, man — halt there!" he called, as he made his hasty and unsteady way — the ground being slick and uneven. Hugh just slowed enough to throw a glance over his shoulder — and must have liked his odds enough. Or perhaps…

A limp! That's what it was, that skew-whiff gait… The man had a limp, and little chance of running from a pursuer with two good legs.

Which meant it was at least half-desperation that made him unsheathe a big, thick knife and, with a wordless shout, lurch for Tom in a crab-wise charge.

A former soldier, Tom decided, as he drew his rapier and stepped into a defensive guard. Tom's was the longer blade by far — but Hugh was half as big, and half as old again, and knew how to do harm, and had no qualms at doing it, while

Tom wanted the tapster not only alive, but also hale within reason.

He sidestepped as Hugh rushed him, careful to do no more than nick the man's arm. The tapster didn't seem to notice, as he spun around with a roar, and elbowed Tom in the ribs, slamming him into the mouldy wall. Winded and off balance, Tom lost his footing in the mud, and slipped — and had a sudden flash of a helmeted Hugh in battle, charging with a line of pikemen. The pockmarked face was barely a foot away, twisted in thoughtless, spitting rage as the man loomed, knife raised... A pikeman, yes, and hardly a good one — not trained to keep his head in a swordfight... Easy enough to raise the rapier's tip now, let the dunce skewer himself in his madness — but...

Dead men do not talk, Thomas...

A heartbeat before the knife found his chest, Tom kicked out, sweeping Hugh's good leg from beneath him — or at least he thought it was the good one. No matter, though. The man staggered back against the wall across, and Tom lunged, shifting his grip to slam his rapier's hilt in his opponent's jaw.

Hugh the tapster, at last, went down. By the time he blinked himself aware, Tom was standing over him — a foot planted on his knife-hand, the rapier's point at his throat.

"So there!" Tom gasped. Hardly the noble words victorious heroes uttered in Latin poems — but then, one always wondered with what breath they uttered them at all...

"Oy, Master!" came from the alley's mouth.

"Here, Dolius!" Tom called, without taking his eyes — or his sword's point — from the sprawling Hugh.

He let the man raise a hand to work an already bruising jaw, and then to finger the bleeding hole on his left arm.

"Ye wounded me, curse ye!" he cried, in such an ill-used manner that it startled Tom into a snort of laughter.

"Ay, well — curse *you*! What did you expect, charging at me like that?"

Hugh tossed his head — and looked as though he regretted the move. "Asking questions, coming after me like that... What's a fellow to do?" he grumbled, in a most unconvincing show of innocence.

By then Nick Skeres had caught up, looking happier with Tom's handiwork than Tom was with him.

"And didn't I tell you to catch him if he went Tower-way?" he asked, after directing the lad to bind Hugh's arm.

Skeres shrugged, of course. "Ay, well, 'e didn't, did 'e?" he said — and there would have been much to discuss about obeying orders, but by then others were making their way into Culver Alley, including the plaguey ballad-seller and two Watchmen, wanting to know what was the fuss and just who everybody was.

Aldgate Ward or Tower Street? Tom wondered, or perhaps some parish men... Ah well, no matter. This was one of those rare times to make full use of his family name.

"My name is Thomas Walsingham," he announced, sheathing his rapier — and he waited as the Watchmen digested the fact.

One's jaw dropped, the other blinked and swallowed, and there was a small murmur in the gaggle behind them. It was most satisfying.

"Kinsman to Mr. Secretary," he added, for good measure. "And this man is expected at Whitehall. He tried to object, at first — but he doesn't anymore."

He spared a glance for the still reclining Hugh, and found him green-faced and gawping, and shaking his head.

It never failed to give Tom pause to see the power of his cousin's sinister fame. If only Hugh and all these tremblers knew how little store Mr. Secretary set by the efficacity of torture… Then again, if Sir Francis's name must be enough to quell Watchmen, and London crowds, and fractious pikemen into obedience, that particular opinion had better not be known…

Things being as they were, it was a very short matter to pick up Hugh and be on their way to the river, Whitehall — and, most of all, Sir Francis.

CHAPTER 18

The Water Gate was noisy and crowded. Close by, men were working a crane to unload wool bales from a barge, but past them, at the stairs, a clutch of watermen stood waiting for business, their wherries bobbing in the water.

Tom's step lengthened, and he waved to hail the water-men.

Not that they made a very attractive group — spattered with mud and blood from the brush in the alley ... but then again, to a waterman custom was custom, and there was a small scuffle before a big, bald fellow motioned them to his wherry — never mind that it was small for three passengers.

"No shooting the Bridge, my masters," the man announced as he descended into the boat. "A penny each to Fresh Wharf."

And that was when Tom remembered his empty purse, and the thrice-cursed ballad seller. "Ah — Skeres," he murmured trying hard not to grimace.

"Ay, ay." Never batting an eyelid, the lad shoved Hugh at Tom and sat down on a coil of rope to slip off a shoe, and shake a handful of coins out of it. "'Ere," he said, shoving three pennies at the boatman, who smirked and spat in the river, laughing to himself, no doubt, at down-at-the-heel gentlemen.

As stone-faced as he could manage with burning ears, Tom pushed his prisoner in the wherry and followed, as Nick Skeres slipped up his shoe again and hopped for the boat. At last the waterman jumped in, grabbed his oars, and shoved off the bank, steering the wherry in the thick, pewter-coloured currents of the Thames.

They landed at Fresh Wharf, just safely downriver from where the water foamed roaring through the Bridge's arches, and walked around to the other side, to take another, larger two-man boat at the Old Swan — that Skeres had to pay for again, while Tom wondered just what, to the lad's mind, would count as a friend's interest...

By the time they were settled in the wherry, the two boatmen rowing upriver with a will, every church in London was chiming noon, all manners of peals — deep or silvery, bright or jangling — rolling over the grey waters. Tom let himself sit back and take a good breath — only to sit up straight again with a hiss, his ribs resenting their acquaintance with Hugh's elbow. Hugh indeed — curse him! — and time to see what use could be made of the man.

The tapster sat sulking across from Tom, with Skeres beside him at his most mastiff-ish. He sat there, and stared at his hands.

When Tom asked where did he get his bad leg, he just scowled harder, never raising his eyes.

Skeres nudged him none too gently. "You answer, when my master talks to you — you woman-killing cur!"

That had Hugh looking up, at last, in the blackest anger — but...

"No, Dolius. Not him. He did no harm to Nance, did you, fellow? He knows who did, though."

The tapster's eyes went wide, and he darted a sharp look at Tom, before looking down again.

Skeres gave the man another poke. "Then why don't 'e tell, eh? Too scared, is 'e? Like 'is woman said?"

Hugh's fists and shoulders stiffened.

So, after all, Nick Skeres wasn't as thick-witted as he seemed. Unsubtle as they came, but ... Tom swallowed a smile. "Oh, I don't know about that," he said, slowly. "Then again, I doubt Nance was truly protecting him, you know. Going behind his back, more likely, and trying to pull the wool over his eyes…"

This time Hugh's glare burnt with fury, and came together with a start that Nick Skeres quelled by clamping a hand around the man's bad arm.

"Down, you jackanapes!" growled the lad, his other hand on his knife's hilt. "You want to take a swim?"

Hugh whimpered a little and sat back, closing his eyes.

One of the wherrymen turned to look over his shoulder, and Tom met the alarmed glance with his steadiest, coldest, most Sir Francis-like gaze. The man looked away, hopefully cured of any itch to complain to the guardsmen once at Whitehall's jetty…

Tom brought his attention back to Hugh — a grey-faced Hugh, wiping the back of his hand across a sweaty brow.

The man looked up to meet Tom's eyes. "Aye, Nance was a fool," he choked out, Northern speech thickening. "Sharper'n me — doesna take much — but still a daft fool. Thinking she could play men's games … and look where it landed her!"

There was no mistaking the broken speech, the red-rimmed eyes. Little Alice was right: the fool had been sweet on Nance.

Tom leant closer, half-wincing when his mistreated ribs made themselves felt. "It landed her dead, where you knew to find her," he whispered. "Because you know that meeting place, too, don't you?"

Hugh dipped his head.

"That's how Nance came across her murderer — and got ideas above her station. It was through you."

Another jerky nod — and perhaps after all Skeres *was* thick-witted.

"Playing bawd to your woman, and now she's dead, not a word out of you?" Tom asked ferociously, kicking at the tapster's shin.

Hugh reared up. "Playing bawd! Taking her for ma wife, I was!" he hissed, face twisting again as it had back in the alley — before it crumpled, and Hugh lowered his head on his clenched fists.

Skeres snorted, but Tom shook his head.

"No, I believe him. He meant to wed the woman — but then she died, and he's in our man's pay, you see. And he knows in whose pay our man is. Don't you, Hugh?"

The man looked up, took a breath as though to speak, then let it out in a huff. When he shrugged a shoulder, it was a desolate, glum, bitter thing.

Tom wanted to sigh with relief. Instead, he nodded, as though he'd been certain all the time. "Think, Nick Skeres. You haven't worked long for my cousin — but would you go drinking to the White Horse?"

The lad gave a peal of laughter. "What sort of dunce d'you take me for? The White 'Orse — right next door?"

"The King's Head, on the other hand…"

"Ay, well." Skeres scratched his head. "Out of the way enough — and I like their ale."

The ale and other things, quite likely. "You, and my cousin's whole household. So…" Tom looked at Hugh again, making him flinch. "Think well, Nick Skeres: who'd want to put a man of his where my cousin's folks come and go? Think of someone with a different interest in certain … affairs. Because, you see, I think that we've been looking at this whole rigmarole quite the wrong way."

But the lad knew nothing of such interests, and even less of how few, even in the Queen's Council, had both the means and the cunning to play far-sighted games of gathering intelligence... Face scrunched in perplexity, Skeres took a breath like one about to ask questions — and, before Tom could shush him, the wherry bucked under them, fit to disgorge one and all into the river.

A bigger, well-appointed barge — some nobleman's vessel, by the painted look of it — was gliding past them, and far too close. It was a many-rowed affair, large enough to catch the wherry in its wake and rock it madly.

Tom grabbed for the cushioned bench, while the wherrymen exchanged foul language with the barge's rowers. Hugh crouched as low as he could in the bottom, hanging on for dear life, but Nick Skeres, who had been so scared of the sea, leant over the wherry's side, shaking his fist at the bargemen and shouting abuse.

Tom caught a handful of jerkin, and dragged him back to sit. "Aren't you the one afraid of drowning?" he shouted over the din.

"Ay — at sea, not in the river at 'ome!" was the lack-wit's answer.

Still, for a mercy, he sat back, and the wherrymen obeyed when Tom ordered them to leave the barge be.

"A disgrace, that's what I calls it!" groused the younger and burlier of the two. "A wonder, it is, they didn't get us all drowned."

"A wonder, indeed," Tom said curtly — not that he didn't agree. "Now put your back into it."

The boatmen complied — to show once more how much easier it was to make oneself obeyed in England. Or perhaps it was London. Or just when there was no Citolini around to undermine one's authority...

Oh Lord, Citolini! Citolini — apprehended, accused, and, it would seem, quite innocent!

Tom hurried the wherrymen again and sat back, looking across the crowded waters to gauge where they were. The far bank, to the south, was flat, marshy grounds for the most part. London-side, the jumble of narrow houses, wharves and alley-mouths had thinned out, giving place to the river side of the lordly Strand mansions, with their own jetties, their own elegant water stairs, name after noble name… Leicester House, Arundel, Somerset, Exeter past the Strand, Durham…

And indeed, what if… Tom sat up straight. What if his man had gone to report… Should he order the boat brought ashore, demand admittance … on what strength, though? And even if the man was there…

But no. Whitehall. That was where the Court was headed, where the Privy Council would be gathered to await the Queen's arrival. Anyone seeking a Councillor would know to go there.

The Thames curved, wide and dark, speckled with all manners of craft. Not much further now, the towers of Westminster were in sight — and before those, the Palace of Whitehall with its keel-domed turrets, and the jutting gallery that sheltered the Privy Stairs.

Now it remained to be seen: would they be waiting at the Palace proper, or further up at the Star Chamber?

When all else fails, Thomas, serva ordinem, and ordo servabit te. Be well-ordered, and order will stand you in good stead.

Order it was, then. Tom reached to nudge the nearest boatman. "Court Stairs first," he instructed — and then turned to Hugh. "Now hear me well. The man who murdered your Nance, I want to bring him to justice, for her and for two

222

more. You'll have to tell Mr. Secretary what you know of him, though. Of him — and of his master."

The tapster looked up, eyes dark in the pockmarked face, and for the first time Tom observed that he was youngish — six or seven-and-twenty, no more than that. "You understand?"

Hugh looked down and nodded — one small jerk of his head.

Beside him, Skeres pulled a face — not that he was wrong. An injured soldier, a tavern bully ... it was wagering much to have him speak against a nobleman who had the Queen's ear...

Just as the wherrymen steered their boat out of the current to the wide Court Stairs, where men in armour and bright liveries crowded, and torches burnt in the grey day, Hugh spoke, so softly that Tom had to lean closer to hear. "At the Rijmenam, it was," he murmured, head low, one hand rubbing at his left knee. "With Norreys."

Tom nodded. "You fellows did well," he said, earning himself another of those curt nods.

It was a start — or so it was to be hoped. Whether it would hold once they were inside Whitehall, was quite likely another matter.

CHAPTER 19

The guards, the scarlet-liveried servants, pages, squires and porters were not much taken with the three battered men clambering out of a common wherry onto Court Stairs — and, all things considered, small blame to them.

Tom thought of his travel attire, the mud, the bruises he sported — and carefully kept from looking down at himself or brushing the mud flakes from his sleeves. Instead, he offered the letter that Will Wade had sealed with Sir Francis's household seal.

"I must see Mr. Secretary most urgently," he said.

The Yeoman of the Guard who had been called, huge and resplendent in black, scarlet and gold, placidly turned the letter in his hands, and then raised a doubtful eyebrow.

"Sure you must," he said with a sniff. "Half of London must see Mr. Secretary today. You'll have to wait."

"But I'm of his household," Tom insisted.

The man hummed, and nodded his chin at Skeres and his captive. "Them, too?"

"No — yes…! Never mind them. *I* am — and…"

"And you must see him — ay." The Yeoman was unruffled. "But the Royal train is a mile away, see. Mr. Secretary has no time for callers."

"That's why I must…" Tom's patience — what was left of it — was fraying fast.

"Do I trounce 'im, Master?"

"For God's sake, Nick Skeres!" Tom turned furiously on the servant, who stood there glowering at the Yeoman, shoulders hunched and a hand fisted in Hugh's jerkin. All they lacked now…

But look! Beyond the two men another boat was landing, a man climbing out of it. A man in Royal livery — with the Tudor Rose embroidered on his chest, and a well-known face…

"Barnet!" Tom most undignifiedly pounced on the newcomer. "Oh, thanks be — Richard Barnet!"

Dick Barnet, born to Chislehurst parents and something of a Walsingham retainer, had one of those faces that split like a red apple when he grinned. "God save you, Master Tom! But it is good to see you!"

Any other day, Tom would have cheerfully traded news of home — but… "Barnet…"

And he could never call good old Dick slow-witted. The word and a glance was all it took him.

"Come, Yeoman Jones!" he beamed at the guardsman. "This is Master Tom Walsingham! You think Mr. Secretary will be happy that you hold his kinsfolk at the door?"

Let it not be widely known yet that you are back, Thomas…

Tom winced as the Yeoman took another measuring look at him, and then shrugged. "If there's trouble, Dick…" he warned as he removed his towering self from his way. "If there's trouble, it's on your head."

Barnet threw back his head in laughter and caught Tom's elbow, steering him up the stairs with the other two in tow.

"Hasn't been here long, that one." Barnet raised his voice to be heard by the placid guardsman. "Still cannot tell an honest Kentish gentleman from a Spanish murderer!"

He was still laughing at his own wit by the time they stepped inside the Palace proper — or at least a cobbled courtyard where an ant-hill's worth of velvet-liveried Myrmidons scurried this way and that.

Barnet leant closer to wink, and whisper in Tom's ear: "A right Bedlam, that's what it is when the Court moves…"

Tom cut right in. "But I must see Sir Francis, Dick. Right now. Do you know where he is?"

Barnet's face fell of a sudden, as though someone had cut the tenterhooks holding it up. "Cuds-me, but I don't know that you can," he said, shaking his head. "The train's —"

"Less than a mile away, your Yeoman said," Tom spoke over him. "And I must — *must* — see Sir Francis before Her Grace arrives."

"Ay, but…" Barnet pushed his velvet beret back on his head, chewing his lip as he reckoned ills. Clearly, letting Tom inside the Palace was one thing, and letting him in on a Privy Councillor was quite another. *If there's trouble*, the guardsman had said…

"Just tell me where to find him — and I'll give you the slip," Tom insisted.

And poor Barnet, a playmate of Guildford's during long-ago summers at Scadbury, was on the brink of yielding. "Well, they'll all be at the Court Gate…" he said, and went no further when a grey-headed, square-faced man descended on them. He wore a chain of office, and a frown solemn enough for a Roman Senator, that had poor Barnet quaking.

A Household Sergeant of some sort, Tom decided.

"Have you run your errand, Barnet?" the man asked, looking down his nose at the underling.

"Ay, Mr. Digby, and…" Good Dick cleared his throat, fingering the rose on his chest. "And at the Stairs I ran into Master Walsingham, here. Mr. Secretary's cousin, that is."

Digby spared a hooded glance for Tom — and none at all for his companions. "Indeed," he said.

One never knew, with Court servants, and their endless games of rivalries, and factions, and preferment and favour, and bribery and, not least, plain arrogance that came of bearing the Queen's colours. Even the Walsingham name may not be enough with this fellow...

"*Indeed.*" Tom squared his shoulders and held up the sealed letter. "And Mr. Secretary awaits me — on an urgent matter."

The moment he'd said them, he regretted the words. Oh, how the Thomases would laugh at him for this!

Meanwhile, the one amused was Digby. With a gleam in his eyes, he leant close, the picture of solicitude, to ask: "Then he'll have left word that you are to be let through, surely?"

"Most surely," Tom said through gritted teeth, knowing what would come. "But look..."

"Then let us find out," Digby said, in triumph. "Now please to follow me. This is no waiting place." With a flick of his hand, he dismissed poor Barnet, who lingered just enough to give Tom a grimace before fleeing.

Then Digby, pompous idiot that he was, beckoned for Tom to follow, and made for a door across the corner.

Tom lengthened his step to stride apace with the man — and to see the way he carried himself, wouldn't one think him a Peer or the Realm! "Mr. Digby, it could be hours before you find whoever it is who knows of me — but it's essential that I confer with Mr. Secretary, and —"

Digby stopped short — and for a moment seemed to consider and reason... "And so you will," he proclaimed. "As soon as we know that it is as you say."

We? Did the popinjay speak in *plurale majestatis* like the Queen?

Whether he did or not, the man opened the door and pointed.

"You will wait in here, Master … what did you say your name is?"

The bootless atomy, the witless jackanapes…! "My name is Thomas Walsingham," Tom snapped. "And if you think that Mr. Secretary won't hear of this —"

"Yes, yes — we'll see." Digby sniffed, in such triumph one'd think he'd taken Troy all by himself. "Meanwhile, you wait like everybody else."

Seething, Tom strode past the door — with Skeres and his prisoner trooping after him — and the door was slammed shut.

Skeres took a breath to speak…

"No, Skeres!" Tom snapped. "You do not trounce him!"

The lad shrugged and pulled a face at Hugh, as one asking: see what I must bear?

And before Tom could take in the look of the chamber — ugly tapestries, a window and a bench or two — someone jumped up from one of those benches.

"Master Tom!" that someone cried — and it was young Tobias Chandler, the apprentice scrivener that Cousin Ursula must have sent after her husband with Tom's message — but…

"But they won't let me see the Master," the boy squawked in great agitation. "I've asked a dozen servants, that I have. They say they'll send for me — but it's Bedlam here, what with the Court arriving, and the Queen!"

The Queen, indeed. Tom pinched the bridge of his nose, trying to reason things out.

Item: the Queen arriving back from Richmond;

Item: Monsieur clinging to Her Majesty's skirts (and let Father never know of such disrespectful thinking!);

Item: if it failed to occur to Monsieur to ask about the glover, there were those who would do it for him;

Item: Sir Francis unaware...

It was the shortest reasoning of Tom's life.

Audentes Fortuna juvat — and let's hope that Virgil was right, and Fortune had some liking to spare for this particular scrap of boldness...

"Skeres!" And there was some satisfaction to seeing the lad jump up to obey the summons. "You wait here — see that our pikeman has no second thoughts. I'm going to find Sir Francis."

The lad's prompt obedience had, it seemed, very narrow bounds. "I'm coming with you," he blustered, as Tom went to one door and then the other. "Why don't you 'ave 'im locked somewhere?"

"Because they won't do it unless Sir Francis says so," Tom said through gritted teeth as he pushed the door ajar, just enough to see nobody was out there mounting guard. "And besides, I want someone keeping an eye on him."

"Toby here can watch over the fellow."

Tom turned to look pointedly at the two of them, side by side on the bench — big, sullen Hugh, and Tobias, all of fifteen and built like a crane.

"Ay, well..." Skeres grimaced and rubbed at his nose. Even he could see it would take three Tobies to make half a Hugh.

"Not that I should need to explain for you to do as you are told," Tom said — and, as a grumbling Skeres went to sit guard on the prisoner's other side — he slid out into the busy courtyard, closing the door with care and trying to look purposeful.

Court Gate, now... He'd only been at Whitehall once or twice, on Sir Francis's errands, and then only around the Star Chamber — but he knew his direction, if not his way, by the gate's keel-domed turrets, peeking over the great tiled roof that had to be the Great Hall...

To dither seldom helps anything, Thomas...

Right, then. He would not dither. He straightened his back and, looking as confident as he knew, plunged into an arched passage, and into the teeming, sprawling, noisy bowels of the Palace of Whitehall.

CHAPTER 20

Only once, as he strode through corridors, passages and yards with a manner of purpose that wasn't half feigned, Tom was questioned, by a Gentleman Pensioner in a scarlet sash, who had to tilt his head sideways over his ruff to look down his long nose at Tom.

Like a pig's head on a platter — like the fool Middlemore in Paris, which was enough for Tom to take a dislike to the fellow.

Tom whipped out his letter, together with his most arrogant way. "Mr. Secretary's service," he snapped, all haughty impatience. The man frowned at the seal, nodded, and stepped aside.

Tom nodded back and marched past him across the high-ceilinged hall — half a dozen strides before he heard himself called.

He turned, shoulders stiff, an eyebrow raised in question. What would he do now, if… "Yes?"

"He won't be at the Star Chamber now. At the Court Gate, I'd say." The Gentleman Pensioner pointed at a tall, great door, not the passage Tom had been about to take.

Tom caught himself a heartbeat short of grinning in relief. A deeper nod would do as he gave his thanks, and the door it was. A dark panelled corridor, a small square courtyard, and another hall with fine tall windows, some more passages — and then, at last, the Court Gate's long, wide, walled strip of flagstones: one way to Westminster, the other London-ward. And there a crowd of courtiers, City Officials and attendants stood arrayed, attired in varied degrees of splendour, chattering and vying for another inch of room, and smoothing silks and velvets, wanting to be seen welcoming their Sovereign back to London.

At last. Now to find Sir Francis…

A Yeoman stood guard at the passage's mouth and, on being shown the letter, pointed Tom towards the crowd's front, where the Privy Councillors stood in a clutch, graver than most.

As he wound his way through the press — murmuring apologies as he disturbed cloaks' folds and trod on silk-clad toes — Tom could make out Sir Christopher Hatton's ruddy visage and copper-hued silk, and then Lord Hunsdon, and the dark velvets of Sir Walter Mildmay, and the Earl of Lincoln … but no sign of Sir Francis's black robes — nor of Lord Leicester's tall figure.

He was nearly within arm's reach of Mildmay — Sir Francis's brother-in-law — when some Court popinjay in green satin took exception to Tom's progress, and gave him a shove…

And one wanted to appear discreetly at Sir Walter's elbow, and crave pardon in a whisper, and plead the urgency of momentous intelligence … yes — that was what one wanted, not to be hurled forward, and stumble among the Councillors, barely biting off a curse before catching one's step…

"What's this!" Lord Hunsdon barked, grabbing Tom by the shoulder, and the Earl of Lincoln frowned — the iciest, and most disapproving frown — and Sir Christopher laughed merrily.

"Why, that's Mr. Secretary's hatchling, aren't you, lad?" he asked.

And behind him a taller man with a white beard, wearing burgundy velvet, turned around and smiled — a pleasant, warm smile that lit up shrewd blue eyes.

"Young Walsingham, indeed!" Lord Burleigh said, looking much pleased. "Back from France already, I see?"

Tom's heart sank. "I…" He caught himself enough to bow low. "My Lords. Gentlemen…" He turned pleading eyes on Sir Walter Mildmay.

Sir Walter's long, triangular face, cast in a perpetually mournful mien, with its drooping nose, downturned mouth and arched eyebrows, twisted in displeasure as he caught Tom by the elbow. He steered him away from the group of Councillors, back the way he had come — only, the crowd opened for the Privy Councillor as it hadn't for the lowly courier.

"I expect you want to see Mr. Secretary, Thomas," he sighed, as though one sorely tried by youth's whims and fancies.

"Yes! Has he…" Tom lowered his voice when Sir Walter's grip tightened around his arm. "Has he talked to Lord Leicester?"

"They will be talking now, I fear," was the murmured answer, with a shake of the head. "His Lordship just rode in, in a fine rage, and Sir Francis looked very ill-disposed."

"Just rode in? I thought…"

A glint touched Sir Walter's pale eyes. "Lord Leicester thought to travel with the Queen and the Duke this morning, like the closest of friends — but Her Grace, it seems, would have none of it, and sent his Lordship riding ahead."

"Oh!" So much for wooing the Queen's good graces. If word reached the Royal ear now of the Lord Leicester's supposed intrigue…

"Indeed." Sir Walter look grimly amused as he steered them both past yet another pike-wielding Yeoman and through the large archway into the Privy Garden. So amused, in fact, that Tom suspected Sir Francis hadn't told the whole story to his brother-in-law — at least not the worst of it. "His Lordship was none too pleased when Mr. Secretary requested — no, demanded a brief talk."

Tom cringed at the thought of that brief talk — but still it wasn't too late, not until word seeped out to indiscreet ears... "Where are they, Sir Walter?"

There was a shake of the head, most doleful. "Oh no, Thomas. I would suggest you stay out of the way, until the matter is settled, and Her Grace has arrived."

"But I cannot wait... Where is the Royal train now?"

"Less than a mile away, the last time I asked. Going a little slowly, but..."

This wouldn't do. Tom clicked his tongue, turned to look at the waiting crowd through the archway, and...

And found himself observed in turn across the small sea of silk and jewelled hats. Sharp blue eyes over a white beard, and a doublet of the finest burgundy velvet.

"Sir!" Tom took the greatest care in not jolting. In not raising his voice. In turning back with the idlest manner he knew. Not that he expected it to work on his watcher — but... "This truly cannot wait. Where are they?"

Sir Walter frowned, working his mouth the way he always did when considering, as one chewing on lemons.

It was all Tom could do not to dance with impatience, not to peek out of the archway again, not to snap when he spoke... "Sir, please, Mr. Secretary needs to hear what I know, to see this." He whipped out Wade's packet. "Before Her Grace arrives."

Sir Walter frowned at him, chewing a little more — and then, for a mercy... "If you must, then." He pointed to one of the smaller buildings at the garden's far corner. "You'll see Davies at the door..."

If there was more, Tom didn't stop to hear it. Was it foolish on his part to take the first steps, while he could perhaps still be seen from the gate, as though he had no care in this world? And to take the longer way along one wall and then the other, rather than cutting through the garden's centre by the gurgling fountain? Most likely so — but he still he felt that sharp blue gaze on him, the silliest of fancies, surely, as he hastened his step along the gravelled path, between garden wall and box hedge. He was almost running by the time he reached the corner door, and stepped into a dim little hall with a chequered floor of black and white, and two doors. By one, leaning against the jamb with arms crossed, stood Sir Francis's Welshman.

"Davies!" Tom exclaimed, waving his packet. "I must —"

And he went no further when a loud thump came from behind the door, and a shout of "Does he, now, curse his eyes?"

The thundering voice was Lord Leicester's, and Tom had an uneasy suspicion that the eyes that were being cursed might be his own...

The thought must have occurred to Davies, too, who cocked his head and removed himself out of Tom's way to the door. One didn't suspect Davies of wanting to smirk, but...

In the next room, Lord Leicester's voice had dropped to a furious muttering, and then it rose again. "...And I, Mr. Secretary, I'm not used to explaining!"

Oh Lord. Oh Lord. Tom squared his shoulders and knocked on the door — rather harder than he'd meant.

There was silence, and then Sir Francis's voice called to enter. And Tom did — though he stopped on the threshold.

The room was small, cold, and lined with cupboards, with one narrow, lion-footed table in the centre. At the head of this table, in the grey light from one diamond-patterned window, Lord Leicester stood, with the blackest of scowls. Sir Francis, as narrow as Leicester was big-shouldered, stood by the window itself, very dark against the dim daylight.

"Come in, then, Thomas," he said, a ripple of impatience creasing the even, cold voice.

So cold, in fact… Tom swallowed. There. He'd done it now. If he hadn't blundered his way out of the Service in France, now surely, surely he had…

A memory of sharp blue eyes jolted him out of his misery. No time for that. He held out the packet — and could have kicked himself for the way he did it, as though he could hide behind the thing…

"Mr. Secretary, Sir, I bring —"

He nearly bit his tongue when Sir Francis raised an eyebrow, and then turned that raised eyebrow on Lord Leicester.

"I'm sure," he murmured, "Your Lordship will please to let me hear how my cousin explains this most extraordinary entrance."

Tom cringed, all the more when Lord Leicester crossed his arms like one who wouldn't please at all…

"And I'm sure, Mr. Secretary," he said, voice rising, as he glowered at Tom, "that you'll please to let me hear what other rings, or papers, or outlandish tales your cousin has dreamt up."

And wasn't that the rankest injustice — and just when Tom came to free the man of suspicion! Tom opened his mouth to protest — wondering all the time what was he doing, talking back to the Queen's favourite — but before he had the chance to thoroughly disgrace himself, Sir Francis spoke.

"The boy, my Lord," said the steady, grave voice that had grown men quaking in their boots, "has very little inclination to dream up anything but Latin hexameters. He shall be heard, not shouted at. Or I, for that matter."

There was the briefest match of stare against hard stare — and it was Lord Leicester who looked away, with a great show of tossing his head and giving a small bark of laughter.

"Let's hear, then, what he has not dreamt up!"

This Sir Francis chose to ignore, and turned to his courier instead. "You have a letter, Thomas, I believe?"

Tom was a little dazed at being thus defended by his cousin, but caught himself quite quickly — if he said so himself — and with nothing worse than the smallest startled blink, he stepped forward to deliver the thing, now crumpled at the corners.

"Do you know what this is?" Sir Francis asked, turning it in his hands.

Tom unclasped the knife from his girdle and handed it to his cousin, who took it and slid it under the seal in one meticulous move.

"I think..." One deep breath. "I believe that Mr. Wade will have found something in the cipher — something that ties it to his Lordship." One sideways glance revealed Lord Leicester leaning forward against the table. At Tom's words, the nobleman shoved himself upright.

"But..." Tom hastily went on. "But that was to be expected, if the blame was to be laid at his Lordship's door..."

Tom stopped again, with the eyes of two Privy Councillors fastened on him, and swallowed hard. Why, oh why couldn't he discuss his findings with Sir Francis alone?

But perhaps there was no blaming Lord Leicester when he took a step forward, powerful shoulders tilted to loom over Tom.

"What do you mean, at my door?"

Sir Francis nodded. "Go ahead, Thomas."

"Well, it…" Now to say it as clearly and concisely as he knew… "It struck me that no man of my Lord Leicester's would go out of his way to bring up his Lordship's name, and tie it to the first victim. And when the one who did so turned out to know things of the murder — things that he should not… It took me far too long to see this — but once I did, it was quite clear: this man had the chance to murder both Simon Litcott in Halcourt, and Jack Dennis in Calais — and another here in London that I didn't know of back then — and he surely behaved as no man of my Lord Leicester's would."

"Ha!" Lord Leicester exclaimed softly, and crossed his arms again, head thrown back in the very likeness of vindicated innocence. "You speak Hebrew and Greek to me, boy — but I'll take it all to mean that I'm no more the villain of the piece?"

Few things Tom hated more than blushing… "Careful steps were taken to make your Lordship appear guilty," he stammered, striving for his blankest face. "But… But…"

"But it appears, my Lord Earl, that we owe you an apology." Sir Francis held up the papers he had been perusing, the faintest gleam of amusement in both eyes and voice. "Once some of the washed out words were pieced together, the cipher clearly implicates you. And, as young Thomas reasoned, this shows your innocence."

Lord Leicester took a breath and expelled it like an explosion, and the two councillors exchanged small, stiff nods. "But then, who would do this to me?" Leicester asked. "The French?"

To him! Trust Robert Dudley to only see his own inconvenience!

"I rather doubt it — and not just to your Lordship. How would Her Highness like it, such an intrigue from those who do not favour her French suitor? That you so lately appeared to have shifted sides in this, my Lord, would make things more awkward still. Two birds with one stone, as the saying goes. Thomas —" Sir Francis turned back to his cousin — "do you know where this ... this man of yours might be found?"

"His name is Ralph Garrard, Sir, and I rather think that he might be here."

"Do you, now?" asked Sir Francis, mild and unsurprised, just as Lord Leicester exclaimed, "Here? Here in Whitehall?"

So Tom explained of the dead woman — the bare bones of the matter at least — and of Garrard's tapster friend at the King's Head — currently waiting at Whitehall's other end.

This had Lord Leicester roaring with mirth, and calling Tom a clever lad. "Why, men will hardly seek their pleasure next door to Mr. Secretary, will they?" he laughed — merry as a boy, all charm and friendliness now that the storm had passed.

Sir Francis allowed himself a small, rueful smile. "I don't imagine that encouraging the White Horse to brew better ale would help?" he murmured.

Tom grinned. He couldn't help it — never could when his cousin's wit came to the fore — but he had no chance to answer, as there was knocking at the door, and Sir Francis called to come in. He didn't look surprised — rather amused anew — when a pageboy in the red, white and blue Burleigh livery entered carrying a huge silver candle-holder, with six lit wax candles whose golden glow made the dark cabinets gleam dully, and warmed the grey gloom. Behind the boy came Lord Burleigh himself.

Tom could have laughed aloud.

The Lord Treasurer smiled. "It occurred to me, Mr. Secretary, your Lordship, that you might want to know: Her

Majesty's procession is less than a half mile away — but this new bout of rain could slow the progress."

Sir Francis, who always looked all the more sallow by candlelight, allowed a corner of his mouth to twitch. "Or make it faster in the hope of reaching shelter, no doubt," he said. "That was most solicitous of your Lordship."

They exchanged small nods, these two old adversaries, shrewd and knowing — Jupiter with the laughing eyes, and dark, unfathomable Dis, two faces of the same coin of power — and it was somewhat startling to find oneself a man of the Netherworld…

And in this Olympian skirmish, Dis was taking the initiative.

"You would not know, my Lord Treasurer, a man named…" Sir Francis turned to Tom. "What was the name, Thomas?"

Not for a moment did Tom believe that the name had escaped his cousin. But since he was to step into this guarded fray, as the one who had teased apart the joints and flexures of this garboil, he squared his shoulders, and hoped that he looked unreadable enough.

"Ralph Garrard, Mr. Secretary. A merchant of woolcloth, he calls himself."

Lord Burleigh spared him a quick, piercing glance — the sort a man would have for something of no great consequence found sorely out of place — and then nodded to himself a few times, reckoning, no doubt, what better course to steer.

Lord Leicester chose that moment to step around the table, and into the battle.

"A fellow most at home at the King's Head in Fenchurch Street, it would seem," he growled. "As young Walsingham, here, can both attest and prove."

And with that he stood back on his heels, chin high, looking more pleased with himself than Sir Francis looked with him, and waited.

Not that he had long to wait, because no one became Treasurer to Elizabeth Regina by chewing on his decision. Lord Burleigh nodded to the page and, as the boy scurried out, sighed as one whose patience was sadly tried.

"I do indeed know Master Garrard," he said, shaking his head. "A most misguided man."

Oh, this now … this! But there were times it was hard not to gape … well, one didn't become Treasurer to Elizabeth Regina without a good deal of impudence, either — but truly! Look at the vexed, disbelieving manner of the man as he spun his account…

"He came to me this morning, with the strangest tale," he said. "One I hardly knew how to credit. In fact, I meant to dismiss the fellow as a madman — but now that there seems to be some substance to his ramblings, I am glad my son talked me out of it. I don't suppose…" Again the keen blue glance fell on Tom, but with a slant of mistrust to it. "We can be sure, can't we, Mr. Secretary, of this young man?"

All the breath left Tom's lungs. He, an accomplice of Garrard in this affair…? This, now… A gasp escaped him and he knew that he was gawking — but unreadable be damned! How was one to stay unreadable when … when…

And then, "Indeed, my Lord, we can be very sure of him," Sir Francis said, an eyebrow raised, a careful emphasis on the one word. Defending Tom for the second time to Privy Councillors…

Ah, but one would go through fire for Sir Francis! — and, because he knew his cousin would not like it, Tom strove to keep the triumph from the gaze he turned on Lord Burleigh. Unreadable, was what a Service man must look.

Not that William Cecil, Lord Burleigh, would pay the slightest mind to a courier's bruised and restored pride.

"Of course…" The nobleman fingered his well-trimmed beard, looking distractedly out of the window. "Of course, then, I have to wonder at the letter." He looked up to meet Sir Francis's eyes. "I did not mention this, did I? No, well, this fellow Garrard brought to me a certain letter, so startling in its content, that I refused to credit it as genuine. But of course, if Mr. Secretary's own well-trusted kinsman now supports the truthfulness of Garrard's claims…"

Oh Lord — the letter. The thrice-cursed secret instructions to Cobham came to roost at last! Tom's heart sank. Had then the letter itself been Lord Burleigh and Garrard's aim all the time? Otherwise Garrard would have disposed of it — but then, why go out of his way to lay the blame on Leicester? Why kill poor, dim-witted Litcott at all? Surely, the letter in Burleigh's hands and a plot of Lord Leicester's negated each other…?

Whether Lord Leicester himself saw this was uncertain as he took a step towards Lord Burleigh. "That has to be," he growled, "the lowest, filthiest trick —"

"Oh, I don't think we need to worry about this," Sir Francis interrupted, head tilted at the Treasurer. "My Lord Burleigh could go to Her Highness with the letter — why, he could do so within the hour. But then, he would have to explain how it came to be in his possession."

Lord Leicester threw up his hands. "Didn't you listen to a word he said, Walsingham? He's making show that this clothier is some overzealous bedlamite who did all on his own!"

242

Sir Francis nodded and — much to Tom's relief, if not to Leicester's — looked formidably unflustered. "So he is — but this doesn't mean he will be believed. Wagers are a sinful thing — but I would lay you one that my Lord Burleigh isn't any more eager than you and I are for Her Grace to see that paper. Not when we can prove with certainty this Garrard to be his man."

And at that something passed in Lord Burleigh's sharp blue eyes — a cold, hard light of calculation, of... Did the Lord Treasurer feel bits and pieces arrange themselves in shapes inside his head, too?

When someone knocked at the door, it sounded like cannonade in the thick silence.

The door opened, and a small young man clad in black velvet slid inside.

Behind him came a man in Cecil livery, leading a grim-faced Ralph Garrard.

"Father," the young man greeted. He had a thin, sallow face, young Cecil, and a hunched shoulder only half disguised by his cunningly cut doublet, and narrow, sharp eyes that widened just a little when Lord Burleigh shook his head.

"There is no more need for this, Robert," said the Treasurer. "We are all satisfied that the letter must be a forgery."

Garrard took in a sharp breath, and young Cecil frowned — but neither man made a sound.

Lord Leicester did, a snort, just as the bells of Westminster and St. Margaret began to peal in joyous salute. The Royal procession must have come within sight.

Sir Francis held out a hand, palm up. "I'm sure," he said, pitching his voice just above the bells outside, "that there's no need to trouble Her Highness with this matter."

Robert Cecil looked at his father in question, and didn't look pleased to receive a nod — but he only hesitated for a heartbeat. He took a folded paper from his sleeve and handed it to Sir Francis, who took it, never bothering to check it was the one he'd dispatched to France twelve days earlier.

Tom let out the breath he hadn't known that he was holding.

"Nor is there need," Lord Burleigh countered, "for Master Garrard to linger in London, is there?"

No need … no need! "But surely, my Lord…!" Tom bit down the rest when four pairs of eyes turned on him — Lord Burleigh's, quite astonished at the objection; Robert Cecil's just this side of sneering; Lord Leicester's, holding perhaps some sympathy; and Sir Francis's with that blankness that spoke of patience tried.

Tom shut his mouth — if only to show he had at least as much rein on himself as sour young Cecil — but surely, surely they never meant to let Garrard go free, not after he had killed three times?

Garrard, though, it was worth noting, stood there, pasty-faced and unblinking, and seemed to take no great relief at this release.

"No need whatever," Sir Francis said slowly. "And, Thomas, perhaps you will be kind enough to see Master Garrard to the stables, see that he's given a good, fast horse — one for riding far."

Lord Burleigh smiled a little at this, and Tom swallowed.

Outside, past the garden, bright trumpet flourishes and men's cheers threaded through the chiming of the bells.

"Ah well," grumbled Lord Leicester. "What a damnable affair! Shall we go meet Her Highness, Mr. Secretary?" He adjusted his high-crowned, bejewelled beaver hat, and strode for the door, utterly ignoring the two Cecils and their men.

Lord Burleigh followed, and Sir Francis, and young Cecil last — and that was that. Three deaths, and all the ado in France, the adventurers, the break-neck journey, Citolini…

Oh Lord — Citolini!

Tom hurried out after Sir Francis, and caught up with him near the archway. "Mr. Secretary, Sir!"

His cousin stopped. "Yes, Thomas, what is it?" he asked — a sliver of impatience to his frown.

But this had to be done. "Sir, Citolini…"

The frown cleared. "Oh, Citolini, yes. Yes, indeed."

A half turn of Mr. Secretary's head was enough that Davies appeared, and was dispatched back to Seething Lane, and then the Councillors went to take their place in the welcoming crowd, joining their fellows in one imposing group — these most powerful men who ran the realm, moving together through the open gate as though no plots, no threats, no breathless *via media* had just run their course amongst them.

With a sigh, Tom went back to the small room's threshold. Ralph Garrard was waiting, watched by the Cecil servant. He raised his eyebrows at the sight of Tom, and sauntered out to join him, looking rather cheerier than he had — and in all truth, why shouldn't he?

CHAPTER 21

The stables were by the tiltyard, on the other side of Court Gate, so it took some doing to get there around the half-pageant of the Queen's return. Tom had to ask his way twice, much to Ralph Garrard's tight-lipped amusement.

I'd know my way without asking at the Tuileries, he almost snapped — but didn't, because it was childish, and because the notion of being more at home in Paris than in London didn't cheer him at all, and because he wasn't minded to have conversation with this man he'd liked, and even trusted, never understanding until it was too late that he was a spy and a murderer...

"Don't take it too ill, young Mr. Walsingham. After all, you ferreted me out when no one else did," the spy and murderer murmured — the man who hadn't seemed to know how to be less than loud...

And Tom, fool that he was, stopped short, and blurted out: "So you *can* whisper, after all. Even in that, a deceiver!"

Garrard, for a mercy, instead of laughing, pulled a face. "Ay, well, much good it did me!" He shook his head. "Didn't keep you from seeing right through me, did it?"

Tom snorted and resumed his march. "Didn't it! Be pleased with yourself: I had no inkling until this morning..."

"No? Why, bless you, lad!" And Garrard did look pleased with himself, most irksomely so. "What made you think of me, then?"

What indeed! Such a small thing — and it would have been so easy to miss... Tom couldn't keep the note of wonder from his voice. "Something that you said back in Calais, about the gate that had been opened from inside. But you couldn't have known that — unless…"

The laugh, when it came, was the big guffaw that Tom remembered from France, loud enough to fill the small courtyard they were crossing. "Oh, sink me — that? That's all there is to it?"

All there was to it… Tom frowned at the puddles among the ill-kept cobbles as he picked his way. *All there was to it.* But no, not all. "That set me thinking, and once I considered you for a murderer, and that you must have been travelling to Paris and not from there, more and more things began to make sound sense."

"Oh dear, my Lord! And all because I slipped my fool tongue!"

"As you said then, it's the small things." Tom spared a sideways glance for the man. "It also greatly helped that your masters threw you out at sea…"

Garrard gave a grunt, wedging his bulk sideways through a narrow door, and into a dark passage. "Ay, well, learn this, lad: the Cecils and their likes, they're only your masters until you blunder. After that…" He stopped and measured Tom with one of his round, unblinking stares. "You've burnt me out of work, you know that. Had it not been for you…"

He whispered that, almost a hiss in the empty passage, looming big in the grey half-light, and for a heartbeat Tom thought of crushed windpipes and pierced chests. Had it not been for him… But no, there was nothing to gain — and possibly much to lose — by slaying Sir Francis Walsingham's kinsman at this point, and Tom had a shrewd feeling that Ralph Garrard did gruesome things for gain, rather than his own satisfaction.

So he just narrowed his eyes at the man. "Be content, Master Garrard. It seems to me that you are paying precious little for three murders. Let's not tarry, shall we?"

And he strode off, and the man was at his side again in a trice.

"How, three?" he asked, as though the number was some piece of unfairness. "Oh — you know of the young woman?"

"And of your tapster at the King's Head — that's how I knew whose man you are. So you see, you killed that poor woman for nothing."

"Now that!" Garrard chuckled. "That it's for nothing, that's your fault, you know."

"Mine!"

"Ay. And that I killed her at all — the fault there is her own. Nothing as unchancy in this world as being only half a fool, take it from me. Shrewd enough to see that I might pay for what your glover let spill, she was — and yet a boastful goose. She knew what she knew, and if I didn't pay, then others would … so I did pay her, with six inches of good steel. You see that I had to, don't you?"

It greatly disturbed Tom that, in some sort of manner, he did see. He stopped where the passage let out onto an open gallery and looked away, under colour of gauging the way.

"And what my glover let spill was how I carried Mr. Secretary's own papers?" he still couldn't help asking.

And Garrard hummed and nodded, of course — how could he not? — and Tom's heart sank. So it *was* his fault, after all — Nance's death, and Litcott's too. A piece of lining torn on a nail, the glover mending it and sewing the letter back — and lo! Two lives lost. Three, if one counted Dennis, who would have met his death elsewhere, but for Tom's piece of clumsiness … oh Lord!

"But I spoke in jest that you're at fault, you know." There it was again, that same thin smile — half kindly and half mocking, as though Garrard were taking pity on a silly boy and his scantling troubles. "Nance's sort, sooner or later they bite off more than they can chew. As for your glover —"

It irked Tom a good deal to be consoled by Ralph Garrard, murderer and spy. "My glover, ay!" he snapped. "Poor foolish Simon Litcott. Never would he pass for a spy — not alive — would he?"

"No, he didn't fit the part, poor fellow — but then..." Garrard let that trail as they entered the stables proper, eyes wide to find them a-swarm with grooms, and squires, and stable-boys and henchmen scurrying this way and that, leading horses or carrying armfuls of brightly-hued caparisons.

"Some pageant or other," Tom said. "It is Accession Day tomorrow." He beckoned to a man who carried a chamfron of gilt leather, fashioned with a silver horn to look like a unicorn's head... It was faintly amusing to see the merchant gape at the contraption, while the groom listened to Tom's — or rather, Mr. Secretary's order.

A head-groom was fetched to hear it again, and after some more discussion and some gauging of Garrard's size, this more exalted personage and one of his underlings went to comply. Tom and his ... what was Ralph Garrard by this point? Hardly a prisoner, was he? *Foe* seemed a fitting word. Yes, foes were what they were — although Tom would have been hard put to tell which of them was victorious. Tom and his foe, then, walked along a quieter row of stalls — Garrard leaving his study of the preparations to peer at horse after horse, humming now and then in appreciation.

When they passed by a pretty, pin-buttocked Irish hobby, he smacked his lips and went to lean against the stall door to fondle the creature, calling it a fine fellow, before turning to Tom: "You wouldn't tell them to give me this one, would you?" he asked.

Tom didn't bother to answer — how could the man be this flippant? — and asked a stern question of his own instead. "What if you hadn't made it to Amiens before us?"

There was a shrug. "*Then* Nance *would* have died for nothing — but I did. I wasn't many hours behind you, and rode like the devil. Not a bad crossing, either. Fit to sour a man's belly for him, mind — but swift enough. I think I passed you about Abbeville and got to Amiens a good day early. All the time in the world — and in Picardy those bands of adventurers come a penny a dozen."

"Only, by the time we turned up in Halcourt, there were more of us than you expected."

"Ay, well — no matter. I misdoubt those rascals took much fright of you. They knew not to be too rough, to filch a dagger that you'd know again, to leave alone the one in the yellow hat."

So Phelippes had been right. "I'd wondered at that."

This seemed to please Ralph Garrard a good deal. "Had you? Good, good. When he came to give me the dagger and letter, that French rogue said the fellow squawked like a wet hen. What was his name — Litcott? Ay, Litcott was a dunce — but, what with having been Leicester's man…"

So! Tom stared at Garrard. "Was it Leicester, then? All the time?"

"Why, cuds-me, lad!" Ralph Garrard shook his head as one marvelling. "What did you think? Leicester's zeal for the Duke, all of a sudden — who believes that? That he was still playing against the Match, nobody'd be surprised — much less the Queen."

Of course. *Of course.* "Two birds with one stone."

"And besides, his Lordship — pox take him — knows to go after that peacock Leicester rather than your uncle."

"Cousin," Tom corrected without thought, even as his mind busily sifted the merchant's words. Because if Lord Leicester had been the target… "Then … why did you keep the letter? Lord Burleigh could hardly put the blame on Lord Leicester *and* appear to be in possession of the letter!"

Garrard shrugged. "You never know what use you can have for something like that. All the more as you took your sweet time in tying the glover to Lord Leicester."

Well now… "How could you tell what I knew or didn't?"

"Jack Dennis told me — in Calais. He heard you and the Italian talk. He laughed that you suspected him — but otherwise, you had most of it straight, by then. *Except who was behind it…* Don't you know your ciphers, lad?"

Now *this* Phelippes must be told — poor Philippus, poring over that half-washed out scrap of paper … but yes, there it was! Of course — the man couldn't know! Tom laughed — and had the petty satisfaction of seeing doubt darken the merchant's face.

"Next time you hide a paper on the ones you kill, be careful of the rain," he said.

It was Garrard's turn to gape. There was a tremor to the fleshy cheeks, and then a rueful grin. "Good Lord keep a hand on my foolish head!" he huffed. "Should have known that rings are safer than paper."

Tom's first thought was, did the man truly think the Lord would take care of murderers? But there was something else… "Litcott's ring. *You* took it then?"

Garrard shrugged. "Had to, together with the purse. Those French rogues would take it, you see — and so would Leicester's man, to throw the blame on them, and you had that cipher anyway… But then, in Calais, up turns that Jack Dennis, saying that he's going to set you straight on Litcott's death, unless I pay him well…"

Tom nodded, glumly. "And so you did. You paid him — only not in steel, this time."

"Since you had your heart set on him having killed the glover…"

"And you put the ring on him, for both my ease and edification."

"Ay, well — for all I knew, you were being thick-witted on this matter of Lord Leicester. When Jack Dennis said you were a bit of a fool, I was half minded to credit him… I reckon I should thank the man: he thought he'd make some profit, and gave me a way to put that ring under your nose instead."

No spy, then, Jacques Denis — no murderer. Just… "Another greedy fool, was he?"

"Another who thought himself shrewd."

A capital sin, it would seem, in Ralph Garrard's book. "And what was it that had him and Litcott arguing in the stables? Never the ring, was it?"

"Oh, you found out about that? Not the ring, no. Your glover took exception to Dennis teasing him… The ring he'd shown to Nance, back at the King's Head, but *that* I couldn't tell you, could I?"

"You shouldn't have told me about the ring at all." Tom couldn't help a touch of smugness. "You know, had you not gone out of your way to bring up Leicester's name, I might never have tied you to Lord Burleigh."

Garrard gave a groan that was half-chuckle. "But I had to make sure you knew. What if you had not seen the ring? I was disappointed in you, by then. Most sorely."

What — when it was the man's own fault and shoddy work…! Just in the nick of time did Tom bite down the protestation. Fool, letting himself be stung by what the likes of Garrard thought! What would Sir Francis think?

"And besides, for all I knew, that Italian of yours was truly Leicester's man. Why, I rather hoped —" Garrard stopped short, nodding his chin at something beyond Tom's shoulder. And there went the head-groom — Mr. Secretary's business warranting no less than his own work — leading a saddled horse, a big dun gelding with two white forelegs, sturdy rather than elegant.

The merchant huffed a little as he took the bridle, but rubbed the horse's nose.

"Ah well, no beauty, but you look the hearty sort, don't you?" he chuckled, and the horse happily pushed his head into the patting hand.

The same hand that had stabbed poor harmless Litcott hard enough to break the dagger in two… Would anyone ever understandthis many-faced beast, Man?

Tom shook himself out of philosophy and walked with Garrard out to the busy courtyard. He had done this before, back at the Trois Poissons… He'd believed those Frenchmen to have killed the glover then. Later he'd thought Litcott a spy, then Jack Dennis a spy and a murderer — until the Merchant Strangers' man had died, and Tom's suspicions had fallen on Citolini… Hardly a shining feat of reason!

Garrard put foot to stirrup.

"Didn't you think that, if you kept killing everyone else, I'd be left with no one but you to suspect?" Tom asked.

The merchant laughed. "Ay, well, you needed a culprit … and I never meant to kill the Italian — only to make him look guilty. And seeing as you said that he swims like a fish… It worked, didn't it?" He laughed again at Tom's grimace, and hoisted himself heavily into the saddle. "It nearly did. But for that cursed gate, the Queen would be singeing Lord Leicester's ears for him, right now, and holding faster to her French swain. But for that cursed gate — and you." He clicked his tongue at the horse and turned it towards the gate. Free to go. Never to pay for murdering three people…

Tom stepped in his way and looked up at the man, squinting against the milky glow the rain had left behind. "Is it true, what Lord Burleigh said, that all this you did of your own accord, under no orders of his?"

Ralph Garrard, merchant, spy, murderer and who knew what else, smiled again — the tight-lipped smile, half-mocking and half-pitying. "This, I'm sure, you'll reason for yourself, young Mr. Walsingham. In the end, that Dennis was wrong: you are no fool." He raised a hand, palm upwards, most augur-like. "I wish you better times and better luck, eh?"

And with that he was gone, out of the gate, and swallowed by the bustle of Westminster — three times a murderer and free as a lark.

Tom sighed and rolled his bunched, aching shoulders. Lord, but he was tired. The rain had stopped, and the last of the bells could be heard, their slackening peals scattered in the grey sky like the last birds in a flock. The Queen was back, and was never to know — which was, no doubt, greatly to be preferred.

And those poor souls — a tavern maid, a witless glover and, quite possibly, a scoundrel — never to know justice for their deaths. Tom thought of young Alice at the King's Head — a child Justitia, with the serious eyes and grief quivering in her voice. *I tried, Mistress. Tried, and failed…*

No sense in going back to Sir Francis now. Better to send the tapster on his way — and not to the King's Head, if he had any wits — recover Skeres and young Tobias, and head back to Seething Lane.

CHAPTER 22

Darkness had descended, met halfway by a light fog from the river, by the time Sir Francis returned to Seething Lane, and Tom was summoned to the study again.

He had washed away the mud, changed into dry, clean clothes, been fed some more by Lady Ursula, and been ordered to rest. That last had not worked too well, and when he entered the small, dark study — almost a cavern when left to fire and candles — Tom had worked himself to the blackest megrims.

Sir Francis looked up from what papers he had been studying. "Come, Thomas. Sit," he said — and motioned, not to the chair by the fire, this time, but the one right in front of the huge writing table.

There. There it came — the dismissal, the cold disappointment, the calling to task… Tom picked at a loose thread in his right cuff, staring at it until he could stand the silence no more.

"There's nothing I can say for myself, I know," he blurted, and stopped, and shook his head. This was no good…

"Isn't there indeed?"

Far too mild — that's what the three words sounded like — and Tom looked up to find Sir Francis watching him, candlelight flickering off the dark grey eyes.

"I… I…" he stammered. Fool… "I trusted where I should not, I let a man under my charge be murdered, I took all the time in creation to understand, I lost the letter, I travelled with false papers…"

Sir Francis nodded at each item. "An interesting catalogue of sins," he murmured. "And I rather hope you mention them in no deliberate order?"

The blood rushed up Tom's neck and cheeks. Would he ever cure himself of blushing? "No," he murmured, looking down again, like a chastened schoolboy. And then he gathered what fortitude he had left, for surely it was better to have it said and done? "But the fact is, Sir, that I greatly failed you, and I know you can have no more use for me, and —"

"Thomas."

Mild again, and quiet — but that sort of quiet mildness that made a fellow shut his mouth at once, awkwardly aware of having raised his voice.

"It seems to me, Thomas, that matters were arranged with some ingenuity — if in some haste — to take the letter from you, and to make you see things under a certain light. That the culprit saw it fit to murder that poor man to achieve this, you are hardly to blame, are you?"

Tom opened his mouth — not that he knew quite what to say to that — and closed it again.

Sir Francis gave him the smallest of nods and went on. "It also seems to me that, in spite of everything, you unravelled this tangle, so that Her Grace, the good Lord bless her, never needs to know how her Councillors plot and squabble with each other like so many schoolboys."

Deathly schoolboys, at that, when one thought of Jack Dennis, Nance and Litcott. "Do you think, Sir…" Tom ventured. "Do you think that Ralph Garrard truly acted of his own counsel?" He'd asked the man himself, and had no answer. Somehow it seemed important to know.

Sir Francis hummed, leaning his chin against his steepled hands, as one considering in earnest. "It all seems to me rather made up on the spur of the moment — not quite the Cecil way of doing things. But I don't doubt your Garrard must have had some manner of standing orders, to seek ways of brewing trouble amongst those who oppose this wretched French affair, perhaps also of stymying Lord Leicester, whose standing is the most dubious."

And that was all there was to it… "It seems so paltry to weigh against three lives…" Tom blushed. Blathering before Mr. Secretary! "I crave…"

Sir Francis waved the apology away. "I see that this troubles you — as it should, for taking lives is a grievous sin. I misdoubt that Garrard meant to kill more than that poor glover. Not that this lessens his guilt before the Lord and before the Law of men — but I believe that he let the events overtake him… Perhaps Lord Burleigh is well rid of such a fellow. Still…"

Tom listened to the clicking fire for one, two, five, a dozen heart-beats. The fire, and the wind soughing down the chimney as it picked up. Somewhere in the house it made a door slam, or perhaps a casement — but it didn't startle Tom as his cousin's voice did, quiet and even as it was.

"Consider this, Thomas. Had we brought this Garrard to justice, what would have happened?"

Tom frowned. "The matter of the letter would have come to light?"

"Indeed. It would have come to Her Majesty's attention — to her very angry attention — and so Lord Burleigh would have had his way."

"But how could he have explained his having it?"

"With much difficulty, I'm sure — but…" Sir Francis's lips curved in a small, wry smile. "It is true of most women, and even more so of our Sovereign, that it is hard to tell which way their ire will run. What if this —" and he held up the folded letter, the pieces of the seal glittering faintly at their broken edges — "what if it had poisoned Her Highness's mind against our counsel?"

What then? Was it very treasonous to think that without Sir Francis at her elbow, the Queen might choose to mellow towards the French? And then a much younger French consort by the Throne of England, who also was his Royal brother's heir…

"Indeed," Sir Francis said, and Tom knew that his black reckonings had shown plain on his face. "And if you still believe, Thomas, that three lives were a high price to pay — all the more because there can be no justice for them — well, you are right. But call it a lesson learnt, that when the trouble of a few may avoid a general trouble, general respects must be preferred to particular."

"Yes, Sir." Tom looked down again. He'd heard that maxim before, and thought it very wise — but that was before he'd felt the weight of those few's trouble on his shoulders…

"Just as you will have learnt, one hopes, never to travel without proper papers again — unless…" The small, wry smile again. "Unless matters of State require it — and then see that you are not caught."

Tom winced. "On this account, Sir, there's this Lieutenant of the Prévôt…" And he told of the Seigneur de Wacogne, hankering for preferment back in Montreuil, left to persuade himself that he may count on high-placed English gratitude…

Sir Francis looked amused. "A letter of good-will and some flattery will do. There are worse things than having a friend in the Bailliage — the sort of friend you don't overly trust."

Indeed — not like the fools who took a liking to the first helpful stranger… "Another lesson learnt, Sir."

"I'm sure." Sir Francis sat back in his chair, and would have said more, but for a gentle knocking at the door. When Sir Francis called to come in, little Frances peeked inside, smiling like an April morning.

"Father?" She entered and curtsied a little. "Mother sent me to fetch you to supper…" She stopped and clapped her hands once when Tom rose, turning to her. "You are truly back, then, Tom?" Then she caught herself, as one remembering that fourteen is a mature age. "Cousin." She gave another, smaller, curtsey — more of a little bounce, really, and a doll-like smile, the sort that is practised at the looking-glass.

Tom bowed, just as gravely, and then spoiled it all: "Why, Mistress Poppet, you have grown!"

"Silly!" The girl's smile grew and dimpled, and she beamed at her father. "Isn't he, Father?"

"A little, my dear." Sir Francis, who had been watching her with a small, considering frown, smiled back. What would they think, all those who trembled at the Walsingham name across the realm and half of Europe, if they could see him with his only daughter? "A little, but not very much. In fact, your cousin has done rather well, and learnt his lessons. And I always have use for a man who can learn."

It was a few heartbeats before the words sank in — the pieces sluggish inside Tom's head, as though dipped in honey. Did that mean…? Surely, now…?

Little Frances, quite adept at reading her father's moods, took Tom's arm and smiled up at him, eyes sparkling.

When the child smiled, Tom could never help smiling back — and he was still smiling as he turned back to Sir Francis. "Sir, I —"

His cousin waved him silent. "Run now, children," he said. "Frances, my dear, tell your mother that I will join you anon."

Frances tugged at her cousin's arm, and they were at the door when Sir Francis called for Tom again.

"I've been meaning to ask: what of that servant you had with you... Skeggs, was it?"

Oh Lord, yes — that one... "Skeres, Sir. Nicholas Skeres." Mulish, cross-grained, loose-mouthed, graceless Dolius... "The most hopeless of servants, and with a mouth as big as Newgate, and quite possibly a thief — but a most steadfast soul, as loyal as the day is long. Also, not half the fool he looks to be."

"I see..." Sir Francis said. "A not wholly unpromising lump of clay?"

Little Frances giggled and half-pushed Tom out of the study, closing the door on her father's small, considering smile.

Frances must have expected things to go this way, because the servant girl waiting in the corridor carried two candlesticks. Frances took one of them and left the servant to light Sir Francis's way.

She clung to Tom's arm, chattering as they made their way. "Tell me of Paris, now. You can't have had much time to go to Court, this time, can you? And what of the journey? Did you have adventures, to bruise your face like that? With all this rain, we thought of you, Mother and I — thought of you every day, wet as an otter's pocket, poor Tom! I am so glad that Mother had it so that it's just us for supper, what with it being Accession Day tomorrow... I wish I could go to Court with Father! There's to be a tilt. Sir Philip says ... you know Sir Philip Sidney, don't you, Tom? He says it will be the most magnificent thing — and I'll miss it! Mother says I can see the bonfires, though..."

Tom let her chirrup away. What could he tell her of all that had happened? As a rule he always had some story for her — but this time, this time… And besides, his mind had gone sluggish — all the fatigue and worries of the last few days dissolving, Sir Francis's good words for him … all of it brewing into a warm, soft lassitude. Now let the barbed matter of justice and the peace of realms not keep him awake — come night…

He stumbled out of his musings when both Frances's step and chatter came to a halt. She went to the staircase's banister, peering down to see who it was downstairs, crossing the dark hall with a candle of his own.

"*Buonasera*, *Mastro Paolo*," she called softly. Frances was proud of her Italian, eager to practise it.

Downstairs, Citolini came to the foot of the stairs and looked up, hand cupped around the candle's flame to shield it in the draughty hall. "*Buonasera, Signora Francesca*," he greeted. Then he saw who was with the girl, and stiffened. "Walsingham."

Well then — this had to be done. "Citolini, I —"

But the Italian would not let him. "Davies told me that I have you to thank," he said, his stare hard and glittering in the yellow glow from his candle.

Amongst the sketches of Watson's days in Rome, there had been that of a bust with a narrow, severe bronze face full of bitterness. Tom had wondered, what had the fellow ever had done to him… Perhaps he had been unjustly suspected of two murders.

"There should have been no cause for it," Tom said. "For Davies to say that. For me to…" He stopped short, casting a glance at Frances, who stood at his side, baffled but quiet. "The appearance of things was deceiving."

Citolini tilted his head, considering. "I did not help my own cause," he said. "I do not see that anyone would blame you for thinking what you thought. But you kept questioning, at least."

Not *I don't blame you* — but … well — the man had some cause for sullenness, perhaps.

Tom nodded at him, and Citolini nodded back.

Then he bowed, perfectly. "*Signora Francesca, i miei rispetti,*" he said, and went away.

Frances, her father's daughter, raised an eyebrow and asked no questions — not even when Tom sighed.

She nibbled at her lower lip, though. "Is it very un-Christian of me," she asked in a whisper, "that Mastro Paolo always rubs me the wrong way a little? I wish he didn't, and it must be my fault, surely — but…"

And Tom, who had been contemplating much the same dilemma — only in far less gentle terms, couldn't help a laugh.

"Come now, Mistress Poppet," he said. "Let's not keep your mother waiting — and you must tell me about this tilt."

CHAPTER 23

A few days later, at dawn, Tom Walsingham stood waiting in Sir Francis's stables, ready to ride. He rubbed his hands together and shivered. Barely light, it was, and chilly. At least what he saw of the sky as he leant out of the stable door was clear.

Behind him, in the horse-warm gloom, there were snorts, and mutterings, and the clink of buckles and stirrups. A mount was being saddled for the first leg of his journey back to Paris.

It had rained hard the last time he'd stood there, waiting together with a bleary-eyed, fretful Simon Litcott, rest his soul. This time he was travelling alone — so perhaps there would be less of what Frances called adventures?

He reached down to pat the cuff of his right buskin, where Sir Francis's letter was sewn — another letter, also explaining Tom's doings to Sir Henry Cobham. This time Lady Ursula herself had sewn the letter in its place, well wrapped in oiled paper against water and mud. Harder to pilfer — or so it was to be hoped…

Also, he'd be on his guard, this time, and observant, and close-mouthed to everyone. Well, not the Thomases, perhaps — but otherwise, he'd had a lesson in keeping his own counsel, hadn't he? If he was to prove himself, to prove to the Cobhams, the Middlemores, the Citolinis that his merits went beyond the name he bore…

"Oy, Master," came from behind, and Tom moved away from the door, to let the groom pass with the long-legged grey horse. He followed him out to the courtyard, pulling on his gloves, and behind him ambled a scowling Nick Skeres.

"To see you, Skeres, one'd think they'd kicked you in the teeth, instead of hiring you."

The lad shrugged mutinously, and went to pat the horse's hindquarters. "Ay, well, you said you'd keep me."

So! Was this what had kept Skeres so glum for the past week? Not even the settling of Tom's debt had cheered him in the least...

"I said nothing of the sort. For one thing, I can't afford you, and for another, no lowly courier goes around with his own servant in tow."

"You 'ave that old Papist, back there. 'Im you can afford."

"Levieux? A third of him, I can afford. And besides, he has advantages for Paris — one being that he does speak French."

"Ay, because 'e's a French Papist..."

"No, he's not — and he can cook, and keep house, and look after three men's attire, men who now and then must be seen in Court. Can you?"

Another shrug. "Ain't it because you think ill of me?"

"Don't be a fool, I don't think ill of you —"

A snort. "You thought that I'd done in the glover and that Dennis!"

So, there it was, the crux of it, what bit at Skeres! But how was this to be explained, that everyone must be considered ... not that Tom hadn't made a mess of it... "Only for the briefest time, Dolius — and look, I'm sorry that I ever did."

A shake of the head, this time — and the smallest un-jutting of the chin. "Still," Skeres grunted.

Patience, patience! Tom slapped the hat against his thigh, making the horse snort a little. "But you don't even like it, out there in foreign parts!" he snapped. "You grumbled all the way to Paris and back!"

And, would one credit it, the scamp looked up and grinned. "Ay, well, but it was fun, that's what it was."

At times what could a fellow do, but laugh? "Fun! With two — no, three murders … fun? You're a blood-thirsty Minotaur, Nick Skeres!" Tom donned his hat, and put foot to stirrup. There was more than enough light to go, now. Once in the saddle, he walked the horse to where the groom was drawing the bolts from the gate.

Skeres followed, with the look of one chewing on the strange word — Minotaur?

"Safe journey, Master Tom," called the groom.

"Ay, safe — and watch yerself!" That was Skeres, of course, and as he passed Sir Francis's threshold, Tom could hear the lad grumble of how it was a wonder that they sent Master Tom about alone, an innocent who'd take a boat at Smart's Key…

Tom's huff of laughter made a small white cloud as he pushed his horse along Seething Lane, towards Dover, and France, and Paris. As though he needed watching — a courier to the Queen of England, and one who enjoyed the trust of Mr. Secretary!

Lady Ursula Walsingham was fond of well-buttered manchets in the morning. Bread, butter, and sage — the wise woman's breakfast. She buttered one for her husband as he stood, watching out of the window.

Frances, poor girl, was still abed, with the cold that she'd caught on Accession Day, and Tom … well, by now Tom would be on his way to Dover, to France and to Paris — not without a hearty breakfast of his own, rather more than buttered manchets, taken downstairs in the warm kitchen.

"Wouldn't you rather eat your bread while it's still warm, my dear?" Ursula asked. Sometimes, the dear man was so absorbed in his thoughts, that he would hardly eat, if someone did not remind him…

Ursula smiled when her husband came to sit at the table, frowning at the light meal laid down in front of him. Never much of an eater, and now even less so, with those dreadful stones tormenting him…

Still, he smiled back at her. "You were quite right, my dear," he said. "About Thomas, that is."

Ursula smiled some more. At times, she would swear, her husband read her mind like a book. Then again, she was no laggard at reading his, either…

"I think he will derive much benefit from another year or two in France," he mused, taking up one half of that well-buttered manchet. "It will give him more assurance, more polish, a less trusting heart."

Ursula hummed. Somehow, it was hard to picture a distrustful Tom in her mind — hard and somewhat of a shame — but surely her husband knew what he was about.

He was looking quite pleased. "And he doesn't seem to have a bad eye for the joints and flexures of things. Let him hone his reasoning a little, let him trust a little less — and I'll have more than use for him." He nodded to himself once, and then twice.

Lady Ursula Walsingham smiled at her husband, as things shaped themselves in a manner that she liked very much.

HISTORICAL NOTES

They stopped Walsingham and Paulo, my Italian, whom they seemed resolved to rob [... and] another Englishman in his company, called Skeggs, as I remember.

On the twelfth of November 1581, Queen Elizabeth's Ambassador in Paris, Sir Henry Cobham, wrote one of many reports to the all-powerful Secretary of State — and spymaster — Sir Francis Walsingham. It was almost in passing that the ambassador slipped in this bit of information about the misadventure of Sir Francis's much younger cousin, nineteen-year-old Thomas, riding as a diplomatic courier between London and Paris.

Almost a throw-away, these lines sketch a vivid vignette: young Thomas, Paolo the Italian, and the man whose name *might* be Skeggs, held up along the road in Picardy... And from Sir Henry Cobham's half afterthought (clearly he didn't expect Mr. Secretary to be unduly upset by the news), was born *The Road to Murder*, the first book in the Tom Walsingham Mysteries.

So, you see, Thomas, who would go on to be a knight, a courtier, and a patron of poets, is a historical character, and so are Citolini, Sir Henry Cobham, the Thomases, the Sieur de Wacogne in Montreuil, Lord Burleigh and his son, Lord Leicester, several other Privy Councillors — and, of course, Sir Francis Walsingham and his family.

The irrepressible Nick Skeres is also historical — although there is no certainty that he was the "Skeggs" from Cobham's letter. For this identification I'm indebted to Charles Nichols, and his fantastically detailed "The Reckoning". It certainly makes a certain amount of sense, and was good for the story.

The attempts to negotiate a marriage between Elizabeth I and François, Duke of Anjou and Alençon, are also historical fact. François was Elizabeth's junior by 22 years, and brother to the King of France — so it's obvious what the French stood to gain by this match; on the English side of the bargain, the prize was to be an alliance against Spain. It was a long-drawn affair. Elizabeth seems to have genuinely liked her Royal swain, but it's hard to tell whether she ever truly meant to go through with a marriage that met with fierce opposition from many of her Protestant subjects. The idea of a Catholic French prince on the throne of England was very unpopular, and Sir Francis Walsingham, for one, was very much against it. It must have been a source of endless frustration to him that the Queen dithered and prevaricated for years, on and off, exchanging poetry and jewels with her "Frog", initiating several rounds of negotiations, and never really showing her mind on the matter. This was done in part, no doubt, to keep Spain on its toes — but I can't help thinking that Elizabeth must have enjoyed driving everyone to distraction (including her own advisors) on the vexed subject of her marriage…

In November 1581 Anjou was indeed in England, wooing the Queen, and trying to understand where exactly he stood with her. That he sent an English glove-maker to his sister, the Queen of Navarre, is my own invention, as is the plot involving Garrard and the letter — but, with the Privy Council split into factions over the French Match, with Walsingham and Burleigh on opposite sides, and with Leicester shifting between the two in a bid to regain the Queen's favour, I think that something of the sort could well have happened.

There is more to the story, of course — and I plan to follow up in the next books: Tom is not finished with the Duke of Anjou and the French Match — nor, it goes without saying, with murder, espionage, and general mayhem.

A NOTE TO THE READER

Dear Reader,

Thank you for reading Tom Walsingham's first adventure in sleuthing and espionage.

I first met Thomas Walsingham as a literary patron in several biographies of poet and playwright Christopher Marlowe, in whose short life he played a not inconsiderable part. I've always imagined Thomas as an open-minded man with a sense of humour, a love of poetry, and a certain pluck: surely, associating in such a public way with reckless, mercurial genius Kit Marlowe, with all his dangerously controversial ideas and no qualms in making them known, must have been a little like keeping a tiger in one's garden.

Then again, Thomas was not entirely new to dangerous situations, having worked at least since 1580 for his father's cousin, Secretary of State and spymaster Sir Francis Walsingham. Young Thomas served in various capacities, in England and abroad — beginning as a courier, carrying confidential despatches, and accompanying Sir Francis on diplomatic missions, and later helping to run the intelligence operations from the house in Seething Lane. I don't think it's unreasonable to assume that Sir Francis trusted his young cousin, and was grooming him for diplomatic and intelligence work.

A position that, once crossed the line between fact and fiction, put Tom in the perfect place to act as Mr. Secretary's unofficial sleuth. And when I came across a letter describing Tom — all of nineteen — held up by disbanded French soldiers on the roads of Picardy, it all sprang to life for me, into a mix of murder mystery and espionage thriller.

I hope you enjoyed reading *The Road to Murder*… if you did, there's more to come.

Meanwhile, I would truly appreciate it if you'd drop by **Amazon** and **Goodreads**, to post a review, and let other readers know that you enjoyed the novel. I'd also love to hear from you on **Twitter** (where I go by @laClarina) or through **my website**.

Thank you, and meet you again in the next Tom Walsingham book!

C. P. Giuliani

claragiuliani.com

Sapere Books is an exciting new publisher of brilliant fiction and popular history.

To find out more about our latest releases and our monthly bargain books visit our website:
saperebooks.com

Printed in Great Britain
by Amazon